"You smelling anything yet?" I asked Doyle.

"Maybe. I—"

He never really had a chance to finish that thought.

Up ahead, I heard somebody, Mike, I think, call out a warning.

"Hold up, guys…this…whatever it is, it's getting stronger."

"Unless it's life or death, you can figure it out while we move," Pilar said and as I looked up to tell her to stop, it happened.

Time shifted and spun away on me.

It was like I'd been flung straight into the past.

Spikes sprung up, out, from the sides, while something swung down from the air. More of them, mounted on what might have passed for an oversized child's swing, save for those thick, deadly spikes.

All of the shifters reacted with fluid, easy grace, moving out of the way. But in the time it took them to *not* be where there was a spike, more of them came up and arrows started to rain down.

Fast…so fast.

I'd only ever once seen somebody who could shoot like that.

J.C. DANIELS

SHADOWED BLADE

By
JC DANIELS

J.C. DANIELS

CHAPTER ONE

It was just pure dumb luck that I found her at all.

The… Well, I can't say it was a *house*, but it had been her home. She'd left it weeks ago, maybe longer. It was dying, too.

Granted, when I'd been sent out to look for her, I'd thought maybe it was another wild goose chase—the first job had been a pain in the ass, too.

But this one…

Hell.

I was staring at a dryad.

A *real* dryad.

She turned her head and stared at me with eyes the color of good, strong oak. In her hand, she had a branch she used to draw circles in the earth.

After a few seconds of us studying each other, she went back to looking out over the river, her gaze sad.

"What is it you want?" she asked, her voice reedy and thin.

Like she was fading, dying as swiftly as the tree she'd left behind.

As I fumbled for an answer, she lifted the branch and plucked off one of the leaves. They were still green. But the moment she plucked that single leaf away, it withered, shriveled, and then it was dust— even before it hit the ground.

"I…" Uneasy, I licked my lips. "Your tree is dying."

"No." Those dark brown eyes came back to mine. "It is already dead. It died when I left it. It just hasn't figured that out yet. It will. But that isn't what you want."

"Why did you leave it?"

"Because the wind whispered it was time." She lifted a shoulder and the wispy strips of cloth that made up her garments drifted with the movement before settling back into black. She was more naked than clothed—covered at her breasts and hips. Her skin was a mottled mix of brown and tan. She could stand in the trees and scarcely be seen, but standing out here on the side of the road and gazing into the river, she stood out.

That was how I'd found her.

I'd been heading back to East Orlando, carefully thinking through the call I'd have to make, when I saw her. I'd been driving the backroads, mostly because I wanted to think, and all the traffic on the main roads annoyed me.

The last thought I'd had before caught sight of the woman had been…*I never should have taken this stupid job.*

My current client—I now realized—was a self-important, pompous prick. But I'd accepted the contract, and for another three weeks, I was giving him twenty hours a week for work of a *sensitive nature*. His term, not mine.

The first job, I'd been asked to find out if there was any truth to the rumors of a Green Man who might be living in Alabama—he had a locale and a few names; he wanted me to look around and see what I thought. I'd also been asked to talk to the families of a couple missing NHs while in the area. Missing non-humans was why I'd taken the damn job to begin with.

Missing people. He had connections.

There weren't many who had more connections than the President of the United States of America, after all.

When I'd told him I didn't see the connection between a possible Green Man and the disappearances, he'd pointed out that a Green Man would have ways of seeing things happening in nature that I could never see.

Well…true enough.

But if there was something weirder than a shifter in those decaying woods, then I hadn't felt it.

My boss hadn't seemed bothered when I'd been unsuccessful. But I hadn't wanted to tell him I'd found a dryad's tree…and no dryad.

Right now, though, I wanted even *less* to tell him I'd found the dryad.

"The wind told you it was time?" Raking her up and down with a look, I shook my head. "What else is the wind telling you to do?"

"The wind tells me to do *nothing*." A serene smile curled her lips as she plucked off another leaf. This time, when it shriveled and faded, *she* seemed to fade a little more, too.

Oh, shit.

"Is that from your tree?" I asked softly.

"Yes. All that is left, all that is living." She plucked another leaf. "Once it is gone..."

"So why are you *killing* it?"

"Because unlike Albus, I am not strong. I cannot stand up to pain and torture. Even cutting down a single tree would break me, and he has much more in mind than cutting down *trees*."

Abruptly, she wrenched a handful of leaves, four, five, six... Dust blew around me and I rushed to her as she swayed, then staggered. She felt lighter than air as I eased her down. Her skin felt like the smooth bark on a young tree. "What are you talking about?"

She just shook her head. "It's been a long time coming. This...this is best. I'll see Albus soon."

She tried to fumble a few more leaves off but her hands shook too much.

"Please." She looked at me.

My phone rang.

She continued to watch me with those calm, patient eyes. Patient, solid. Like an oak.

I took the branch and stripped the remaining leaves off as the phone rang again.

By the third ring, she was withering away, turning to nothing but dust and ash that blew away in the soft, chilly fall breeze.

I answered the fourth ring.

"Ms. Colbana, I was calling for an update."

"I found her." Dragging a finger through the dust, I rose to my feet and stared down. Even the branch was gone. "She's dead, sir."

"He's pissed."

Shanelle Maguire was a beautiful bitch and she delivered the words in a stark voice as she dropped into the chair across from my desk.

"I gathered that." I'd just finish talking to him myself. Whitmore was a pain in the ass. "Did he send you here to snarl and snap at me in

7

J.C. DANIELS

hopes of making me do better?"

She snorted. "Like that'd do any good." She skimmed her hands back over her hair in what I'd come to realize was a nervous habit. Beautiful bitch or not, I'd come to sort of like her over the past ten days. She was blunt and didn't hold back the truth, something I could definitely appreciate. She was also manipulative as hell—something I less appreciated—but she knew how to make things happen. "Look, I was standing out—"

"This is my shocked face."

"Shut up," she said, sighing in annoyance. "I heard you explaining what happened. What were you going to do? She wanted to die. Although...wow. Picking leaves off a tree branch—that's *crazy*."

"Dryads have a connection to their chosen trees." I shrugged and thought of the forest giant I'd gone back to look at before returning home. It hadn't turned to dust, but it was dead. It had been an oddity, standing there in the middle of the forest where so many trees had already gone brilliantly orange and yellow, but its leaves had been green...mostly. Some, though, had been going brown. Not yellow or orange, the way you'd think.

But brown.

All the leaves had been gone the second time I saw it and the branches hung despondent, as if the tree's strength had simply drained out of it with the life of the dryad gone. I'd touched the bark and it had crumbled under the light pressure.

A few storms, a few hard rains, and it would come crashing down.

"So she just lay there, plucked the last few leaves and died, huh?" Shanelle wasn't even looking at me. She was staring off at nothing, looking about as tired as I felt—although I doubted it was for the same reason.

"Faded into dust," I said, carefully dancing around the fact that I wasn't telling the complete truth. I'd had to do the same with Whitmore, but for some reason, I was reluctant to explain that *I* had been the one to strip away those few remaining leaves.

Whitmore had *really* wanted to talk to that dryad.

My gut was all twisted and hot as I remembered what she had said.

"Because unlike Albus, I am not strong. I cannot stand up to pain

8

and torture. Even cutting down a single tree would break me and he has much more in mind than cutting down trees."

Who was Albus?

Who was the *he* she'd been referring to? I had a bad feeling it might be my *client*—but there was no way I could even try to figure that out without questioning him; everything in me was saying *Don't*...

I thought of asking Shanelle, probing gently. I knew how to dance around things and be subtle. It wasn't my *greatest* skill, but I could do it.

While I was debating, though, the door swung open.

The sight of the man standing there was enough to distract me, though.

"Justin..."

I hurtled across the room and caught him up in a hug so hard, he was laughing and wheezing at the same time. "Careful there, Kit...I break."

I didn't care. "You're awake."

"Seems that way. Although if you keep squeezing the life out of me..."

Two weeks ago, Justin had almost died. The first week, he'd been in a coma. He'd started to stir, but another friend of ours, Colleen had used her healing to put him back under.

"The swelling in his brain has gone down, but there's still a lot of healing to do—the area of the brain that controls magic has been heavily damaged and the longer he rests, the more likely it will be that he'll regain full control."

We'd agreed. He needed to stay asleep for a bit longer, but Colleen could only hold him for a few more days before she had to bring him back.

"I didn't know she was letting you up today."

He patted my back when I sniffed.

Absently, I'd realized Shanelle had left and I still needed to talk to her. But that could wait.

Chapter Two

The tent was crowded.

Outside the tent wasn't much better.

"I really don't want to be here," I said tiredly.

Next to me, Justin stood there, his face emotionless but there were tiny lines of strain around his eyes. I knew he wanted to be here even less. The stink of death and pain around this place was hurting me—I couldn't imagine what it was doing to a witch.

I *could* have pointed out to him that he'd been the one to insist he come along, but what was the point? He'd spent the past couple of weeks sitting around doing nothing. I would have been bored too.

"I think we need to make Colleen brew us up some margaritas, whip up some tacos and such, that sort of thing." Crossing my arms over my chest, I stared the opening of the tent that yawned open in front us. "It's her fault we're here."

Justin didn't respond.

"Are we going in or not?"

Finally, he turned his head and looked at me. "You realize she really is healing people?"

The sharp green light of his eyes cut into me.

"I…" I stopped and huffed out a breath. He'd made it clear more than a few times, but I'd done my best to avoid thinking about it. *Healing* people. That was why we were here.

There was somebody inside that tent—she called herself Frankie. And according to what people were saying, she could heal cancer, broken bones, HIV, lupus. I didn't care what *people* said. But Justin had seen the people there—one of the *healed*. He'd lain eyes on some of those sick people, he'd *seen* the sickness inside them. Then a day later, he'd seen the health.

"You can't cure cancer with magic," I said. Just as Colleen had said to Justin and I a few days ago, before we'd left Orlando.

We—no, *I* had been sent north on a job. Justin had been slouching around the office, going out of his mind from boredom, if you ask me. He'd had come along not long after the details of the job came in, had started nagging me about following along, but then he'd been there when Colleen called, all but hysterical.

And that that sealed it.

"No." Justin frowned, his mouth going tight. "You can't. So apparently, she's doing something that's either more than magic…or something totally different."

He jerked his head toward the tent. "Come. They're getting restless."

Crouched on the floor, surrounded by the stink of vomit, I remembered few things clearly.

Colleen's voice, practically pleading…*She's telling people she can cure them, Kit. Magic doesn't cure cancer!*

A woman's laugh. *You'll want to enjoy this.*

Pain. It sliced through my head.

Justin. In my office. There had been a job—I remembered that. When? A few days ago? A few weeks? A lifetime? *Let me come with, Kitty. I'm going crazy sitting around here.*

My head.

Another thought—no, memory, worked free. Justin. *She's doing something that's either more than magic…or something totally different.*

Something moved in front of me and I tried to swing out instinctively. "Easy, Kit. Easy…"

Justin.

That was Justin.

"Well, hell." A woman's voice that time. I *knew* that voice…

I swallowed as bile rushed up my throat and the taste of vomit was enough to make me start puking again—almost.

I didn't want to throw up again.

Especially not here. I'd just thrown up on her shoes and I didn't want to be anywhere around here.

"Get your friend, boy," a deep, intense voice said from behind me. The sound of it made me flinch and that made me want to cry, but

11

I feared doing even that, the pain was so severe. "You must go, both of you."

I tried to wobble back onto my heels, the first step in getting to my feet, but it took more effort than I'd expected and I wasn't even close to steady when I finally managed a somewhat upright position. I could see the man now. Recognition flickered, stirred. Big and dark haired and lean, deadly eyes.

Deadly.

They narrowed on me for a ponderous moment and it occurred to me that I should be smart and get away. That was what I should do. But I couldn't get my body to cooperate.

Justin knelt by me, eased me upright. "Come on, Kitty."

I did manage to sneak a look at him, but he was too busy staring at the other two in the room. The woman had dismissed us, her back to me, but the man...he was still scrutinizing us like a couple of bugs.

"Go," he said again, the order clear.

We went.

Something akin to real fear was knocking in my belly and I didn't want to be anywhere around this guy—or the woman. As Justin eased me toward the door, I glanced at her.

My heart froze.

She was staring at me from one of the reflected images cast by a mirror on the wall.

And she was smiling.

"It didn't work, did it?"

It was the first time Justin had spoken in nearly two hours.

Thanks to the delay we'd taken at Colleen's request, we were a few days late in starting this job and we hadn't gotten to our destination until well after midnight.

We were parked in front of the building we'd been told was ours to use for the duration of this current *assignment* but so far, neither of us had made any attempt to get out.

I was personally a little afraid of moving. My stomach had finally settled and my head no longer felt like a melon that had been split open with an axe. Now it just felt like somebody had installed an automated battering ram in my skull.

Absently, I reached down and touched the hilt of my sword. More than once during the drive, I'd done that very thing, reached for my blade. Her grip felt warm and I resisted the urge to curl my fingers around her, pull her into my lap and stroke her—the way a scared child might pet a dog.

"Nothing's changed, Justin," I said tiredly. Then I did grab my sword. With my free hand, I shoved the door open and braced myself before standing up. My entire body protested the movement and my stomach threatened a savage revolt, but after a few seconds it quieted.

Damn good thing. I wasn't sure if I could have handled a session on my knees. If I'd started throwing up, I might have just thrown myself on my sword and gotten it over with.

Eying the dark shadow of the building looming over us, I started forward. My steps were unsteady lurches that sent the world spinning around me. If I ever got my hands on that woman…

Frankie's face flashed through my mind and despite the bravado, a shiver of uneasiness worked through me. She'd been freaky. Freaky, fast, scary, and the big guy with her had been just as bad. Justin joined me and when he slid a steadying arm around my waist, I didn't have the energy to tell him to leave me alone.

The building hadn't seemed so far away when I'd looked at it from the car, but now…

"I feel like calling in dead," I told him sourly.

"You are looking rather corpse-like."

"Yeah, well...I blame you for that. I'm tempted to make *you* look rather corpse-like." The grim humor in my voice didn't make him smile though.

Justin actually looked away. "I thought..."

He didn't finish, but I heard the things he didn't say. Once we'd mounted the crumbling concrete steps, I eased away from him. "It's okay, Justin. I know what you thought. But I already told you...it's done."

Turning from the guilt I saw in his eyes, I dealt with the locks on the door—one of them was newer and I didn't have a key. That was just a minor hitch, not a deterrent. After I'd picked the lock, I slid a hand inside one of the pockets on my vest, coming out with a small flashlight. Sending a stream of light shining inside, I waited for Justin to join me. "Once we clear the place, you can put your car down in the garage."

We had the code to open those doors, but neither of us were going to put away our means of escape without clearing a building. Maybe we were getting more paranoid, but despite the fact that I'd been assured that the building was secure, we'd both agreed we'd ascertain that fact for ourselves.

After we did that, I was finding someplace horizontal, even if it was only for about twenty minutes.

"What's your boss going to think about me horning in on this with you?" Just asked after we'd cleared each floor, checking every room. He'd already moved the car into the garage, facing out so we could blast the hell out of there in a blink if need be.

If that happened, I just hoped it didn't happen today.

"Funny that you'd ask that now." I collapsed into the only chair in the small kitchen and eased my head down onto the cool surface. It felt like heaven against my overheated flesh. "I mean, you were nagging me to come along, whining about how bored you were."

"Well, yeah. But that's not answering my question." He opened the small refrigerator. "He definitely didn't plan on feeding you. There's water. That's it."

"I don't want food." I didn't want *anything*. Why had I told Colleen I'd swing by and check out that so-called *faith healer*?

Although she had been *healing* people…sort of.

For a few blind, hopeful seconds, I'd thought maybe she'd find a way to heal *me*, too. Fix the bond between me and my sword—but that hadn't happened.

It was still as broken as it had been before I'd seen her.

Another series of vicious pulses went through my head and I wanted to curl up in a ball and die.

Justin came over and pressed his hand to the back of my head.

I went to bat him away, but he was doing…something.

Cool energy radiated out from his hand, seeped into my skull.

I groaned in relief as some of the pain eased back.

"We can start tomorrow," he said. "You're useless right now."

"Somehow, I get the feeling this didn't go as planned."

Justin stood over me, blood dripping from a gash that ran from the corner of his eye down his cheek. It was deep and blood had flowed freely until he had staunched it using magic. It wasn't healed, though so he was just sucking up the pain.

The lines around his mouth cut deep grooves into his cheeks as he held a hand out to me.

I was in marginally better shape than he was, but that was just luck.

And that was kind of my fault.

Luck always tended to play in my favor—and sometimes his, if he happened to be around me. It was something coded into my DNA, just like my affinity with weapons and my ability to go invisible. It wasn't the kind of luck that meant I had an easy life—don't I *wish*— but it did mean shit like what we'd just gone through didn't end up with us dead.

Justin held out a hand in lieu of answering and I took it, letting him help me to my feet. Pain streaked my side and when I sucked in a breath; it only got worse. I winced, pressing a hand to the area.

He shot me a look.

"Ribs. At least one is broken."

"You're going to have to suck it up." He turned his head and stared up at the smoking ruin of the building we'd been watching.

Keep it under surveillance for a few days and report back. I have reason to believe that individuals with connections to Blackstone are carrying out meetings there. I want faces—pictures, if you can get them. Don't try to approach them. They are...sly.

That was the last assignment I'd been given, four days ago.

So far, I'd seen *one* individual.

In the weeks since the dryad I had died, I'd had a few other jobs that felt like...bullshit. Although I *had* gotten the name of several more missing NHs, tracked down four NHs who were actually *working* with the bastards to help capture loners and the like. Nobody high up the food chain—and while the other jobs had been strange, none of them had been like the dryad.

I hadn't *liked* any of them. I'd walked away from one because it hadn't felt right.

This one, though...

Blowing out a breath, I stared out at the blazing remains of the building.

If Justin hadn't come along, *I* might be a pile of blazing remains.

"You said you pissed him off on the last job?" Justin asked as we studied the smoke rising into the sky.

"Eh. Yeah." Grimacing, I swiped the sweat from my brow.

I hadn't gone into any details, mostly because I didn't know how Justin—or one other man in my life—might take it if I mentioned I thought there was something on that last job that wanted to eat me.

I'd related my concerns to my boss. He'd implied I was being paranoid. I'd told him I'd go if I could take my own back-up. He'd refused. I'd politely told him where the job could go.

Four hours later, I was given the specifics for this job.

"You think maybe he wants you dead?" Justin shifted around restlessly, his eyes flicking all over. He didn't wait for an answer, his gaze moving to the north. "We need to move—*now*. That fire wasn't natural and there's no witch close enough who could have started it and kept it burning—which means she used something to do it."

"Something like..."

Justin just grabbed my wrist and yanked as something hit the back of the building. I'd felt the power spike in the air, but not in time to recognize the threat. Justin, being what he was, had—and that was what saved us. We were running by the time we hit the crumbling frame of the doorway, all that was left from the first explosion.

It wouldn't survive this one, but maybe it would give us some protection.

The world turned to flame around us and I crouched down, arms over my head as Justin closed his eyes and magic began to pulse out of him.

Everything else faded away my very existence narrowing down to the man in front of me and the fire that raged just past the shields he created with his magic.

If those failed…

Eons seemed to pass before Justin's body slumped and the shields fractured, then fell around us. The smoke was so thick in the air, I could barely see past it. The silence around us was so thick and pervasive, I fancied for a moment that I had gone deaf.

I wanted to find a deep, dark hole and sleep…for a month. The lingering headache that had persisted ever since my encounter with Frankie the Freaky was no longer *lingering*. It was a monster rattling around inside my skull and chewing on my brain matter for a midday snack.

But there wasn't any time to curl up in a ball and whimper.

I lurched to my feet and then bent down, grabbing Justin's hand. It was cold, a sign of how much energy he'd expended. "Rock and roll, hotshot," I told him, hauling him up.

About half way through, he started to put some muscle into it.

We were ten feet from his car before he really started to show signs of life, but by the time we climbed in, there was awareness in his eyes. "Gotta move," he said, voice rough. "She's not done. I feel her."

We were pulling away when the next wave of fire came. "How in the hell..."

"That's why I said we gotta move." Justin punched the car into action, and we took off while what looked like a dragon of fire chased it. "Kit, my friend...I think we just came into contact with a salamander."

My question was lost in the rattle and roar of the car as the fire below and behind us blazed hotter and tried to wrap around the vehicle as we fled. Justin's eyes began to glow, the silver on his sleeves blazing as he fed more of his magic into...something.

The roar faded.

Slowly.

I shot a look behind us, staring at the flames that punched into the air, impossibly high, impossibly tall.

"That's..." In between one breath and the next, the fire was gone. Just gone. "Crazy."

The rundown little no-tell motel we'd ended up in was a pre-pay affair; the kind where they didn't ask questions and you didn't, either. We'd stayed at this sort of place before. Between Justin and me, we probably knew every semi-safe spot in the south—and he knew quite a few outside of the region, too.

While I couldn't claim we'd never had trouble with one of these spots, we tended to do a lot better out in the middle of nowhere than we did trying our luck in cities outside of Orlando.

Both Justin and I attracted attention.

There was just no help for it.

I could blend in and pass for human as long as we were in a heavily human populace, but Justin didn't do that as well; even then,

17

both of us just looked...well, we invited trouble.

Neither of us were very good at walking away from it, either.

Since we needed to lay low, heal up, and get back to Orlando, places like this were best.

Plus, they had another benefit.

It made it a hell of a lot easier to pick up on the presence of *others*.

I came awake in the blink of an eye, no lingering grogginess, all the adrenaline rushing to the fore. *Get ready...get ready...*

That had me flexing my hand, even though there was no point, not now.

The sword I still tried to call leaned against the rickety excuse of a nightstand, waiting patiently. I reached for her.

That simple movement had Justin stirring.

A moment later, he was sitting up.

Already at the window, I shot a quick glance his way as he rubbed at bleary eyes.

Get ready...get ready... That little voice of warning, my instincts, all of those were still in perfect working order. Not quite a year ago, I'd been kidnapped and the skill of a witch who is no longer alive had damaged something inside me. The bond he'd broken still hurt, but I was learning to live without it, function—fight.

"Get dressed," I said softly. Not that Justin had much dressing to do. He had been working as a hired fighter ever since he'd left Banner, a government branch where he'd hunted down rogue NHs. Technically, I guess he'd been a hired fighter then, too—one paid by the government.

He'd left them a while back. Lately, we'd been working together a lot.

I was a jack-of-all-trades and while I used to make most of my money as a courier, lately, I was doing a lot of jobs that made me think I needed to find another way to make a living.

Something that let me sleep naked more often than not, instead of just taking my boots off when I needed to sleep.

Hearing the stamping of feet behind me, I went about gathering up my weapons.

He had his boots on.

He was dressed.

I strapped my sword into place and slid the various blades I always carried home.

Justin didn't ask what had woken me.

I didn't offer any insight. At that point, I didn't have any. I just knew we needed to *move*.

We were outside when Justin grabbed my arm and started to drag me along behind him. "Hurry," he said grimly. "It's her."

I didn't waste time asking him what he meant, just tore away from him and flung myself toward the car, drawing my body tight and then leaping over the hood. Behind me, I heard him mutter, "Show-off."

Once we were inside, I pointed out, "You're the one who said to hurry." I was staring into the woods and it made it easier to see.

Something red, fast…

"Is that—"

"Don't know. Don't care. Getting out of here."

CHAPTER THREE

Sleep fogged my brain and I was so tired, it hurt to move, but the sound of my phone made me do it anyway.

We'd been on the move for close to forty-eight hours, zig-zagging across the northern part of Florida, in and out of Alabama before circling back around. We'd collapsed to rest less than two hours ago, and even the thought of moving made me want to scream.

The number didn't immediately come into focus and when it did, I had to force my brain into functioning.

I didn't know the number. How had this person gotten my personal line? If it were a forward from my business, it would have gone to voicemail this late. Groaning, I flopped onto my back and answered.

"Yeah?"

"You need to move."

The sound of the voice cleared away the fog of sleep, and adrenaline chased away the heaviness in my tired muscles.

I didn't *know* that voice. It was low and clipped and hard to determine the gender of the speaker. Uneasiness tripped down my spine and I shot a look at Justin. "Move."

"Yes. As in get your gear, get your friend, and leave. You have little time."

Justin was already sitting up, looking at me, his sleepy eyes clearing. Neither of us had slept much in the past few days—dealing with this salamander-toting witch had us both on edge. We couldn't go back to Orlando with some fire-breathing, pocket-sized monster still tracking us.

We were trying to keep a few steps ahead of her, and that's about *all* we were doing—staying a few steps ahead.

Justin frowned at me as he swung his legs around, the question in his eyes clear.

I lifted a hand to indicate my confusion as I kept most of my attention focused on the phone.

"Just who is—"

The phone went dead.

Justin and I studied each other for a span of two seconds, then without either of us speaking, we both got up and started grabbing our gear.

We were out the door in under three minutes.

We'd settled down inside an old, abandoned building on the outskirts of a town that had pretty much shuttered itself up after the war between the species. The few who still lived here did so in an uneasy truce. We'd seen signs in the yards and in a window of the one still remaining business. The store sign had read *HUMANS ONLY.*

The signs on four or five houses had varied from that simple sentiment to *GO AWAY, MEAT.*

That sentiment, while not quite so simple, made one thing clear. There were non-humans living in the pathetic, dying little town. I'd felt the prickle and crawl of some weak power as we battened down the hatches—so to speak, grab some rest before we got up and tried to come up with another game plan. But it was hard to think up a way to smoke out a witch who could send a little bitty lizard into your hidey-hole from miles off and *burn* you out. All without blinking an eye or showing herself.

Once we were in the car, I tugged out my phone and pulled up the log. I studied the last number that had called me. After a few seconds of trying to prod loose some memory that didn't exist, I did a search on the internet, hoping to find out who the phone belonged to, but no joy there. The phone number was assigned to a throwaway, one that had been purchased in the past couple of months. Most likely it had been bought with cash and registered under a fake name. Burner phones.

I doubted whoever it was would answer, but I called back.

To my surprise, I *did* get an answer. That same, sexless voice. "You are no fool, so I assume you are calling from the road."

Glancing out the window as Justin shot off into the night—via the sky—I said, "More or less. So, why am I leaving and who the hell are you?"

"You are leaving because—"

The rest of the words were lost.

I'd dropped the phone.

Justin had swung the car around and he was hovering. I hadn't noticed anything out of place until just that moment. Now I couldn't look away. "That bitch," I said softly, staring at the flaming remains of the building where we'd been staying. *Sleeping*, up until maybe...shit, I doubted ten minutes had passed.

There was another blast of fire—this coming directly toward us. Justin yanked hard on the steering controls and hit the power. We jerked to the right as a thin whippet of fire reached us.

"Son of a bitch," Justin said. "If you go fucking with my car..."

I managed a weak laugh. "Something is pelting us with fire and almost burned us in our sleep, and you're worried about your car. Priorities, Justin. Get us on the ground. We're sitting ducks up here."

He nosed the car down one-handed while flipping at one of the gadgets on the dash. "That will help some," he said with a mutter of disgust. "You know, I really... *really* want to know who this bitch is and why we were put on her tail."

That was something I'd like to know myself, something I'd be asking about as soon as we managed to shake her off our asses.

Yeah, so maybe he didn't like questions, but I didn't like having buildings blow up around me.

"We've got a problem."

I'd been watching the rear view mirror, but now I looked forward.

I didn't have to strain myself to see it. It was pretty obvious. A road block, made of trashed cars and dumpsters—all of it shoved into the road. Those responsible for the roadblock were loitering in front of it, sitting in a couple of plastic chairs, trading a bottle back and forth.

I'd imagine the fumes coming off that bottle would be as strong as the shit used to fuel a jet, and although the bottle was half-empty, the eyes of the men watching us through the windshield were clear and sharp.

Slowly, I reached down and fished out the phone I'd dropped.

The line was still open.

"It seems we've run into a roadblock," I said, keeping my voice calm. "Just an FYI...if you have any hand in this, you better hope both of us die. We're really good at tracking people down."

"I would hope you are," the speaker said. "If you're...trapped in a rock and a hard space, I suggest you stop speaking and deal with your troubles."

"It's trapped *between*," I said. But the phone had gone dead.

A loud clanging came from behind us and I glanced over to see Justin eying the rear view mirror. "Boxed us in from the rear," he said, tone almost bored. "Most of it's metal. I can deal with that. There's one guy back there, too. I can handle the blockade and him. You?"

"Sure. I'd love to handle a couple of shifters on my own." I focused as I stared out the window, trying to gauge their power level. Not terribly strong.

"Kit?"

"Son of a bitch. It's the best we got. Nobody else too close, I don't think. You feel anything?"

"Nope." He shot me a look.

I nodded, resigned. This job sucked. Disgusted, I reached down and drew the gun from my thigh rig. After checking the cartridge, I reached for the handle. "I guess it's too much to hope we can talk our way out of this."

I came out fast, gun high. While the two shifters in front of me were focused on that, I flicked my left wrist and sent a dagger into my hand. It flew through the night and lodged in the throat of the shifter closest to me—he'd been tightening his muscles, ready to lunge. "It's silver," I warned. "If I were you, I'd be very, very careful about how you pull it out."

He went to his knees, face already white.

The other man whipped his head around—he'd instinctively turned when his friend's breathing went to wet bubbles. Now, though, he was glaring at me, eyes glowing. He was solid, through and through, face mostly hidden behind a grizzled gray beard, eyes a muddy brown and the teeth he'd bared at me were yellowed—likely by a lifetime of smoking. Even asshole shifters like these were big on hygiene.

"There's silver in the cartridge," I warned. "Semi-automatic and yes, I'm just as fast with the gun as I am with a knife. You even think about moving toward me, I'll open your guts up."

Behind me, I heard the hiss of metal against metal, magic rolling through the air. Justin had that end covered.

The shifter in front of me growled low in his throat and a prickly sort of heat emanated from him. But it was...muted. Not weak—he could rip me apart limb by limb if he got his hands on me. But he didn't have the kick to him, power-wise, that some of the shifters did.

I held his gaze, not even blinking.

"You want to tell us what's with the new road decor?" I kept my eyes focused on the man who didn't have silver in his throat. He'd have an easier time speaking. Hopefully, I hadn't thrown the knife at the wrong man.

"Ain't telling you shit," he said, lip curling.

Lowering the gun, I squeezed off one round. He jerked, but not in time. "I told you I was fast," I said over the sound of his harsh screech. He was now on his side, blood and smoke curling up from the ruin of his knee. The silver in the ammo would have shattered on impact, tearing into him. He would have to get it all out before he could heal completely.

"Bitch..." He gasped out, eyes going wolf green on me. "Fucking stupid bitch..."

"Come up with something that hasn't been used a hundred times." I chanced a look over my shoulder and saw that Justin had his man rolled up in the threads of silver that normally decorated Justin's jacket. That silver wasn't decoration, though. The metal had a deadly purpose and Justin now had the man hanging in the air, the thin chain cutting into his mouth, effectively—and cruelly—gagging him. Without looking away from the man, he flicked one hand toward the mess of cars. One of them gave way with a screech of metal. He'd already moved two of them. He added a third car as sweat broke out on his brow.

From the corner of my eye, I saw the man with the knife still in his throat reaching up. I swung my gaze to him. I palmed another blade and flashed it, letting it catch the light of the rising moon. "Want another? I can send it through your hand. You look like a lefty. I do that, you'll have trouble pulling the knife out without shredding your jugular. You won't bleed to death, but you'll be damn weak."

His hand fell to his side. Blood had turned the front of his shirt red. It was a slow stream instead of the river it would be once he pulled the blade out. Of course, once it was out, he'd heal. But he'd have to do it with care if he didn't want to seriously shred the vessels in his throat.

Satisfied he'd be still for a few more minutes, I focused back on the other man. His dull brown eyes kept flickering to wolf green and back as he fought to control both anger and pain. "Let's try again. Why the roadblock?"

His lip curled, but he glanced over at his partner and something he saw on the man's face made him shrug. With a pained mutter, he said, "What the hell. Money. We was told you might be coming through this way. Lew saw your boy there driving his car inside the old Shaeffer garage. We saw you shut the door. Call went out to some folks to be on the lookout for you and him. A blonde and a witch, in that kinda car." He jerked his head toward the vehicle, his gaze lingering briefly on the lazy twirl of the third shifter. Likely a packmate. "Whoever managed to slow you down would get cash, lots of it. Once we knew it was you, we sent along word."

He shot a look toward the burning building before shifting his glaring fury toward me. "If we'd known you'd be this much trouble, we would have asked for a lot more."

I moved a couple steps closer, still keeping a good ten feet between us. Holding his eyes, I crouched down in front of him. "I'm not sure if you could ask for enough to cover the kind of trouble we're going to give you."

His nostrils flared as he dragged in a deep breath, and I saw a flicker in his eyes. That alone made me smirk. I could only imagine what his nose was telling him. Damn shifters and their sense of smell. If I'd gone into a pizza parlor a week ago, one of them could probably tell—and I'm fastidious—okay, maybe *obsessive*—about my hygiene. But their noses are beyond sensitive.

Smiling, I ran my thumb down the rough material of my vest. When I wasn't wearing it—and if it wasn't covered in blood or brain matter or something to that effect—it was stored in the closet at the Lair. At least, that was where I'd been storing it for the past few weeks, along with my other clothes. I'd recently moved in with Damon. He's my...lover. Boyfriend doesn't quite describe him.

During the day, I'd sometimes catch his scent on my clothes, so it wasn't any big shock that somebody with a nose far more sensitive than mine had just picked up something.

The shifter's eyes dropped to my vest, lingered on my hand where it stroked the placard of buttons.

"Who you got after you, girl?" he asked, pain drawing deep grooves around his mouth.

"Well." I offered a one-sided shrug and a wink. "If you're hoping it's some big cat shifter, you're out of luck. See, he's already caught me—that's why you smell him all over me. But enough about that...who is it that offered to pay you?"

I saw the *oh, shit* look fade from his face, replaced by resignation. The indecision, the minor inner struggle had been brief and obvious—he could either hold out and hope he could get the money, or just talk and hope whatever cat shifter he scented wasn't going to get too pissy. Apparently, he figured the witch was the lesser evil.

The man was not an idiot.

Grimly, he set his jaw. "I don't know. We never spoke to anybody. It was all done through text."

"See, that's pretty sad for you." I straightened and sited on his undamaged knee. "This close, I'm going to do you a lot of damage—"

"Wait. Wait..." He started to shove upward, pain twisting his features. He gingerly put weight on his damaged knee. "I'll give you information. I don't want no more trouble—I ain't getting paid that much." Face folding into a sneer, he muttered, "Skinny little thing like you, shoulda been easy."

"People always think that." I didn't lower the Glock. "Come on, man. Give me something...a number, a name."

For the first time, Justin spoke. "Money doesn't do you much good if you're dead."

"Ain't that the truth." He set his jaw and jerked his head toward the man on the ground, the knife still jutting out at an obscene angle. "I can't give you a name. I never knew it. I got a number—and information. You get that information if you take the knife out of him—*without* killing him and you let my other man back there go."

Some of the lazy country boy drawl had disappeared, leaving somebody with sharper eyes and a grim attitude. He still wasn't all that strong power-wise, but it was becoming clear he wasn't quite the bumbling yokel he'd pretended to be.

"What kind of information?"

"You think we're the only ones who were interested in the kinda money being offered for your skinny ass? I can tell you, we ain't. The notice went up and shit went wild at that kinda cash. We was just the lucky ones who saw you first." The sneer on his face deepened before fading, leaving him looking tired and in pain. "You make sure my men don't end up dead and I'll give you as much information as I can, and I'll spread the word that you two probably aren't worth the money being offered."

"And why would you be so helpful?" Suspicion choked me. I didn't trust anybody who pulled this kind of one-eighty.

"Shit." He spat on the ground before answering. Eyes slid to my hair, then to the sword at my hip. "We were told to look for a witch with brown hair and his bitch—cute girl with blonde hair, likes weapons. That's what the bulletin said. Didn't say shit about a sword. If it had, we woulda just stayed back. People know who you are— you're that girl who's hooked up with the outfit down in Florida. I ain't gonna fuck with that Alpha."

"Damon's reputation proceeds him," I murmured. I still wasn't quite ready to lower my guard; although I had a feeling the man was being straight. It would explain the change of heart. "How do I know you boys aren't going to change your mind the minute I lower my weapons? What if your Alpha decides *he* doesn't want to just let things ride?"

The man's eyes narrowed. Something that looked like affront crossed his features. "I don't lie, girl."

"Can you speak for the others? What about your Alpha?"

He hitched up the shoulder and shifted, wincing as the movement sent pain shooting up his leg. "Ain't no Alpha here. I'm the strongest of us, so I make the calls." He gave a short nod. "If I say we're done with you, we're done. Those two ain't going to try to take me on."

As he spoke, Justin moved up to stand beside me. His wolf trailed along behind him like a bizarre balloon, drops of blood falling from the gashes the silver had to dug into his flesh. Meeting Justin's eyes, I saw the answer to the question I hadn't even asked.

I pulled my phone out, snapped a picture of the man in front of me, and sent it off to Chang. The object of my attention scowled. "What was that for?"

"It's called insurance," I said dryly. "If I end up disappearing, you better hope you have nothing to do with it, because people will come asking questions."

The thin smile I gave him had him clenching his jaw. "I told you, I got no desire to mess with them cats down in Florida. I'll be straight with you."

"Think of it as incentive."

He looked as if he wanted to tell me to shove my incentive up my ass, but he just nodded at the man dangling in the air behind us. "Let Lew down. Get that knife out of Jimmy's throat."

I looked at Justin. His eyelid twitched. Behind us, there was a *thump*.

"Lew is down. Justin will free him and I'll deal with that knife once you give us something. Show of trust."

He dragged a hand down his grizzled face and muttered. The words weren't particularly flattering but I hadn't expected us to become friends. "We got the information about you from a site online—people go asking for...jobs to get done. Messes to get cleaned up, that kind of shit. The poster gave a dollar amount and your description. A few others responded right after we did. I don't know most of them, but a vamp from a house south of here, right near the border? One of their top men had a few questions. He's probably got men out looking for you. And a couple of freelance witches chimed in. All of them are nasty pieces of work."

He hesitated a moment, then added, "The vamps, they're the biggest problem. Nasty. Meaner than a pit full of rattlesnakes. Not exactly...civilized."

I could have laughed at the phrase civilized being applied to vampires. I chose not to. "And you've got no idea who put the word out?"

"Nope." With a shake of his head, he said, "We was just told to look for you and if we hold you long enough, we could get money. We were given that number—" He recited it off and then made a grand show of looking at his bare wrist. "Now I ain't wearing a watch, but you've been standing around here chatting with us a while. I put in that call maybe half hour ago, once I thought it was likely we had the right people. If you talk to us too long, I might get that money after all.

Justin bumped my shoulder with his. "We need to move. I'll deal with this one." He slid his hand down my arm and plucked the knife from my hand. I didn't ask why.

As he backed away, the blade rose slowly into the air. It hung there, a silent threat as I walked over to the man on the ground, still bleeding. He was pale now and he was going to need some serious recovery time. At least for a shifter.

He flinched when he saw me reaching for the blade and a fresh trickle of blood flowed free. "You should probably be still," I advised. "I'm just going to take it out. Don't move."

His whole body tensed, but he was still as I closed my hand around the blade, withdrawing it slowly. More blood flowed and I took his hand, pressing it to his neck. "Pressure. I assume you know you lost a lot of blood. But now that it's out, you'll heal."

Rising, I met the eyes of the older man. "He'll need rest, liquids—*lots* of liquids. Food as soon as he can manage it."

"I've been a wolf longer than you been alive, girl." The man's yellowed teeth bared at me in a mockery of a smile. "I think I can deal with it."

I didn't waste time saying anything else. Reaching up, I wrapped my hand around the knife Justin had left hovering in the air. His ability to control metal was nothing short of amazing and if he hadn't let me pull the knife out of midair, I wouldn't have been able to. Not turning my back on either of the shifters in front of me, I backed away until Justin was in my line of sight. Silver was spinning in the air and in the span of a heartbeat, it burned white hot. Charred blood and flesh fell away, and then Justin held out his arms. The silver wound itself back into place on his sleeve. On the ground at our feet, the man who'd been trussed up like a pig was covered in ugly black and red welts from head to toe. Blood seeped from some of the deeper wounds. He was going to hurt. Bad.

Rage leaked from his eyes, mingling with the pain. "Let's go," I told Justin. This guy was going to heal a lot quicker than the one who'd all but bled to death. I didn't want to be anywhere near this one once he was healed up.

For a response, Justin jabbed a thumb at the car. "You're driving."

I might have asked him if he'd been hit in the head if I thought we'd had the time. But once we were in the car, speeding away from the dead little town, I figured out why he wanted me in the driver seat easy enough on my own.

As the miles sped away, he busied himself on his handheld computer—sometimes switching to the in-dash computer if he wasn't getting results quick enough. I was pretty decent with tech and was getting better, but Justin had grown up using it and he'd also spent a few years in Banner—the government entity that policed...problems between humans and non-humans. Tech was drilled into his head.

"Trying to find whatever forum he was talking about?" I asked as we sped deeper and deeper into the night.

"Already did. I know a few—use some of the less unsavory ones. Used to have to watch the more disturbing ones in Banner." He made a disgusted noise in his throat. "Now I'm trying to connect this bullshit to the witch after us."

From the corner of my eye, I saw the look he gave me. "It would be easier if I knew more about her."

"*I* don't know anything about her. I was asked to watch the building and follow those who came and went."

"She was the only one who came and went." Justin sounded disgruntled. I couldn't blame him. I hadn't told him everything about my new client. He'd been busy being all comatose when the man had approached me, and I wasn't certain just how much leeway I had when it came to informing my partner of the pertinent facts.

We were slowly making our way south, but not directly. Going to Orlando when we had a witch of unspecified powers and grudges trailing after us just wasn't an option. What we knew of her could fit in a tin can—she used a salamander that made big-ass fires and she was as good at tracking as I was. Maybe even better, because I'd had no luck in trying to turn the tables on her.

My phone buzzed indicating an incoming call and I looked down. The sight of the blocked number made me want to grit my teeth. I didn't have *time* to talk to him. "I swear," I muttered. "You've got the worst..."

A suspicion started to form in my head as the phone rang again.

She was tracking us somehow. Whipping the car off the side of the road. I grabbed Justin's phone from the console.

As I shoved the door open, he demanded, "What are you doing?"

"Desperate times, desperate measures." I threw both phones down and smashed them under the solid heel of my boot, grinding until I felt certain they were pulverized. Justin had climbed out behind me and stood watching in silence.

Because I wasn't certain enough that any and all electronic bits inside the phone had been fried, I pulled the weapon from my hip and shot each of them.

"Are you going to burn it with fire next?" Justin asked.

"I can't." Giving him a considering glance, I said, "You could."

"I don't think it's necessary. You destroyed any battery left inside so it can't give off any signal." He paced forward, hands in his pockets, green eyes narrowed. "You think somebody had locked onto our signal?"

"Don't know, but somehow, she keeps turning up like a bad disease." Turning away from the remnants of the phone, I said, "Come on. We need to find new phones—or at least some way to put in a call to the Lair. Otherwise somebody is going to get antsy."

Justin snorted, although whether he was amused at the idea of me calling a six-and-a-half-foot Alpha shapeshifter *antsy* or if he was just amused by my understatement, I couldn't tell.

"I've got an idea where we can stop and grab some throwaways, maybe some rest." He rolled his head toward me and the shadows under his eyes probably matched mine. "Might as well put your theory to the test. If she doesn't show up by dawn, we should be in the clear and we can start working on how to trip her up."

"Yeah, because that's been so successful." Sourly, I circled around the car.

He climbed in behind the wheel and I ducked inside, glad I wasn't driving this time.

"That's because we're hopping, trying to stay two steps ahead of being made into barbccue. But I've been thinking...and we're heading in the right direction for what I need anyway."

The undertone in his voice had me wary. "Just what are you talking about, Justin?"

In the dim light coming off the dashboard, I could see him smiling. "Relax, Kit. It's all good. I've got a plan."

CHAPTER FOUR

In the watery gray dawn, I stood in the doorway of a house that had been abandoned so long ago; only the skeleton of the walls remained. The floor was stable, mostly stone, nothing that would have rotted away. We'd been able to sleep, and the fireplace had worked so we hadn't frozen.

Fall was turning out to be a cold bitch. I had thought I'd been prepared for the weather. Of course, I hadn't foreseen us making a trip into the higher elevations of Alabama while trying to evade somebody who still remained nameless.

My breath came out in visible clouds as I braced my shoulder against the door. I hadn't had a shower in three days. I hadn't had a cup of coffee in two. I wasn't sure which one pissed me off more.

Justin was behind me, crouched in the dark shadows, grumbling to himself as he continued to dig into the murky cyber shadows online and ferret out information.

We'd had twelve hours of silence. I think maybe we'd managed to throw her.

She wasn't done, not by any means. The last update on the forum had mentioned an additional five grand for somebody who'd point the original poster in the right direction.

"I think we might have a ghost chasing us." Justin's voice sounded oddly disembodied, catching me by surprise.

Running my tongue across my teeth, I thought that through, but I couldn't quite figure out if he meant it in a literal sense or not. "Explain."

His boots scraped over stone as he moved to join me. "There was a cell phone number left on the update. I'm going to call it. Chances are it's just a burner phone, but if this person knows how to use the forums, chances are he knows how to protect himself—herself. We won't be able to track anybody down that way."

"This tells me nothing about any *ghost*."

"I'm getting to that," he said sourly. He took up a position across from me. "You're going to level with me about this job, Kit. Once we're free and clear, you're going to level with me."

I held his eyes, not responding.

Justin came off the door frame and bent over me. "I might have to help take down somebody I used to call friend—somebody I thought was dead. If I end up having to do that, the least you owe me is an explanation."

The bite in his voice was nothing compared to the fury in his eyes. Sighing, I hooked a hand over my neck. "Okay. Okay."

He remained where he was for a long moment, watching me closely. Finally, he nodded and then shoved back, bracing his back against the wall. "I started focusing on the salamander. Should have done that to begin with. Not many witches who have the power and the control to handle one. The thing is…salamanders are rare, but not *that* rare. It's finding a handler that's the big problem. Salamanders are social little creatures and they'd cuddle up to any old witch who can help them spark their fire. They are kind of…" He blew out a breath. "Think of them like a teddy bear that doubles as a flame thrower. Their owner is the on/off switch. A weak witch will turn that power on and then burn out, leaving the salamander stuck in the *burn it all* position."

"That's…problematic," I said slowly.

"Most of them shut down once they realize their handler is gone. It's kind of shocks them." Justin jerked a shoulder in a shrug. "Since getting a salamander *and* finding a witch with the right kind of magic and control is pretty damn rare…well, I started working through those I knew."

"How many is that?"

His mouth twisted. "Five. I thought one of them was dead and I started going through my list and it turns out, one of them died about six months ago—documented death, no question about it."

"There is a question about one of the deaths, though?"

"Nobody ever found her." His gaze slid away, then back to mine. "She just…disappeared. Left her house one day, claiming she was trying to track down a kid who was coming into her magic and she just never came back."

He stopped speaking for a moment. Eyes closed, he blew out a breath and just stood there. After a while, he started to speak again. "She was in Banner for six months, then up and left, said if they wanted to throw her into Blackstone, they could do their best. She left and a few months later, she was gone. Her name was Chaundry."

"What's her house have to say?" I asked, wishing I could offer him something more. But he wouldn't want empty comfort. He'd want what I would want—answers.

That's what we could focus on.

"She's dead. That's what they think. Their…connection to her splintered two weeks after they last saw her."

I knew too much about witches not to understand what he meant by *splintered.* A connection among witches who shared a house went deep—almost soul deep. They had ways of reaching out that defied explanation. Once she pledged to a house—not a physical structure or even a *home*, something almost spiritual—her fellow witches should have been able to reach her.

Only death could break those bonds. Or so I thought.

Judging by the look on Justin's face, I had a feeling his thoughts had gone down the same ugly path mine had gone.

"Okay," I said, nodding slowly. "So you have an idea who could be behind this. And we have an idea of *why*. Now what?"

His smile bordered on deadly. "Now we get on the road. While we drive, I tell you about my plan."

CHAPTER FIVE

Relax…I've got a plan.

I can still remember what Justin had told me as we barreled out of that miserable little town.

Famous last words.

As plans went, this one had sucked and I was going to withhold judgement on whether or not to call it a success.

I had to give it to Justin, it had been an interesting experience. The brackish stink of swamp water filled my nostrils and permeated every inch of my clothes as I hauled myself out of the swamp. The dock was still in one piece. I couldn't say the same for the house across the murky surface of water. Shaking water out of my face, I slid into the pirogue tied to the dock and started to make my way over to the other side. It took too long even though logically, I knew it was only a few minutes. By the time I was able to climb out and haul the little boat up on the land next to me, I felt like hours had passed.

The man lying on the ground hadn't moved since I'd laid eyes on him. "I'm going to kill you," I said to Justin's still form, refusing to acknowledge the knot of fear forming in my gut. "I swear, I'm going to kill you. I had to dive into that swamp and one of my guns is *still* down there."

By the time I fell to his side, my voice was shaking. "It's probably nothing more than gator food now, you dumbass."

His hand twitched.

Some of the fear inside dissolved.

Oh, shit. Oh, fuck.

Bending closer, I put my nose on level with his. "If you try something so stupid as dying, I'm going to tell Damon to skin you and do whatever he wants with your corpse."

"The…" Justin's voice came out in a rasp. "Your boytoy's a pervert. Better…not…risk it."

He cracked open an eye and groaned, one hand reaching down. He'd been inside the cabin, a lure for Chaundry, but she'd realized something wasn't right. I'd been across the swamp, waiting for my shot.

She'd blasted the house into nothingness. I'd screamed a warning for Justin just as I squeezed off a round.

Whether or not he'd heard me, I didn't know. I'd seen his body flying out the back only seconds before the explosion turned the tiny little cabin into nothing more than a memory and smoke. He'd hit the water as I took aim again.

That was when she'd focused on me.

Justin had opened up the earth under her. He had a weak gift for earth magic, weak enough to create a chasm that sent her plummeting down into a pit some six feet deep. A hole that close to the swamp was going to turn into a mud pit pretty damn quick.

I shot it a look before focusing my attention on Justin.

A piece of wood almost twice as thick as my thumb skewered him. "Thinking of masquerading as a shish-kabob?" I quipped as I checked the location. Could be worse. Hadn't hit the gut or kidney. Instead it had gone straight through two ribs and the sickening sound of his breathing made my chest ache in sympathy. Or it could have been my ribs—they still hadn't healed.

He made a groan, wet and thick. "Take it out," he ordered.

"Justin..."

"Take it out," he said again and he opened his eyes, focusing on me. Pain wracked him. "Otherwise you have to move me around with that inside me and it will take too long and hurt like a motherfuck."

I shot another look at the pit. I could hear…something.

"Hurry." His voice was low, urgent.

Swearing, I grabbed the ragged piece of wood and hauled it upward. I came with a sucking, wet noise. He screamed, the sound echoing in the desolation around us.

I had the smallest of first aid kits tucked in the cargo pocket on my hip and it wasn't going to do shit for a punctured lung, but it was all I had for now. Tearing it open, I grabbed the biggest non-stick bandage and pressed it down, leaving one end up. The adhesive clung to his bare skin and I tried to block out the sickening sounds coming from him as he breathed. "I'll do better once we're secure."

"It's fine." He was pale, eyes half wild. "Get me up."

I wanted to hit him. I could have pointed out that he did need to breathe, but I knew as well as he did that it would take more than a punctured lung to kill a witch. At least right away. It would sure as hell slow him down though and the more he moved, the weaker he would get.

But if I didn't help him, he'd get up on his own.

"Bastard," I grumbled, awkwardly helping him up and propping myself under his shoulder. I was so short, it wasn't the easiest solution, but it was the best we had to go with. Knowing he wouldn't go to the car without looking, we made our way to the pit.

She was down there.

In her cupped hands, she held something so small, it could have been overlooked, but it glowed red and as if it sensed me, it lifted its head and stared.

The salamander.

Its handler looked up next.

I had to bite the inside of my cheek to keep the words in my mouth from spilling out. I had no idea what might have come out, but it wouldn't have been polite.

Her eyes were red. Everywhere that should have been white was pure, blood red. Compared to the pale gold of her irises, it was freaky.

She blinked at me and cocked her head, the movement strangely alien.

"Chaundry," Justin said.

She shifted her bizarre gaze to him. He didn't stiffen or react, but I felt his uneasiness.

"Chaundry."

She didn't even seem to realize he was talking to her; her attention flicked back to me.

The little salamander danced about, looking agitated, and she leaned down, whispering to it.

Justin barked out something harsh, one word I didn't recognize.

He flung a hand toward the swamp, the movement knocking us both off balance, and I struggled to keep him upright as a fat stream of swamp water came blasting toward us.

It flooded the hole, deepening the mud and muck until Chaundry was buried in it to the waist.

She was shivering and shaking when he ended the stream of water and the little salamander had curled up in her hair, gripping at it with little claws that too closely resembled hands for my comfort.

Its red skin had lost its brightness and it made a weird trilling noise.

Chaundry shuddered, her eyes blazing bright red as she lifted a hand, prying the scared little thing from her hair. It made another one of those trilling noises.

Without taking her eyes from us, she placed the salamander on her chest and fell back against the wall of the pit and started to slide down.

"Chaundry!" Justin swayed forward, as though he'd reach down and haul her up. He might have tried, if I would have let him.

She pressed the salamander to her chest.

"Stop!"

I didn't realize what was going on until it was too late. Justin had already figured it out.

It was over in seconds, the stink of charred flesh now overlaying the scents of water and earth and mud. Chaundry started to slip beneath the surface of the muddy water in the bottom of the pit, her eyes blind…lifeless.

There was a perfectly round hole twice the size of my fist in the middle of her chest—her skin melted, blackened…burned. There was hardly any blood, because the heat of the salamander had cauterized all the vessels as she sent him through her chest.

A flicker of movement caught my eye.

The salamander, trying to crawl up the slick side of the wall.

Justin wavered again, almost taking me down with him. He lifted a hand and a second later, something round and covered with mud came out of the pit. It spun around dizzyingly, sending mud flying.

It was a cage, I noticed dimly. It scooped up the salamander and came drifting toward me.

"Take it," he said hoarsely. "Can't leave him here. Not safe."

I snatched it out of the air and managed to turn us around, the two of us lurching toward the copse in the trees where Justin had stashed his car. "One foot in front of the other, you sorry jerk. We need to get out of here."

I had a split second of warning—just a shiver of awareness and that was it. Coming to a sudden stop, I jerked my head up and looked around.

"That would be ideal."

At the sound of that voice, I tensed. Only for a fraction of a second, but the small voice in the back of my head kicked me for allowing even that. *Move, girl…why are you so slow?*

I dropped, steadying Justin as best I could while drawing the Glock from my hip. I couldn't see anybody. *Shit.* Why hadn't I heard her—him—here???

"Come out," I said, keeping my voice level.

Nobody moved and after a second, I said it again. *"Come out."* Adrenaline kicked in, sharpening my hearing and my vision. While nothing stood out in the dappled shadows cast by the moonlight through the spindly trees, I could hear something.

A heartbeat, breathing.

I focused on it. "If you have eyes—and I expect you do—then you can see the gun I'm pointing at you. Come out. Now."

"A gun." There was a dry chuckle. "A gun, really? That is the weapon you choose?"

"It goes with the moment. Come out."

A prickle raced down my spine, eerie and full of awareness. The shift in the shadows caused no noise. She was in front of me so suddenly, if I hadn't known somebody was there, it would have scared the life out of me.

Although she was utterly sexless, I knew without a doubt I was facing a woman—and although.

Although I'd been waiting, I was still caught off-guard.

She slid into the dappled moonlight, clad in a motley mix of gray and brown, looking like she belonged to the night. She bladed her body, presenting the smallest target possible. Still, it was hard to guess at her body weight, even her height, thanks to the way she'd layered her clothing and I knew it was intentional. She was slumping as well. She could be tall and thin or average height and dumpy—I couldn't really tell.

All of it done intentionally, but I had no idea if it was an effort to mask what sort of opponent she'd be or if there was another purpose.

"Who are you?" I asked. Still crouched by Justin, I kept my gun leveled on the spot between her eyes. Bladed or not, at this range, I couldn't miss and with the Glock. It really *did* go with the moment.

"That isn't your concern, I don't think."

"I'm going to have to disagree." Next to me, Justin shoved himself upward with a pained grunt and there was another one of those wet, sucking sounds that made me cringe internally. "Who are you?"

But she continued to speak, ignoring me completely.

Snapping my jaw shut with an irritated snap, I listened.

"Your area of concern *should* be getting out of here. As your friend is injured, you have even less time." Those eyes glittered as she jutted her chin toward the pit where Chaundry's body remained. The dirt walls were slowly crumpling around her and she'd likely remain there, for always.

That would be her tomb, a pit of dirt and mud.

"She wasn't working alone. She is not the one hunting you. She was just the one they thought would to get the closest. Should you really remain here?"

Alarm started to shriek down my spine. Instinct screamed at me, like a siren in my head. *Go, go, go…go.*

I could have argued, disagreed. Chaundry had spent the past ten days chasing after us with a lot more success than I cared to admit. She *had* been hunting us. But was she alone?

Justin hadn't been able to figure out why she'd been after us.

Neither had I.

It only stood to reason somebody had been manipulating her.

The knowledge blooming in my brain made my skin crawl, though I wasn't surprised. Part of me head already clicked onto this bit of knowledge. There were other players at stake. One possible idea filled me with a fury so potent, I could almost feel his neck giving way under my blade.

But that didn't make sense.

Slowly, I lowered the weapon in my hand. It only dipped a fraction, but it was enough to signify something important to the woman. She shifted to face me fully and when she did, I saw moonlight glint off a blade. She didn't lift it though.

"Go." The word came out clear and full of command.

I'm not big on command, but there was something so intrinsic in that word that it made me pause and in that pause, my instincts started to scream at me.

Hell yes, I'd go.

But only because *I* wanted to. I'm contrary that way.

"Come on," I said to Justin, helping him up. Fear chittered inside me as I realized just how weak he'd gotten. As we backed toward the car, both of us watched her and I saw that his hand was flickering with red. Fire. His most basic magic. Every witch, even those who didn't have mastery over fire could use it to some small extent and he was expending what was left of his energy to give us that extra weapon.

"It's okay," I told him.

I don't know if he heard me.

We were ten feet from the car when she turned her back to me.

By the time we got in the car, she was lost to the night.

She was quiet. So quiet. My ears hadn't even picked up a footfall, not even a heartbeat this time. And I knew she was gone.

CHAPTER SIX

"I'm getting really tired of constantly having my hands in your guts," Colleen said.

She was absolutely not joking.

It had taken me entirely too long to get Justin someplace safe.

That was an hour south of the armpit where we'd trapped Chaundry, and each moment I'd feared would be his last.

Once I'd been certain nobody was following us, I'd called Colleen and demanded she tell me where the safest, closest witch house was and how soon she could get there.

She'd sworn at me like a sailor and then told me about a Red Branch house that was on good terms with Green Road.

It was just past the Florida State Line and to be honest, I wasn't really surprised it was part of Red Branch. They were warriors, almost all of them and if somebody were going to be that close to the Georgia/Florida border, it would be Red Branch. They weren't afraid of a fight.

Even though Justin was the one who was spilling blood all over Colleen, he didn't respond. Then again, he wasn't even conscious. He was so pale, I could practically see through him.

His head lolled to the side and even when she jabbed a needle through the torn flesh, he didn't move. He was lost to the pain and whatever brew Colleen had given him. It wouldn't last long, but whatever respite he'd have I was grateful for. Witches couldn't handle real pain meds—too often they turned out to be more harmful than helpful, but a good witch could mix up herbal brews that would offer some relief.

Justin's heartbeat faltered. I could hear it.

Colleen would sense it.

I saw her mouth flatten out. I rubbed her shoulder. "He'll be fine. And you do know that we don't *try* to get into these scrapes."

"You don't have to try." Colleen slanted a look at me. "I think these scrapes hunt you down and jump on you."

She had a point. Shifting my attention to Justin, I focused on his face, all but willing some of my strength into him.

"Okay…" It seemed forever before Colleen was finished and when she lowered the tools she'd used to close the wound, her hands were shaking. She was almost as pale as he was. We shared a grim look before she turned her attention back to him. "I'm saving my strength to deal with the rest of him, that's why I stitched him up rather than healed this. His lung is a mess. *All* of him is a mess by now."

A sharp pain hit me square at the base of my skull, a painful reminder of the headache I'd been ignoring.

Colleen sensed something and she shot me a look.

"I'm fine," I said sourly. "He needs you more than I do." There was a remnant ache in my ribs from the two I'd broke, but they were mostly healed and I felt worn to the bone. Beyond that, there was nothing wrong with me that some rest and food wouldn't cure.

Something else washed over me, something that almost made me forget the pain in my head—a heated rush of prickling warmth that slid across my skin. Focusing my eyes on Colleen, I asked slowly, "Did you bring company, Coll?"

"I wouldn't say I *brought* company." She had her hands on Justin's torso, one above the now-closed wound just off the midline of his torso and the other over his heart. "I'd have to go with *company* brought *me*."

Finally, she looked up. "I was racing out of town like a bat out of hell. Somebody must have reported it back to him—which, by the way, pisses me off. Let him know that. He sort of…pounced down in front of me and asked if he could join me. I guess he figured only one or two people could have me moving like that."

"She figures right."

That low, rumbling voice had my heart—and other parts—of me tightening. I turned to see a familiar form filling the doorway and I had to admit, the sight of Damon Lee was almost enough to chase away the fog of exhaustion that kept trying to overtake me.

He came around the bed, eyes never leaving my face. I wanted to jump up and grab him. Before I could put thought into action, Colleen's voice cut through the air and I whipped around to see Justin arching upward, mouth open in a silent scream.

"What the hell?" I caught his shoulders and held him down.

Damon pinned his thrashing legs.

"Infection. Already settling in. Burning it out." Colleen's voice was brusque. "The tonic I gave him is burning off, too. He's hurting."

Damon's hands were as effective as steel clamps. Over Justin's taut body, he and I stared at each other. "Hi, honey," I finally said. "I'm home. Well, almost."

A wry grin twisted his lips. "So I see. Funny that the local neighborhood witch gets the call, but I don't."

"Well, my hands were full." Justin made a strangled sound deep in his throat and I flicked my eyes to my friend before looking up at Damon. "As you can probably tell."

"True enough."

Colleen murmured to Justin as she shifted her hands, placing both of them over his ribs. The words coming from her were low, making no sense but I doubted they needed to. They were intended to soothe, comfort. She probably wasn't even aware she was doing it.

Damon studied me closely, no doubt searching for whatever injuries might be hidden under my clothes.

"I'm fine." Now really wasn't the time to discuss what had happened in Tallahassee, so I went with the safer version. "Busted a few ribs, but they've healed. There are some bruises and I'm exhausted and hungry."

Damon's eyes probed mine and I suspected he didn't entirely believe me, but he didn't call me on it, either.

"Finish the job?"

"No." I couldn't keep the disgust out of my voice and my hands tightened on Justin's shoulders until Colleen had to tell me to ease up. Focusing on a spot on the wall, I thought about just how far left-field this job had gone. The target we'd been assigned to watch was *dead*. Did that count as finishing?

Damon quirked a thick, black brow. There would be questions later.

"Okay," Colleen said, her voice heavy with exhaustion. "Wounds are closed and he's stabilized, or as much as he can be since he's running at about sixty percent of his blood flow. I'm going to have to start an IV."

I shot her a look. She held up a blood-stained hand. "I don't like it either. But it's nothing more than saline—that's a fairly natural component and typically, our bodies accept it rather well. If we don't restore the fluid balance, he's going to take three times longer to heal."

"I should have gotten him here quicker."

Damon came up behind me and stroked a hand up my spine.

"You got him here quicker than anybody could expect." Colleen shook her head, looking disgusted. "The two of you have to go around chasing trouble."

On the bed, Justin groaned, the sound almost nonexistent.

"The tonic's worn off," she said wearily.

I eased closer, but a soft murmur escaped him.

I straightened, sliding a look back at Colleen.

It wasn't a wordless noise that time. It was her name.

Her face flushed and she moved in, settling down at his side. "Save your strength, big guy," she said. "You went and watered half of Alabama with your blood. You need to recover."

But he was already asleep.

I left in silence, Damon falling in step at my side.

The stone floor echoed hollowly under my feet and I moved on autopilot for a few seconds before realizing I had no idea where to go. I'd gotten inside the walls of the local Red Branch house and we'd immediately been whisked away to the medical ward.

House was disingenuous.

Fort was more like it. I had a feeling the end of the world could happen outside these walls and those inside Red Branch would carry on unaffected. They raised their own crops, had their own livestock and didn't give a damn about anything outside their walls.

The words *self-reliant* came to mind.

Damon stopped next to me and I said levelly, "I have no idea where I'm going."

"With me." He slid a hand down my arm and linked our fingers. "Come on, kitten."

Listless, I let him guide me down one hall after another, so turned around now that a trail of breadcrumbs wouldn't have done me any good at all.

We ended up in a sizeable room, one with a bed to match and that bed looked like nirvana. I stared at it longingly before searching the rest of the room. There was a door on the far wall, and behind that wall there was a bathroom. I could have whimpered in relief.

Hearing the faintest noise from Damon, I turned and stared at him. "I need food. I need a shower. I need sleep." He took another step toward me. "You're going to have to grill me after that."

He came up to me, face impassive. When those big arms came around me, a hundred knots seemed to unravel and I pressed my face against his chest.

"You, you, you," Damon rumbled in my ear before pressing his face to my neck. "How about what I need?"

Weakly, I laughed. "And what do you need?"

"This. So be quiet a minute."

That was easy enough. Just standing there in his arms took away some of the raw edges that last few days had dug into me. When he scooped me up into his arms, I didn't even protest.

He shouldered the bathroom door open and I tipped my head back to study him. "If you're thinking about engaging in some sort of watersports, big guy, I'm not sure I'm up to it."

"You can close your eyes and sleep if you want. I don't mind."

My snicker turned into a gasp as he let my lower body drop to the floor, keeping me pressed up against him in a way that made it clear I wasn't likely to sleep. "If you don't mind..."

He smiled against my mouth as he slid his hands under my shirt. It was ruined—stained and ripped and it smelled of swamp water—but that didn't keep him from stripping it away as though it were made of gossamer. When it fell to the floor, he lowered his head and pressed his lips to the curve of my shoulder.

"You getting sleepy yet?" he asked after skimming his lips across my torso to my other shoulder.

Under the sturdy material of the bra I'd pulled on, my nipples were hard and tight.

Down lower, I was aching.

No. Sleepy didn't touch on what I felt.

"I'm not sure...you aren't putting much effort into this. I probably should catch some rest."

His mouth closed over mine. It took less than thirty seconds for him to deal with my cargo pants and boots and not even that long to maneuver us into the shower.

I was shoving hair out of my face when he tore off his clothes, right as he turned the shower on, he said teasingly, "You ready to get some rest, Kit?"

I thought I was going to say something. I had no idea what. But I thought I was going to say something. The words died on the tip of my tongue as he lifted me up and braced me against the wall, thrusting deep, deep into me.

I felt like I was home.

Food was waiting in the room when we came out. I was more than a little embarrassed by the fact but clearly, Damon wasn't.

Not that I was surprised…by any of it.

He might as well walk around showcasing the scratches I left on him, he was that proud of them. That somebody might have overheard us in the bathroom didn't bother him at all. He nudged me toward the bed. "Sit down before you fall down."

"I'm not eating in bed."

"Wanna bet?" His brows came down in a hard, straight line over his eyes. "You are about ready to fall asleep on your face. How long has it been since you had any real sleep?"

"A few days." With an evasive shrug, I made my way over to the bed. I wasn't even sure when I'd eaten last. I didn't want to point that out, either.

His mouth drew into a flat, hard line. "Exactly what all went wrong with this job?"

"That's a question." Bunching the blankets up to my lap, I rubbed at my throat. I'd taken some tonic a witch had offered me earlier— she'd said it would help with the smoke. I'd stared at her blankly and she told me I smelled like smoke and my voice was raw.

Up until I'd drank the brew, I hadn't realized how raw my throat was. Now that it was wearing off, I wanted more.

"Maybe I'll let you sleep." He bent over me, braced his fists on either side of my hips. "As long as you take the medicine they brought in for you."

I made a face at him. He kissed the tip of my nose.

"And as long as you agree to tell me once you get some rest."

"As long as I get food to go along with whatever poison they are giving me." Glum, I stared at the simple tin mug they'd put on the tray. I had no doubt it was the brew for my throat. I think it was their way of torturing people. Making the tonics and brews and potions taste like shit. There *were* herbal remedies that didn't taste bad. Not that I knew how to make them.

Damon returned with a plate loaded with vegetables, meat, and cheese. Heavy on the meat. My cat was a big believer in the benefits of protein. Rolling up a slice of cheese and some of the roast beef, I nipped off a bite and accepted the cup he put in my hand. I drained half of it.

Damon lifted a brow.

"Better off to get it over with. Is there some water? I feel like I'm dying of thirst." I was probably dehydrated, considering how hard we had been running.

I scraped at an itchy spot on my right arm and took another bite. He came back with water, but withheld it until I finished the toxic sludge in the cup. Once I had that down, I guzzled the tall, cold glass of water and then pushed the food away.

I couldn't eat any more. I was fighting to keep my eyes open.

"You need to eat more."

"Give me a minute," I said, the words coming out slurred. Adrenaline had kept me going until Justin and I were safe, but there was nothing left.

"Yeah, right. You're about to fall asleep."

"Am *not*." But I was.

And I did.

CHAPTER SEVEN

Justin no longer looked like death warmed over.

Now he just looked like he'd been living at a refugee camp for a couple of months.

Colleen had kept him in bed for hours. I had no idea how she had done it. It was possible she'd tied him to the bed—or threatened to. His eyes were sunken as he glanced up at me from over the rim of the bowl he held.

He'd lost weight in the past week. Typical for an injured NH who wasn't able to eat to keep up with the demands being put on his body. He'd powered through his reserves like a kid in a growth spurt, only faster.

"You look like shit," he said bluntly.

"Looked in a mirror lately?" I sat on the edge of the bed. "At least I don't have shadows under my eyes thick enough to hide in."

He started to shrug but stopped with a wince.

"That hurt?"

At his baleful look, I just gave him a serene smile. "You had a piece of wood the size of a cue stick inside do you. You might want to take it easy."

He flipped me off.

Behind me, Damon curved his hand over the back of my neck. "Your pretty witch isn't so pretty today, Kit. Somebody kicked him around a little too hard, I think."

"Kiss ass, furface," Justin said, unperturbed.

Damon didn't respond, dropping soundlessly into the chair near the window.

"It's so nice to see the two of you getting along. It just warms my heart." I drew one knee to my chest and rested my chin on it. Focusing my eyes on Justin, I asked, "How are you feeling?"

"Like I had a piece of wood the size of a cue stick going through me." He gave me a wry grin. "I never understood just how good it felt *breathing* until I was drowning in my own blood. Collapsed lung, Kit. I don't recommend it."

"I'll take that on advisement."

He laughed. "How long you been here? You still get your phrases twisted up. You'll take *it under* advisement."

"I've been here long enough to know that the English language is one of the stupidest ones there is. The rules don't make sense and the phrases are weird. A month of Sundays—what's that mean? And how about the pronunciations? The words comb and tomb? Fish and pharmacy?" With a roll of my eyes, I shrugged his comment away.

I'd spent more than half of my life at Aneris Hall, located on a remote island, protected from mortal eyes. Set apart from even the closest country, it might as well be trapped in a time from centuries past. Modern comforts, technology, none of that had any sway.

"Colleen says you're good to travel. Do you feel up to it?"

Instead of answering right away, Justin finished the soup and set the bowl aside. His vivid green eyes locked on my face and he eased higher up in the bed, pinning me in place with his gaze.

"I can travel. But I want answers. I think you owe me that." His gaze slid from me to Damon at my hesitation. "Your man got any idea how close you came to being flambé, Kitty?"

"Don't." I pointed a finger at him. "You're not going to wield him over my head."

Still, I felt Damon's gaze cut toward me. I'd managed to put him off, because I knew I'd get it from Justin and I didn't want to get hammered twice today.

Justin eased a knee up and braced his elbow on it, staring me down. The intimidation factor would have been considerably more if he hadn't looked so sallow. He was considerably paler than normal—his mixed race normally gave him a nice, warm glow, but he looked rough and raw.

His eyes, though, they were unblinking. "For the record, I'm not threatening anything. I'm just wondering if he can offer some insight about this bullshit job. He hasn't ever come running quite so fast before—protective as he is, he knows you can take care of yourself. Which makes me think he's worried about this job."

Now he slanted Damon a measuring look.

Damon's face was an unreadable mask, but I had a bad feeling that Justin's logic was right on the mark.

"I don't think it's the *job*." I resisted the urge to pull out a knife and make it dance. "I think it's my client—he doesn't like him."

Neither do I.

"Okay. Give me some more insight then. We were supposed to be providing surveillance." Justin's voice grew hard. "*Surveillance,* Kit. You see only one person coming and going and two days into the job, things go sideways and the target turns the tables on us. Turns out she's a witch with a very unique power and somebody I'd written off as dead. When we finally get her cornered, she looks at me like she doesn't know me, then she commits suicide right in front of us. And then—"

"Okay." I cut him off. I don't know what drove me to interrupt him before he could mention the nameless woman who had had sent us a warning—not once, but twice. I knew in my gut she was the woman who'd called me with that vague warning to *move*...right before the salamander came calling. "Okay. Just...shit, Justin. Breathe before you make Colleen come in here and throw us out."

Shoving off the bed, I paced over to the window. I wanted more time to think this all through, but I didn't have it. Damon watched me from under his lashes and I knew I was going to get a whole lot of questions from him. Every time I thought I might be able to avoid dragging him into what I did, something else happened.

"I wasn't—" I stopped and shook my head. I didn't even have any idea to go about explaining this. We were in a place that was a secure as I could hope to find. And yet, I didn't want to *talk* about this here. Or *anywhere*.

He deserves to know why.

Squaring my shoulders, I turned to face him. "While you were taking your week long beauty rest, I took on a very unusual...client. He wanted to hire me exclusively, but I told him that wasn't happening but he did put me on retainer—paying...insanely well."

"At this point, I've worked two other jobs; both were simple surveillance jobs, lasting no more than two days. He's told me most of the jobs would be in that vein, odd jobs, surveillance jobs, typically. But occasionally he would send me after people who might be able to offer some insight on Blackstone."

Justin's eyes sharpened at that. I now had his undivided attention.

Blackstone had been on our radars for months now.

"I'll admit, the only reason I found it at all appealing was because of the possible connections to Blackstone." Crossing my arms over my chest, I turned back to the window. Misgivings had shown up fast and hard, especially once he'd tried to get me to work exclusively for him—he'd even offered lodgings closer to D.C. Right in the thick of things, he'd claimed, would be more *convenient*. My gut had shrieked a warning at that.

"If it wasn't for the hope that I might get closer to Blackstone, I would have told him to fuck off. Albeit a bit more diplomatically."

"Kit, you wouldn't know diplomatic if it bit you on the ass." Justin snorted.

"True enough, but this time I would have managed. You see… this client was somebody who could cause trouble for a lot of people." I looked back at him, slicking my suddenly damp hands down the sides of my trousers.

Justin canted his head to the side. "Yeah, who was it? The president? I don't see anybody else making you go for *diplomacy*." He flicked at something on the sheet.

No doubt, Justin had expected his sarcastic comment to be met with an equally sarcastic reply.

"Yes."

The absolute lack of humor in my voice caught his attention and slowly, he looked up.

A few seconds of dead silence passed. Finally, he tried for a smile. "You're bullshitting me."

"No."

"I only wish." Now I moved closer to the bed, unconsciously hugging myself. "And you want to hear something else? The man is *not* human."

Justin came off the bed, moving too quick for his injured body to protest the movement, although the moment his brain registered it, he was pale and clutching his ribs. Swaying on his feet, he floundered for something to steady himself.

Damon was already there, nudging him down none too gently. "Stay on your ass, you idiot." He remained where he was, eyes on me.

Justin didn't even respond, clutching at his side, face pale from strain—but I don't think he really registered the pain. He stared at me in dumbfounded shock. "That's not possible, Kit. Whitmore *is* human."

"No, he's not."

Justin shook his head. "I've *met* him, Kit. He bleeds red, white, and blue and has a great big *fuck you* to anything not human."

Now it was my turn to look dumbfounded. Shifting my attention to Damon, I tried to make the adjustment from what Justin was telling me to what I'd seen for myself.

A discreet knock on the door kept me from thinking too long.

Head spinning, I tried to make myself move over to open it, but Damon got there before I did.

One of the witches from Red Branch stood there. She gave Damon a deferential nod and held out a phone. "Your second in command would like to speak with you. He tells us that you're not answering your cell."

Damon just nodded and took the phone.

She hesitated a moment and then offered, "The line is secure, Alpha. We respect the privacy of our fellows."

Then she left, pulling the door shut behind her.

I dropped down to sit on the edge of the bed, shoving my hands into my hair and tugging at it rhythmically in hopes of jarring loose some key bit of information.

"You're sure, Justin?"

"Yeah."

Damon spoke in low tones to Chang, but we could both hear him—Damon at least. I heard Chang, too, and they weren't even a minute into the conversation when my gut went cold and tight.

Slowly, Damon looked up, pinning me with a grim look. "Apparently your client is having trouble getting a hold of you, Kit. Any reason why that might be?"

"My phone was damaged." By my foot. I didn't add that part in.

Damon gave a nod and repeated that back to Chang.

I heard Chang promising to relay the message.

"Is he getting pushy?" I demanded.

"Nothing I can't handle, Kit." I heard the polite amusement in his voice as he answered my question before resuming his conversation with his Alpha. "Damon, will you be back soon?"

"Yeah." He focused on me, eyes thoughtful. "Do me a favor, Chang. Start trying to see what you can uncover about her…client. Everything. But be very, very quiet about it."

"And here I thought traipsing about like a bull in china shop would be more fitting," Chang said calmly. "As it would happen, I've been reaching out to my sources already. Some unsettling information has reached my ears. I thought it would be best to see what is going on."

Damon's response was a grunt. He disconnected without saying anything else and then he tossed the phone down.

"How was your phone damaged?"

"It met an unfortunate ending with my boot heel." With a nonchalant shrug, I flicked the question away as though it meant nothing. "I haven't gotten around to replacing it yet."

"Unfortunate. I guess that explains why you haven't touched base with me, either."

With a brilliant smile, I said, "It does."

The smile faded, though, and fast as I focused back on what Justin had said. "When did you meet him?"

"Before he became our esteemed president. He was just a lowly congressman." Justin shifted around and braced his back against the headboard, eyes dark and grim. "But he was most *definitely* human, Kit. I was brought in back when I was still with Banner. He'd had somebody sending his office...well, we can't call them threats. They were more ominous warnings than anything else. The writer was smart, knew how to walk the right line. Turns out it was somebody who worked for him—kid's mother was a witch, she'd died in the wars. The kid had ended up in the foster care system...long story short, hid all this hate and ended up getting an internship for the guy. When Whitmore found out, he belted the kid before any of us could stop him, attacked him. The look in his eyes..."

Justin shrugged. "As it was, because of the way Whitmore had acted, the kid ended up getting a slap on the wrist. Now leads one of the larger activist groups for NH rights. But I had my *hands* on Whitmore, Kit. I touched him. He's all human."

The taut silence was so thick, I thought it would choke me.

Damon was the one who broke it when he asked, "Did he know you were bringing Justin?"

"No." Shaking my head, I crossed my arms over my chest and tilted my head back, staring upward. "Justin showed up about an hour after the call. I almost told him no, but I had a feeling..."

Justin swore.

I leveled my head and stared at him.

But he had closed his eyes. "You and your damn feelings, Kit."

I didn't have anything to say to that.

CHAPTER EIGHT

Hauling ass to Orlando didn't really appeal, but sitting within the confines of the safety of Red Branch didn't appeal either.

They'd been decent enough to take us in, but Justin and I—or at least *I*—had some weird sort of target on my ass and if I was going to draw attention to myself, better to do it somewhere else.

So I'd do it at home. With other non-involved parties.

That idea didn't settle all that great either, but home was where you went when trouble came calling, or some shit like that. I thought. Besides, something weird was going on and neither Justin nor I could hope to untangle it if I kept my head tucked down.

I'm pretty sure Damon would rather me untangle things back there anyway—then he can tear off the heads of anybody who decides to try to come at my back, and damn the consequences.

Granted, that wasn't the way to handle this.

And Justin thought I couldn't be diplomatic.

Once I'd gotten back to East Orlando, I'd made him stop so I could get a new phone. Colleen and Justin had broken off some miles behind us, Colleen driving Justin's car. One of the witches from Red Branch had promised to deliver her car within a week or so after she'd voiced some reserve about letting him drive alone.

I doubted he'd pass out behind the wheel, but I wasn't going to point that out to a healer. There were some people you just didn't argue with. Ogres. New mamas. A healer with her charge. A woman in love. I wondered if she'd ever tell him.

Of course, once or twice, I'd seen him looking at her in a certain way and I had to admit, I wondered if it was necessary. He didn't let her see it, though. Maybe Justin was determined to keep himself closed off. He and I had once had a thing, but I'd been…safe, I think. He'd known what we had wouldn't last. If he let himself fall for Colleen, *that* would last.

And love was scary.

Screw facing psychotic vampires or sociopathic first-water demonesses. Love was the thing that could do a person in.

I should know. The biggest weakness I had was eying the piece of shit phone I'd bought with the same look I might have given a dime-store knife.

"You plan on using *that*?"

"Yes. Because if I end up having to trash it, I don't want to be out a decent phone." I sliced through the packaging and popped the device out. While it wasn't *exactly* a throw-back to earliest days of cellular communication, it was the very bottom of the bottom line. That was fine. It would take calls and make calls. It would take texts and make texts. No video. That was fine. Right then, it seemed wise to keep my communication with one Mr. Whitmore—or maybe one pseudo Mr. Whitmore—very limited.

"What's the issue with the phone?" Damon asked, his level voice not quite hiding the tension inside him.

I caught my lower lip between my teeth, let it roll out as I pondered my answer. Finally, I said, "If it wasn't for the fact that you can scent track, if I wanted to hide from you, you'd never find me."

His hands blanched. That's how tight they went on the steering wheel. Something cracked, and I reached up, resting my hand on his arm. "Relax, I'm not trying to say something here."

"Then out with it," he said, voice ragged.

"I…" Blowing out a breath, I rested my head on the pillowed back of the seat. "If I got in a car and drove and drove and drove, made sure to not stop long enough for my scent to catch, just kept on moving, eventually, it would be impossible for anybody to find me, except for Doyle. Even he would have to have help right now."

Doyle was Damon's ward—and oddly enough, somehow kin to me. I didn't understand that; maybe I never would. But he was the only other person like me—*aneiri*—outside my native home that I'd ever met. That he would be *here*, in the place *I* had decided to call home after years of running was beyond unsettling and I was starting to wonder if maybe it wasn't just coincidence.

My kind had been created to hunt, to track…to kill. Assassins, thieves, we moved in the shadows, lived in them. We were as home there as a fish was in water. At least, the good ones were. But I'd never been a very good *aneira*.

My half-human side had made me repugnant in the eyes of my kin and that was why I'd left. Still, I couldn't leave behind the parts that were ingrained.

"Nobody has ever been successful in hunting me down if I didn't want to be found," I said softly. "But that witch?"

I looked over at Damon. "She found us. Both Justin and me."

Damon frowned, shooting me a look before focusing back on the road. He slowed, taking the final turn that would lead us to the Lair. "Any number of reasons could explain that."

"True enough. But not long after I ditched those phones, she tried a new tact. I don't think it was just coincidence. It's possible she could have locked onto the cell signal being emitted from the phones, but both Justin and I use scramblers. It wouldn't be that easy for the typical Jones to locate somebody using their phone."

Damon's lips quirked up.

I rolled my eyes, already suspecting I'd messed up the phrase, but I didn't care. "Justin could do it. I doubt I'd be able to. Would this witch have the knowledge? Would *you*?"

"Is that your subtle way of asking if I track you?"

"No." As the car slowed to a stop in front of the Lair, something in me relaxed. *Home. Safe.* I could breathe for a little while. Could think. Plan. "If you wanted to track me, you'd put Chang on it. Then I'd find out and kick you in the balls."

"Exactly. But no…I couldn't figure it out. I'd have to put Chang on it." He slanted a look at me. "No, I've never asked him. I know you'd find out and kick me in the balls."

I smiled at him as I reached for the handle. "You understand me so well." Before I could get out, he reached over, caught my hand.

"You need to think long and hard before you accept any more jobs from this guy, kitten."

"Technically, once tomorrow comes around, I'm not required to."

"He's going to try to twist you up. Be ready for it."

Tension gathered at the base of my neck, pulsating like a bomb waiting to explode. "I already am."

I put off calling Whitmore. I needed a good night's sleep in my own bed—without stressing about things—and I needed to think. I *could* put him off too—because, hey, he didn't have my number.

That wouldn't stop him from knowing I was in town if he had goons watching—assuming the goons were any good, so I opted to err on the side of caution. I assumed they *were* good and pulled out all the stops, leaving Damon's without telling anybody, including him the next day.

When I didn't want to be seen, I simply wouldn't be seen. Although it didn't work all that well if I decided to drive.

Cars being driven by invisible people caught attention.

There were remotely operated vehicles, but they weren't often seen driving around in East Orlando. The licenses to handle such a vehicle were pricey, and NHs were deemed to *unreliable* to responsibly use much of the drone-operated tech that existed in the world.

That was fine.

Most of us preferred to be more hands-on with things anyway.

But it did mean I couldn't get into a car and pretend it was driving itself.

It wasn't an issue to take the distance to my office on foot. I had some work to do, and I wasn't going to do it at the Lair.

Circling around and watching for those who might be watching for *me* was more time consuming than the five-mile jog to my place of business. And yes, there were two cars. One on the main cross street, another in the miserable armpit of a strip mall across from me. The strip mall mostly stayed in business because of a 'massage' parlor where a couple of female shifters and one male offered their services to anybody willing to pony up the dough. They ran a clean ship and I was well aware of the fact that they kept an eye on me, thanks to my relationship with their alpha.

The other businesses were a tax office—they were everywhere—and a diner.

There used to be a bookstore, but it hadn't been able to stay open. That kind of sucked because I loved to read. I know one of the girls from the massage parlor had gone in there pretty often, too.

A hooker and a smart-mouthed swordswoman had been their best customers. Probably not enough to keep them rolling.

The men watching me had opted for a beat-up car of indiscriminate color, and a make that didn't particularly stand out. And yet, standing there with one shoulder braced against a utility pole that hadn't been connected to anything in operation for over a decade, my gaze zeroed in on that car as if it had been a brand new Rolls Royce, fresh off the line and painted some atrocious color like lime-green.

"Does the alpha's pretty lady need a distraction?"

The voice came from behind, low and discreet.

I glanced back, knowing that whoever it was couldn't see me. I was still hiding behind the veil of invisibility. But that didn't keep whoever it was from smelling or hearing me.

It was Jana, the girl from the massage parlor who liked to read and her male counterpart, Rogan.

They sauntered up the sidewalk at a slow pace, without a care in the world, looking at each other.

But the question had been directed at me.

"Did the Lair call you?"

"Hmmm..." Jana twirled her hair around her finger. "We were told you might be heading this way. Should we distract them?"

Well, it might be easier. "Sure. Have at it. But don't needle them."

Rogan flashed a wide grin, one that made his too-pretty face even prettier. It was no wonder the massage parlor was in no danger of going under. It had been my experience that the cats were rather...odd about their sex lives. They weren't at all prudes, but it seemed like until they were ready to settle down, most of them avoided getting involved sexually with any one person. But they were also intensely...well...sexual.

Jana had once told me that she provided a service and nothing more. That was *all* she was interested in, too. She'd had a mate, and now that he was gone? She didn't want anybody else.

They moved past me, Jana's hips swinging while Rogan rested a hand at the base of her spine, just above her butt. She wore a pair of shorts so brief they could barely be called that. Panties was almost more accurate. The tank top was form-fitting, while her hair spilled down strong, sleek shoulders. She was beautiful and sexy, and undeterred by the stoic faces of the men staring out at her when she paused by the car.

"Hello, gentlemen. Now you boys do know that this isn't exactly the kind of establishment meant to...cater to your needs?"

While she was providing a very, very tempting distraction, I

SHADOWED BLADE

shoved away from the utility pole.

I didn't go in through the front.

They might notice the door swinging open, no matter how intriguing Jana's bust line was.

There was a window on the side—in the narrow bathroom stall—tucked up high. It was so small, it didn't look like anybody but a child could fit through it.

I could.

I'd done it before, several times over, just in case.

I liked having escape routes.

Or in this case, entry routes.

Getting the window to open from the outside took a little more finesse, and I mentally scolded myself for not making such plans. I'd have to put some thought into this, but then again, I hadn't foreseen I'd have to break into my own office.

Regardless, I was inside in under ninety seconds. Closing the window behind me, I stood there for a few seconds, taking everything in. Nothing moved. Nothing breathed.

Everything was as still and as quiet as I'd left it.

Except for the note taped to my mirror.

"What the—" I bit back the near soundless whisper as I eased closer, staring at the note.

As you've demonstrated considerable intelligence thus far, I will assume you came in through the window. Please exit the same way immediately. Your office has ears. Do not go home. Those same electronic ears are there as well.

The script was elegant and flowing, an old-world style that didn't belong on the ripped-off sheet of recycled paper.

A shiver went down my spine and I grabbed the note, immediately turning back to the window.

Ninety seconds to get in.

Getting out took far less.

It didn't matter. The car across the street was already whipping around and speeding my way.

They wouldn't see me, but that wouldn't keep them from searching and now they'd know—*Whitmore* would know—that I was

61

leery of something. Of course, if Whitmore wasn't up to anything, it wouldn't be a big deal. I'd have egg on my face for doubting somebody who was paying me damn well.

But if he was up to something...

Fuck.

I didn't leave the area.

I could have. Maybe I should have. But I wanted to know what was going on. Circling around, I cut across the street, keeping a wide berth between me and the shifters at the massage parlor. When one of them casually glanced my way, I said, "Stay back. I just want to know what they are up to."

My phone buzzed.

Damon calling.

I ignored it.

No doubt somebody had notified their mighty ruler.

No doubt that same somebody could let him know I was all hale and hearty.

I was also pissed off. Two hard bodies in custom suits had broken down my door when nobody had answered it.

"I'm over here, dumbasses."

Across the parking lot, Jana hid a smile behind her hand. Rogan ran his fingers down her thigh. "It's a beautiful afternoon, Jana."

"Yes. Too bad they're human. I could have used some company until my next client comes in."

My hearing was acute and over their playful banter, I could hear disgruntled voices. "The alarm went off. The bathroom window— voices."

"I know, I know. But there's nobody here!"

"Son of a..." The speaker bit the rest of his words off as a phone rang. I had the pleasure of listening to a one-sided conversation, because the distance was too far for me to pick up the caller's voice. "Yes, sir. We...no, we came inside. Nobody's here. We...ah, well, we busted the door down. Nobody answered—yes. Yes, there were witnesses."

Panic lit up inside me and I looked over at Jana.

Pulling out my phone, I punched in one message, then another. Jana's eyes came to me before going back to the men across the road. She gave a lazy shrug after reading the phone.

She got another message a few seconds later and her response to it was far from lazy.

Both she and Rogan was stiff-limbed as they stood up and retreated inside the parlor.

I punched another message into Damon.

Tell me you've got people close—too many to make it worth their while to do anything.

Damon's response was short.

I'm on it. I don't want you there.

I bet he didn't. Too bad. Instead of answering, I shoved my phone into my pocket and continued to glare across the street. One of them had come out and was slowly crossing the street. The other one was still on the phone.

If he even *thought* about making a move toward Jana—

A long black car pulled up right in front of him, and arrowed its way into three spaces, taking up much of the parking room boasted by the massage parlor and effectively blocking it.

At once, I felt better…and worse.

The door opened and a familiar dark head appeared.

Damon stared out over the hood of the car and unerringly, his gaze came my way, lingered for the briefest of moments.

He must have been heading this way when I called. I had little doubt as to why, either. Jana had notified him.

Slicking my palms down the sides of my pants, I hoped the mortals didn't do anything to escalate this.

"Jana, Rogan. Your presence is required at the Lair." Damon said that statement flatly and without emotion, barely sparing a look. When the others from the parlor appeared in the doorway, looking confused, Damon nodded at them. "You too, ladies. Sorry. You'll have to close up shop for a bit."

"But..."

Jana raised a hand. "Of course." Her smile was strained. "Whatever our Alpha wishes."

The others must have picked up on her tension, because they meekly agreed.

"Excuse me, son." The man came around the car, smiling a

smarmy smile. "I had an…appointment."

"Son?" Damon rounded on them, big arms folding across his chest.

The smile wobbled, then died entirely as he fell back a step.

"Appointment has been canceled," Damon said, his tone so condescending, even I felt the sting. "Get out of my town."

The man jerked back as if he'd been slapped. "How *dare* you—"

Damon took two slow steps forward and dipped his head. "You're in East Orlando. Know whose word is law here?" He raked him with a scathing look. "It's mine. And I'm not your *son…boy*. I'm the Alpha here and I was fighting my way in this world while you still had your mama's milk on your chin."

Now the human's face was a mix of embarrassment and rage. "Now you listen here—"

"It doesn't work that way…*son*." Damon smiled, but there was nothing pleasant about it. "Again…I'm the Alpha and it's *my* town. You want your words to matter, drive about ten miles west and find somebody who gives a damn. Here? *I'm* the law."

"I had an appointment," the man said, his voice stiff.

"That a fact." Damon smiled. It was a smile that would have warned even the most foolish to get the hell back. "See that sign?"

Owned and operated by a person of non-human blood. Proceed at your own risk.

"I'm tempted to *give* you an appointment even though I know you're lying. You reek of it. But if you want to go on record saying you've paid money…" He slanted a look at Jana as if questioning her sanity.

"He hasn't, Alpha." She kept her chin up, eying the suited man as if *he* was the contagious one—not the other way around.

"Nice to know. As it's illegal for any NH to offer skin to skin services to a human—and it's illegal for you to *request* them." Damon lifted a straight black brow. "We are being recorded. Did you request them?"

"It's…this…" Now he was fuming, shooting a dark glare at Jana. "This *is* a massage parlor, isn't it?"

"Absolutely." Jana didn't bat an eyelash. "But many humans think it's possible to catch the virus simply through touch. Thus…we advertise our services as skin to skin."

Red in the face now, he backed up a step, but he wasn't quite ready to back down.

The arrival of his partner that ended the standoff.

"Alpha." The second man offered Damon a polite nod.

The first one looked over at him, his mouth opened in outrage, but he was ignored.

"My apologies. My partner doesn't seem to understand the…intricacies involved here." He gave a modified, stiff bow. "We'll be on our way. We meant no offense."

"Offense has been taken." Damon cracked his neck one way, then the other. "I don't know why you've been watching the office across the street? But you should know…she's part of the Clan."

"You—we—*what* are you implying?"

"So noted." Again, the second man spoke over the first. He all but dragged the other one to the car.

As they retreated, Damon settled in, arms crossed over his chest and making it clear that he wasn't going to leave until he saw their hides peeling out.

They got the message.

Once they were gone, Jana and Rogan breathed a sigh of relief.

"Don't go getting too relaxed," Damon said. "You're going to the Lair for the time being."

Rogan stiffened.

"Argue with me and I'll knock you senseless, Rogan." His eyes flashed gold. "Don't like it? Too bad. I don't blame you. It sucks and you got caught up in some kind of mess, but you either go in or you get your ass left out to dry. FYI—there's really no *or* here. You're going in even if I have to take you in."

He waited a beat to see if they understood. Then he nodded toward the building. "Pack up what you want to take with you."

While they were doing that, Damon turned and unerringly faced me, despite the fact that he couldn't see me.

"You sure as hell found a mess this time, didn't you?"

CHAPTER NINE

"Are you trying to get me killed? Are you mad at me? Or are you just still jealous that I slept with Damon before you did?"

Shanelle and Scott were standing side by side at my front door.

"It's not who he slept with first." I gave her an easy smile. "It's who he's sleeping with now. And it ain't you."

She rolled her eyes and leaned against the door jam. "Hurry it up. He put an *all-eyes-out* on the radio earlier and he had that snarl in his voice. That snarl only comes out for you, honey."

"I'm touched." Damon hadn't lingered long at the massage parlor. Doyle had shown up to take over escorting the shifters—and presumably, *me*—in.

I'd told Doyle to pass the message to Damon that I'd be along very shortly. I was telling the truth. I *would* be along very shortly. But that didn't mean I was going straight to the Lair.

Since apparently whoever—mostly likely Whitmore or his possible impersonator—knew that I'd been in my office; there was no reason not to go by my house. It didn't matter if it was being watched. I had things that couldn't be left there unprotected.

I'd gone to a diner right in the thick of shifter territory and called two people I figured would be useful to have with me. Shanelle had no reason to think Whitmore was up to anything. She still thought he was digging into all the evils behind Blackstone. Maybe he was. We had gotten some useful information on that hell, thanks to him. But maybe he wasn't. Getting her to go with me served a dual purpose. He wouldn't suspect me of taking her along if I no longer trusted him, I figured. Hoped.

And Scott was one of Damon's most highly trusted men—that translated to *one of his most deadly pieces of work.*

My gut told me that something wasn't sunny with the man who'd hired me, but the man was also crafty. He would have done his homework on the Alpha, and he'd know that Damon Lee wasn't somebody to fuck with. He also wouldn't want to show his hand to Shanelle—somebody he'd been cultivating for a long time.

All that put together made me think I'd be safe enough to go to my place and grab few essentials that hadn't already been taken to the Lair. With the exception of the apartment itself.

It had been my home longer than anyplace else and leaving it ripped at me.

Damon was home now, though.

That was what I had to focus on. There was no reason to keep delaying the inevitable, so I had to move certain…items.

I definitely didn't want to leave those items alone since I had eyes watching my place.

Scott had stared them down when we climbed out of the car and every so often, he made a display of looking back at them with a certain amount of contemptuous disdain in his eyes.

They hadn't moved.

They hadn't even made a phone call.

Shanelle had noticed the device planted near the doorframe and pulled it down, frowning as she pointed out, "This is high end— military issue. I've only seen the like a few times."

I didn't ask her where. I had a good idea already. If she put two and two together and came to the same conclusion, then I'd answer her questions…should she ask them.

For now, I had a weapons cache to unload.

It was secreted away in my room, hidden from prying eyes by both man-made means and witch-made. Once I broke the charms that protected it, the power was enough to make my teeth ache but I ignored the gut-deep instinct to just pull back and leave these ugly treasures be.

Weapons had once called to me, whether they were the kind of weapons I should *use*…or the kind I should *hide*.

These were the kind that needed to be hidden.

Once I had them all laid out on the floor, including a blade I knew only as Death, I swiped the back of my hand over my forehead. Sweat had formed there, a side effect of exposure to their power and from resisting the call some of them put out. It had nothing to do with my lost connection to weapons, and *everything* to do with their particular magic.

These weapons were deadly—their power ranging from a dose of cyanide to that of a nuclear bomb…well, a bomb with a limited range. The spells that had kept them hidden had been crafted by Justin, subtle and quiet, refined over time, until nobody but those who knew these weapons were here would even know to look for them—or possibly a witch stronger than Justin looking to cause a lot of trouble.

Since trouble didn't *typically* run in a witch's blood, I'd always felt safe leaving them here. There were a few bad eggs out there, but they were rarer than one might think.

But then again, Chaundry had been quite a bit of trouble.

The concealment spell simply kept the weapons hidden—but if anybody had managed to seek them out, the destructive spell would have made them wish they'd have left everything alone. It would incinerate anybody who triggered the spell, but the spell couldn't be triggered without intent. Nasty business, true, but decent people wouldn't want go trying to steal weapons like these. On a base level, they'd sense the first defensive spells and avoid going any closer. Decent people wouldn't even want them existing, save for maybe the Druidic bow.

Death whispered to me, but I ignored him.

You need me, he crooned, his voice a seductive, sly whisper. With me, your enemies will know only pain.

The blade was too sentient for its own good. It had fed on blood in recent months and ever since, he had been determined to make me feed him *more*. Death wanted to come out and play.

Hearing a noise at the door, I looked up.

Shanelle stood there, mouth open as if to ask a question.

Her gaze darted over the weapons, face freezing.

"Get back," I said.

Some of these weapons had odd effects on other NHs, including shifters.

Shanelle didn't move.

"Get back!" I snapped.

A hand appeared in the door, hauling her out of the way. Scott's voice drifted to me. "Is everything okay, Kit?"

"It's fine. Just…both of you stay back."

Flipping a cloth over Death, I shifted my attention to one of the other weapons—the Druidic bow. Warmth flooded my hand and after a moment, I let myself grip the bow.

I'd spent months researching it, had even talked to several less-than savory folks who had run with a Druid pair or two—or so they claimed. If there was anything elven-like in our world, it was the Druids and they were a secret, reclusive lot. From what I'd heard, their weapons were prized above all others, known for striking true, even in the hands of amateurs.

Not that I'd ever needed help hitting my target, but even knowing I needed to hurry, I ran my fingers along the carved surface, felt the weight of the weapon's age crashing into me.

Her song had been...wild.

Blood, tears and death. Raw magic pulsed from her.

I'd keep her out.

For some reason, I had a feeling I'd need her.

The last of the weapons were a few charmed blades and one short sword that had been crafted to poison whatever blood it tasted. I really didn't like that one.

If I could find a way to destroy it, I might have already done so.

After I had all the weapons out, I packed them up in a trunk, each going into a spot made just for it. I'd spent a fortune having that trunk made and Justin had already set basic protections on it, but he'd have to do more. I had no idea where I was going to put this thing in the Lair and I didn't want curious noses poking around it.

After I snapped the lid shut, Scott glanced around the corner, his eyes wary. "What do you have in there? Mustard gas?"

"No." I crooked a smile at him. "Death on a stick, a little bit of wolf's bane. Hemlock, eye of newt, that sort of thing."

"Eye of newt and hemlock wouldn't have me wanting to tuck my tail and run off and hide," he said bluntly. With a shake of his head, he added, "I hope you plan on keeping whatever that was locked away in the chest."

"It's staying locked up." Taking the bow, I hooked it over my chest and fastened the quiver full of arrows to my belt, opting to carry my blade for now.

"Can you help me carry this?"

"Shanelle." Scott stepped aside as she came in and he jerked his head toward "Let her get it. I want my hands free."

Shanelle snapped off a smart salute, but there was no real irritation in her eyes and when I stepped forward, she cut me off. "I'll get it." A faint grin curled her lips. "Probably not a bad idea for you to keep your hands free, too."

"Are you two aware of something I'm not?" I asked, tightening my grip on the blade.

"No." Scott's reply was level and easy. "But I'm being careful. The Alpha will have my ass if I'm not."

I gave him a long, lingering look before I nodded and shifted my attention back to Shanelle. "You square now?"

She didn't pretend not to understand. With a stiff shrug, she said, "I smell death. I don't like it and the cat in me wants to get the hell away. But it's not screaming at me anymore. I'll deal."

We were out the door in under two minutes.

It wasn't until the car rolled into the solid protection offered by the Lair's underground garage that I breathed easier.

Even then, it was too soon. I just didn't know it yet.

CHAPTER TEN

Now that I had my weapons cache stashed in the Lair—apparently Damon had a place in his dungeons for *special cases*—I breathed a little easier. All of my other weapons, books and clothes had migrated over here in the past few weeks, but I'd been reluctant to move the deadlier items.

That solid, stone tomb that Damon showed me proved to be ideal.

Apparently he paid an arm and leg once a year to have a freelancer come in and lay the works on it. In a magic not dissimilar from the spells that had protected my weapons cache, the wards around the stone bunker were fed by the energy of the shapeshifters. Their power was a form of magic and it pulsed in the air around the Lair. If magic were light, this place would be lit up morning, noon and night. There was no lack of energy, even if for some reason the place managed to empty out a few hours at a time.

The Lair would have to be abandoned, left empty for weeks, or even months, before the spells powering the protection around this room would falter.

"It's perfect," I said wryly, shrugging. "But you're overpaying whoever is handling the wards. Justin would do it for half that. Might even be able to do it better."

"Sure. Your pretty witch does *everything* better." Damon rolled his eyes.

"Not everything." I made a face at him. "But as far as magic goes…" I let my hand hover over just a few inches above where the wards started. "This is loud. It's showy. It's kind of like putting iron bars covered with gold over the windows of a tacky jewelry store. You're telling people there's something expensive in there—something valuable. Sure, you might have a pit bull inside and a man with a .45 Magnum waiting to blow the head off any would-be thief, but you could have made the place a little less obvious—and attractive to the thief to begin with." Sliding him a sly smile, I added, "Trust me. I'm a thief. I look for showy things."

Damon studied the stone walls, the plain wooden door skeptically, but shrugged. "I'll talk to him. Will this work for now?"

"Yes. Although you probably need to put somebody on the door to make sure nobody comes in until Justin can tone things down some." Rubbing at my neck, I asked, "Will you need another…tomb?"

"I've got two. If we end up with a couple of assholes who need special treatment, they can share. Or I'll just kill one of them." He gave me a toothy smile that made it clear he wasn't concerned with the idea.

On our way up the stairs, he sent word to Scott about having somebody on the door. Doyle's name came up and I gave Damon a vehement *no* on that, but he was already declining. So nice to know that he'd figured out that Doyle would share my same sick fascination with the weapons…and Doyle wasn't mature enough yet to get how dangerous some of those were.

Once that was done, I was tempted to take his hand, tug him to our room.

Chang stepped out of nowhere.

At least that was how it seemed.

"Kit, you have a call coming in…" He checked the slim watch on his wrist. "Four minutes. If you and Damon could please move along to his chambers?"

"Don't you have someplace else to be?" I said sourly.

"I do." With a close-lipped smile, he inclined his head. "And I'd much rather be there. But things being what they are, it seems wiser to deal with this…client you have acquired."

He said *client* the way one might say *cancer* or *disease*.

"I'll make sure he has my new cell," I said tiredly.

"Perhaps hold off doing that." Chang's mouth went tight. When I went to ask, he simply shook his head and indicated that I walk. Damon would wait for me and if that kept Whitmore waiting…well, fuck it.

Damon wouldn't give a damn. Most of the NHs in the country wouldn't for that matter. Our voting rights were strictly limited and each election year stripped away more of them. Currently, NHs who had a minimum of fifty percent human DNA, who'd been *born* human and forced to change or those who had actively served in the military for a minimum of eight years could vote. Of course, if it was determined that you were NH while serving, you could be discharged. The military went back and forth on that one. What a conundrum.

Frowning, I thought back to Whitmore's platform. Had I paid much attention?

I doubted I had. There was no point.

The bottom line was that the US was as far as I could get from my native home since they still hadn't colonized the moon or Mars, and that made me an illegal alien. One with very convincing papers, but I wasn't about to register my status as anything other than an offshoot and if I even wanted to consider trying to vote, I'd have to prove my human parentage.

I wasn't giving them blood for anything. I didn't want to make it that easy for my kin to come looking for me should they ever decide to try.

Like so many other NHs, since I had no voice, I'd grown...apathetic about so many things. It was dangerous to be that way, but after years and years of being told you don't matter...after growing up *being told you don't matter*...apathy is just easier.

But now, I had to wonder.

NHs rights, the *NH problem*...all of it was always a big issue with politicians.

What had been his stand on it?

It hadn't been anything pushing for us.

He's human, Kit. I had my hands on him.

"Kit?"

Chang's voice cut through the tangle of my thoughts and I looked up, realizing we'd arrived inside the rooms Damon and I shared without me even realizing it.

Chang shut the door behind us, closing the world out.

More often than not, Shanelle was on hand to take notes and answer any tactical questions I might have, but Chang hadn't ferreted her out this time. I would have asked him about it, but the phone rang before I had the chance.

"Just made it," I said, wondering why my heart was racing. Without thinking about it, I reached up, took the Druidic bow off, and laid it on the couch—adding the quiver of arrows as well.

A voice came on the line before I finished, and Chang was the one to answer since I was half way across the room.

"You told me that she'd be available when I called *this* time," Whitmore said, his voice biting and cold. The phone's visual display was active, but Chang had adjusted it to a narrow window so that only those standing right in front of it would be visible.

He caught sight of me from the corner of his eye and without addressing the man on the screen, he turned—and in full view of President Whitmore—or the wannabe, I still hadn't decided—Chang gave me a deferential nod. Then, still ignoring the man on the screen, he stepped out of view.

When I took his place, I saw Whitmore's face was slightly flushed, temper burning in his eyes.

Chang's subtle slap hadn't gone unnoticed.

"I *am* here," I said mildly. "Chang moves a little faster than I do. He got to the phone first. Should we have let it keep ringing, sir?"

Immediately, Whitmore's face was all smiles. "Of course not, of course not…" Hands spread wide, he leaned in closer to the screen, oozing sincerity. "Ms. Colbana, I've just been trying to get in contact with you for days. Surely you can understand my urgency. You went completely off the grid."

"Yyyeeaahhhh…" I averted my eyes, reaching up to rub at my neck as if I wasn't quite sure how to proceed. It wasn't entirely an act. Lying to an NH was an art form. Telling an outright lie could be read, almost like the lines of a book, even on something like a phone call. Granted, taking away something like body chemistry made it trickier. The body chemistry changes a person's scent with each and every lie, but there are other differences—slight fluctuations in the voice, in the breathing, and heart rate. All of those are signals that something isn't entirely as it should be. But sidestepping the truth or presenting *your* version—or just answering a different form of question? That's where the art comes in. "There wasn't much choice there. That easy job you sent me on ended up being not so easy. It's a good thing I'd taken a friend along for the ride—my partner, sir, and I trust him implicitly before you get upset. But if he hadn't been there?" I lifted a shoulder. "I wouldn't be here."

That faint red color came and went. "You had your…partner. I wasn't aware you *had* a partner."

Bullshit. Talking about lying being an art form—he'd just gone and used his own version of the truth there, I'd bet my eyeteeth on it.

It was pretty damn common knowledge that I frequently worked with Justin Greaves when the need arose. Whitmore either hadn't heard that Justin had come out of his death-like sleep or he'd decided I wanted all that green for myself, but if he knew jack about me, then he knew about Justin.

A knock at the door, quiet and discreet, distracted me for a moment and I looked away, watched as Chang opened the door, frowning at the sight of Scott standing there. He beckoned him in, though, one hand up, indicating for silence.

"Ms. Colbana," Whitmore said, tone sharp, severe.

"Don't worry about it. It wasn't anything important." From the corner of my eye, I could see that Scott had eased over to the far side of the room and had all but gone dead, breathing so shallowly, I could no longer hear him. "You have my undivided attention, sir."

"I'm not sure I do." He leaned in even closer, as though trying climb through the screen. "You see, when I hired you on, I thought I made it clear I was hiring *you* on. I do not want the risk of exposure that comes with extra...bodies. I can't risk others being made aware of my endeavors."

Heat began to pulse to in the room, along with a growing tension that I couldn't quite place. I couldn't take the time to do it either, not when I was playing a very strange game with the man on the phone. "See, this is where it gets tricky, sir. When you hired *me*, what you basically hired was Colbana, Incorporated. And Colbana, Incorporated sometimes takes on a freelancer by the name of Justin Greaves. It's in the contract you refused to sign." I plucked at a non-existent thread on my sleeve. "The contract that you wanted *me* to sign, the one *I* refused to sign that would have leased my services to you *indefinitely* might have prevented me from bringing along aid when I deemed it necessary, but again...well, I didn't *sign* it. We ended up agreeing to a term of four weeks."

This time, I was the one who all but tried to climb through the screen. "And since I was the one who was almost fricasseed, fried and flambéed not once, but *several* times over by that quiet, low-power witch you sent me to watch? Forgive me if I don't give a rat's ass if you're pissed. I signed on to help you with *work of a sensitive nature*." I said it mockingly and watched his mouth draw tight. "And *during* said time, you and I would also work to uncover information on individuals connected to the facility known as Blackstone—and

FYI, we didn't turn up half the information I would have liked. *That* is what I signed on for. I did *not* sign on to die for you."

He wasn't red faced. His eyes were icy, expression so stony he might as well have been a statue.

"Is that quite enough, Ms. Colbana?"

Lips pursed, I cocked my head to the side as though I were thinking it through. "Well...I got a hell of lot more questions, like why that woman was running us down like there was a price on our tails, but...she's kinda dead and I doubt you have the answers to that. I've got other questions, too, like why it was such a big fucking deal that you send me to the caves in Alabama—caves you insisted I explore and I said hell no, not without backup and you shut down like I'd asked if you wanted to catch the virus. I'm curious why some pretty little dryad decided she'd rather die than talk. She was pretty convinced that she'd be tortured if she lived. I'd like to know why you sent me looking for a Green Man, yet I can't find shit-all information on one *ever* being reported in Alabama, but...well. Yeah, that's enough for now."

"Indeed." He sniffed, sounding as outraged as some prissy little debutante who'd gotten her dress soiled by rain—the outrage. "Are you *finished*?"

"Some tea, Kit."

The presence of Chang at my side was disconcerting, but I managed to hide it. I took the cup he presented me and lifted it to my lips, taking a drink to wet my throat—it had gone as dry as the desert. When our eyes met, I saw the warning there. *Be careful...*

Then he angled his head toward the screen, stared Whitmore dead in the eyes and I understood why he emerged.

Chang stepped away.

Damon, as if they'd choreographed it, came up and stood behind me. He placed a hand on my spine and stroked up, then down—just that one touch before retreating and taking up a spot on the wall behind me. It was the only spot in the room where the person on screen could see anybody besides me.

I knew why my growly cat had decided to emerge from the shadows. He had no desire to speak to the man who'd hired me. But there had been an implied threat hidden somewhere in Whitmore's voice. I couldn't quite place where it had been, but the cats had heard it, too.

Whitmore wouldn't think twice about making me disappear.

I was just a lone woman, some strange offshoot. If one dug deep enough, it could be discovered that I was unregistered—which meant I had no rights here at *all*.

It was a bigger deal when I was a woman affiliated with the leader of one of the larger shifter clans in the country. Whitmore could make *me* disappear, but doing so would cause a lot of problems—a few thousand, and all of them roared.

Damon had just reminded him of that.

But I didn't want to be responsible for the hell it might bring down on the Cat Clan—or the wolves, either. Damon was the leader of the largest shifter faction here. By all appearances, he was the leader of the shifters in this general area. In reality, what he shared with the wolves was an alliance. Alisdair MacDonald wouldn't take it lightly if something presented a huge threat to the cats, because if they were threatened, the smaller wolf clan was also threatened.

I hated having to be reasonable.

But I gritted my teeth—mentally—and managed to give Whitmore a level look. "The bottom line is I often end up on jobs that go sideways. I often end up deciding to take backup and if I hadn't, I would be dead. I'd think you'd be pleased with that."

"Of course I'm glad you're not dead."

Another play on the truth there…was he lying or prevaricating? I couldn't tell.

There was no time to question further though because a flurry of pounding erupted on the door, causing me to jerk my head around in surprise. Somebody flew inside—nobody *ever* did that in Damon's chambers.

"I'll have to get back to you, sir. Emergency!" I cut him off before he could say anything. An odd buzzing rippled through my skull and I felt a pang at the base of my head where those weird headaches always originated. The buzzing only got worse as I turned to the door and in the split second it took for me to do that, hell broke loose.

Hell took the form of Damon shifting to his half form, over seven feet tall, his muscled pelt covered in a golden pelt and spotted. His clothes fell in shreds around him as he launched himself at Scott.

My mind denied what it was seeing.

Scott flung up a hand and Damon flew to the far side of the room while Scott leaped toward me. I whipped up my sword, my mind furiously trying catch up with what was going on. "Stay back," I warned.

A grin—one that seemed both insanely out of place and strangely familiar—twisted Scott's lips.

"Now, now, Kit…is that any way to say hello to an old friend?"

The voice—oh, *shit*.

Those words had no sooner left his lips than a growl ripped out of the shifters who'd burst into the room like their lives depended on it.

And one of them was…*Scott*.

Damon was off the floor and moving again.

Instinct screamed.

Move now—think later.

I swore as I dove for Damon and the Scott-lookalike. "I'm going to kill you," I told the man who'd somehow managed to sneak into the Lair. Of *all* places.

He chuckled, his visage starting to waver. "You won't be saying that in a minute. I'm here for a reason…you know that."

He leaped up and in a movement that defied physics—and the human body—as he flipped and sailed through the air, placing his body behind mine.

Damon made a deep, deep noise, one that spoke of fury—and I heard something else, too.

Perhaps Chang would recognize it, but I doubted anybody else would.

It was fear.

He saw only some unknown enemy and the man was now at my back.

I held up a hand. "Stop…Damon…stop. He's not…" I heaved out a breath before I said the one thing that might keep the man in front of me from trying to kill the man behind me. "He's a friend. He's saved my life twice now."

Damon slowed for a split second, but nothing changed the animalistic set to his features.

Behind me, there was a faint whisper. "You'd think I'd remember how sharp their noses are, wouldn't you?"

"I hope you enjoyed yourself," Damon said, his voice a predatory growl. "Every man should have a little fun before he dies."

"Oh, I don't do *this* for fun, son. Trust me, *this* is a pain in the ass."

"Don't be a more of a moron than you already are," I snapped over my shoulder.

Chang was staring at the man behind me with eyes that promised death. This was going to be ugly. The man had breached their home—their safehold. Unless he had a good reason for doing that...

Damon made another move toward me, green-gold eyes locked on the intruder.

"Damon...I know him." I reached back, daring to risk one quick glance—my eyes connected with eyes of pure *white*—all white. No pupil, no discernible iris and whiter than any mortal eye should be.

And Nova, for all intents and purposes, *was* mortal.

A freakishly powerful mortal with psychic skills that weren't supposed to exist, but still, he was mortal.

"Hello, Nova."

He looked at me and grinned. "Kit."

Damon took a step forward.

Chang placed a hand on his shoulder and they shared a look. The subtle nod Damon gave the other man unsettled me and I pondered ripping my hair out when Chang was the one to move forward to meet Nova.

I wouldn't call Damon the more *reasonable* one of the two, but there were times I could get Damon to listen to me. If Chang made up his mind...

Nova slid to the side, shifting so that he faced all of us, although he was clearly keeping his focus on the shifters. "Come on, boys...let's all take a deep breath and calm down." He shot them what was considered his...less crazy smile. "I've been here *three times* today and I've called *five* asking, then demanding then *begging* to speak to Kit. It's urgent, I said. It's life or death, I said. And I'm told to leave a message at her office."

He snorted and shot me a sidelong look. "Kit, how often do you check messages at your office?"

"Get to the point, Nova."

He hitched up a shoulder. "I'm trying to be polite and explain why I felt the need to take drastic measures, Kit. In a minute, you'll be just as pissed as I am. The third time I came to the gate and said I absolutely had to see you..." The whites of his eyes started to glow.

Oh, fuck...

"See, I was told, *We don't listen to urgent messages from the likes of* you, *meat. Get out.*" Nova's smile went cold. "The guards you have at the door really should show more courtesy—I could have turned *them* into meat. But I showed restraint."

Chang made no response, just took another slow step toward Nova.

"You really should have left a message at her office," Damon said.

"Kit sucks at checking her messages. I thought this kind of thing—the lives of some friends and all—was a bit more important." Nova cocked his head. "But if not…well, we can get downright nasty in here."

Lives of some friends…?

"Nova?" I whispered.

Scott—the real one—had circled around. I whipped my gun out and leveled it at his knee. "Don't. I like you, Scott, but if you even think of trying to move me out of the way…I'll put you on the ground."

Nova chuckled. "Now it gets *fun.*"

I fought the urge to turn and punch him in the nose. "One of these days, I'll find a way to thank Justin *properly* for introducing us, Nova."

"You can do that by saving his life, Kit. Now..."

I spun to stare at him, the gun falling limp to my side. I was the one to lunge for Nova. And he didn't try to stop me. "What?"

"Now…ask me why I'm here," he said gently.

"Nova."

"Somebody grabbed Colleen and Justin, Kit."

CHAPTER ELEVEN

My hands tightened on his shirt.

"When?" I demanded, my voice ragged, my knees temporarily trying to go weak under me. It lasted only a split second and Nova casually bolstered me with a mental nudge, not even touching me.

He flicked a look past me.

I didn't even bother. I could feel Damon and the others drawing nearer.

In a flat voice, I said, "He's a friend of mine, he came trying to talk to me and he was *turned away*. Is this my home or not?"

There was no answer. But I knew they backed off—a bit. There would be a reckoning over this, but some of the tension eased from Nova's body and he reached up, gently tugged my hands from his shirt, holding my wrists in a way that made it clear he was offering support as much as anything else.

Nova and I had what one might call an uneasy friendship—in truth, he went from freaking me out to scaring me shitless, but that wasn't through any fault of his own.

He was just a dangerous piece of work—Justin had once said he was a walking time bomb. The only comfort was that Nova knew when he'd explode and his goal was to take out pieces of shit when he went, not friends.

"Come on, Kit," Nova said, a grin tilting up one corner of his mouth. "You know me. I wouldn't be here if I didn't think I could help. So…take a deep breath, then we can talk. Friendly-like."

Nova had a deep, lazy drawl, pure Southern charm and if one didn't know any better, it might be easy to get suckered in by the slow rhythm of his speech. I knew better. Still, I knew panicking wasn't going to do shit.

"I'm breathing, Nova. You need to be talking. *When?*"

He angled his chin toward the table. "Maybe we can all sit down and talk. Like I said…friendly-like."

"Fine." I chewed the word off, feeling like it was nothing but broken glass in my throat, but in the calm, logical part of my mind, I understood. Nova didn't know the shifters. He felt like he had to keep his eye on them for his sake—and mine. He'd feel better if he had a birds-eye view of everything, and if I didn't have my back to them.

I wasn't worried about having my back to them. What *I* was worried—no, *pissed* about was finding out who'd turned Nova away.

I gestured to the table, angling my body as I did so. Damon and I had a brief stare down before he finally looked at the men who'd torn into his chambers. "Scott, Bayou. Go back to your posts."

I almost called out to Scott—demanded to know *who* in the hell had turned a friend of mine away. But I held my tongue. I wasn't going to countermand an order from the Alpha in front of his men— he might not be *my* Alpha, but there were certain *courtesies* to be followed. I'd follow them—then bust balls later.

Once the door closed silently behind Scott, Damon—staring at Nova unblinking—slid seamlessly into his human form, leaving behind the upright, powerful half-form that was more monster than anything else. He stood there nude, hands at his side, unperturbed by the fact that he wore nothing but his skin.

Nova didn't blink.

It took quite a bit to throw Nova.

But I was too pissed to point that out.

Knowing that the stare down could last forever, I swore and turned away, stalking over to the chest of clothes and grabbing some jeans for Damon. "Either get something on your ass so we can talk or Nova and I will go to my office—I'm sure he'll be happy to talk to me *there*."

Damon's gray eyes cut to mine, fury lighting the darkness there. I could see the response trembling on his tongue.

But he simply pulled the jeans on and strode over to the table. His tone was pure, silken death when he spoke. "After you…Nova."

Chang didn't sit, simply taking up position at Damon's shoulder. Such a good little soldier.

I was so pissed, I couldn't see straight.

I was so scared, I couldn't *think*.

Once Nova sat down, I focused on him, ignoring the cats. They were no threat to me.

Nova didn't block them out, but he seemed to finally get that I was here because I wanted to be. Once more, I felt that weird buzzing in my brain and I sighed in pained resignation, realizing what it was.

Nova.

He'd done that earlier, just before everything went to hell. He'd been 'knocking' of sorts. Letting me know he was around.

My shields weren't like a psychic's or a witch's and I was close enough to human that he could read me, but it was…different, he told me. Like translating from a learned language to your native language. Different.

And he tried not to intrude. He could power through my shields in a heartbeat, but that would be painful.

Right now, I was wishing he'd powered through—a *lot* earlier.

Are you safe here, Kit?

Passing a hand in front of my face, I said wearily, "Nova…I'm fine. Just, please…what's up with Justin and Colleen?"

His mouth tightened slightly and I realized he would prefer that I keep his ability to speak to me mentally quiet, but oh well. Leaning forward, I jabbed a finger at him. "Talk."

"Yes," Chang said from his position at Damon's shoulder. "By all means, talk. The Alpha and I are very…interested in what he has to say."

"Shut the *fuck* up!" I shouted.

The outburst had Chang slanting a look at me.

Damon never once turned his eyes from Nova.

I was going to explode. I could feel it.

That pulsing ache at the base of my skull, the worry in my gut. All of it. I was going to explode.

Nova leaned forward, bracing his elbows on the table. Out of everybody in the room, he was the one who saw how close I was to the edge. "They were almost to Colleen's, Kit, as near as I can tell. I tracked them as far as the city edge and then I decided it would be best to have somebody other than me on hand."

"If you're strong enough to turn some of Damon's men into…meat," Chang offered a cool smile, "why didn't you stop whoever took Justin and Colleen?"

Nova turned his head slowly. It was eerie how he did it. Nova *was* human. At least under that mad power, he was. But the *human* part was almost…superficial. It was like somebody had decided to shove a crazy amount of pure, volatile energy into a casement of human skin. Nothing about him *seemed* human, not the way he acted, carried himself, not the way he fought, lived, breathed.

And the way he turned his head was almost alien, more like a predator sighting its prey from a far-off distance.

Chang recognized it, too.

The cat in the slim, elegant man stirred. I saw Chang's eyes flash gold in eerie warning…or perhaps awareness.

"Perhaps I would have," Nova said, his voice deep and echoing, resonating throughout the large chamber. "Had I actually *been* there when the abduction went down. As it happens, I was approximately twelve hours and six minutes too late."

"Twelve hours and six minutes," Damon said, deadpan.

"And thirteen seconds. If we're going by the time the abduction started. The whole process took under three minutes." Nova cocked his head. "If you'd like the time from when it ended?"

"You seem to have your times rather…pinpointed." Chang's eyes were all gold now in his face.

"A knack of mine. Just as I can tell that you have…" Nova's lids drooped and then he smiled. "Eight shifters lined up in the hall just outside this door. You've yet to decide if you'll need them, because you believe you can handle me yourself. One of them is the young blond that Kit is fond of. You believe you'll use him as a distraction, should you need him—should Kit prove to be…intractable."

I closed my eyes.

This was already going very badly. I thought very hard toward Nova, knowing he'd pick it up as clearly as if I was speaking to him aloud. *We have to get them to focus, now.*

That was going to take something…unsettling.

There was only one way to get through to Damon—at least if I wanted to do it fast.

He slanted his head toward me. *Really.* His voice, as clear in my head as if he'd spoken out loud, sounded terribly amused. *If that's the way you want to handle this. Your cat will not like it, sweetheart.*

At the same time, Nova smiled at Chang. "The more interesting question is just *how* did such an undertaking occur on the Alpha's territory? After all, *all* of East Orlando is his territory…is it not?"

Damon rose slowly, one hand slamming down on the table. It hit with enough force that I felt the reverberation clear up into my arms.

The threat in his eyes promised death, blood, and very bad things.

That's it. I pushed my thoughts toward Nova, felt his understanding echo back.

"Enough." I stood up, making sure all eyes were on me. "I'm tired of the dick-wagging."

Without blinking, I drew the Glock from my hip.

In quick succession, I fired off four rounds.

One at Nova.

One at Chang.

One at Damon.

One at the underside of my chin…from a few inches away.

I was staring straight in Damon's eyes the whole time.

The flickering of emotion was…surreal. Amusement. Stunned shock. Betrayal. Blankness…followed by denial.

And each emotion played over and over and over, none of them ever having the chance to fully manifest, because not a single round hit its target.

Each one spun lazily in the air before drifting over to Nova. He kept them spinning until they came to rest in his palm, clinking against each other. "For the record, it's got nothing to do with metal." His smile was grim and humorless as he angled his chin across the room.

I glanced over, unable to help myself, and saw that the mattress was hovering several feet in the air, bed hangings and all.

That wasn't the only thing.

Water began to run in the bathroom. Within seconds, it came *out* of the bathroom, in a narrow stream. In mid-air.

It splintered in four separate rivulets and each one went to a different person. I lifted a finger and touched the water that spun in a lazy circle around me. Not a drop fell to the ground. If Damon had still been in his half-form, his fur would be on end. But while Chang was staring at the dancing water slipping and spinning around us like some strange ballet, Damon only had eyes for me.

After a full sixty seconds, Nova folded the stream of water back in on itself, turning the faucet off in the bathroom.

"There's no mess," he said to Damon. "I try not to be rude when I'm in another's home."

For the first time since I'd pulled my weapon, Damon's gaze left my face. "So appreciated," he said, his lips barely moved.

Nova shrugged as if Damon had paid him a huge compliment.

"Now that I have your attention," I said, my voice low and furious. "Will the two of you jackasses listen?"

Nova stepped forward and lifted his hand. In a steady stream, each round fell from his cupped fist, striking the table with a force that seemed far, far too loud.

Damon flinched each time. At the fourth one, his eyes closed and his mouth went tight.

"Damon," I said softly. But he didn't answer. "Damon!"

"What…" He blinked, shaking his head. "You…what…"

"Look at me," I said. "Are you looking at me?"

Dark, stormy gray eyes—as dark as I'd ever seen them—finally met mine. His throat worked as he swallowed.

"You two need to listen to me. This bullshit, macho, super-alpha shit doesn't *work* with Nova. He's not a shifter and he's not *afraid* of either of you. He already picked you up, Damon, and *threw* you like a ragdoll."

Damon's lids twitched. I think his brain was starting to work.

I flung a hand toward him. "I already told you that he saved my life twice. One of those times was when I ended up neck-deep with a rogue pack in Alabama. There were *thirty* of them. Nova showed up and when he was done, not *one* was left standing—or alive."

Chang's eyes flicked to Nova.

Damon was still staring at me, his chest heaving like a bellows. He took a step toward me.

"No. We're not doing this right now," I said, backing up. "I'm talking to *him*. Which I should have done *hours* ago, if one of your men had let me know he was looking for me."

Damon still took another step.

There was a light *thump* from across the room—the mattress settling back into place. Chang and I noticed.

Damon didn't.

"I'd like to mention," Nova drawled. "What I can do? It's got nothing to do with metal, water…the element, the item, the weight, size…number. None of that matters to me."

"Then what does?" Chang asked, sounding politely interested. But his eyes were on Damon who was moving closer and closer, like a man in a dream.

He wasn't the only one watching the Alpha either.

I was watching Damon.

So was Nova.

"Me. *I* matter," the man in question said. "I'm the most psychic piece of shit you're ever going to meet."

"Well, you are often a piece of shit," I muttered.

"Thanks, Kit. Love you, too."

Damon growled.

"Don't," I said, snarling back. I was about ready to punch him in the nose.

Chang moved up, possibly risking life or limb—both. He rested a hand on Damon's chest, spoke to him urgently. Damon all but vibrated on his heels, eyes still locked on my face.

Damon closed his eyes after a moment and Nova took that opportunity to continue his one-man cheer squad. Although it was more like a doom and gloom squad.

"Psychic piece of shit or not... What I am is... well, call me a tool." Nova braced his hands on the edge of the table and leaned forward, eyes moving ceaselessly between Chang and Damon. "I can tell you that you have exactly thirteen hundred and twelve shifters in the Lair right now—no. It's thirteen hundred and twenty. More are en route. You're calling in the troops, Alpha. I guess I've got you good and riled up. I'm flattered."

"Don't be." Damon's voice came out hoarse, like he hadn't spoken in months. He shot me another look and I had the feeling he was fighting the urge to come for me again. "Right now, I'm holding off on having you torn limb from limb but that can change in a heartbeat."

"You don't *get* it, Damon," I said, risking drawing that primal attention all over again. "Remember how I told you he came after Justin and me when it was like...oh, thirty to three? Only it was more like thirty to one, because I was injured and if Justin turned his back for a second, we were done for." I stared at him, hard. "Thirty rogue shifters. Have you never heard about a group of rogue wolves running anywhere near here? Maybe you might have once been concerned about them, but were told to leave them alone?"

Damon's lids flickered.

But Chang straightened, drawing himself rigid.

"They called themselves the Devil's Angels. Not terribly original, I don't guess. But maybe the name will ring a bell."

Damon's shoulders went tight, but that was his only reaction.

Chang, however…for once, his reaction was instantaneous, and obvious. Almost all of the malice drained out of him and he reached up, dragging a hand down his face. "That was you," he muttered, swearing under his breath. "Kit, *you* went in after that idiot brat?"

I inclined my head. "That idiot brat was fourteen and I thought she deserved a chance to live long enough to know she'd made a mistake."

It was one of my biggest regrets to realize we'd wasted our time—and nearly our lives. Sometimes evil lurks even in the heart of supposed children.

Her name had been Magdalene and of that group, she was the only one to survive. She hadn't lived to see eighteen though. Her own family had been forced to put her down six months after her rescue. A very reluctant rescue. She was the reason Justin and I had needed Nova's help to begin with.

She was the reason those thirty men had ended up with their insides liquefied by the power Nova carried inside him.

None of us ever took credit for taking out what would have become one of the ugliest threats in the south. It was Nova's kill, but he didn't want to be known for killing *thirty* in the blink of an eye. Neither did we.

So we'd said nothing.

That didn't keep people from talking about it.

Chang stared at Nova, his face impassive now. After a moment, he turned away and paced over to a bookshelf, staring at the volumes there without seeing a single one.

Finally, he looked at Damon. "If he's the one who took them down, perhaps we owe him the courtesy of…listening?"

I didn't care what they thought they *owed* him.

Turning back to Nova, I said, "Stop it with the bullshit. Ignore them. Talk to *me*. My two best friends are missing. What's going on?"

Nova talked.

I listened.

A few minutes into it, Chang started to listen…reluctantly.

And somewhere in the blur of it, so did Damon.

CHAPTER TWELVE

"I've been trying to catch up with you and Justin since the deal with Chaundry and the salamander, Kit. I'm...fuck. I'm sorry."

Hands over my face, I tried to take in what he'd told me but I felt like I was about to *explode* from it. Just *explode*. Taking in anything else was just going to be that one final bit that pushed me over and I'd lose it. Lowering my hands, I made myself meet Nova's pale eyes. "It's not your fault. Although, hell...next time, pick up a fucking phone."

"You think I'm going to put this kind of information on a phone?" He scoffed.

We both pretended to laugh, but I understand why he hadn't, even assuming I hadn't destroyed my cell sometime last week.

"Mister..." Chang paused, a frown on his face. I realized it was because he didn't know Nova's last name, and a brief thought danced through my mind. This whole thing had to be frustrating for him.

He was used to knowing everything about everybody.

He knew *nothing* about Nova.

"Just Nova." The psychic's lips curled in a wry smile as he spun the chair and focused his eyes on the shifter in the dove gray suit.

"Nova, then. You're telling us that you were a...guest of Blackstone. For two months." Chang's jaw tightened, his liquid black eyes unreadable. "Just *how* were you able to escape? And if you're the most psychic piece of shit—such a charming turn of phrase, mind you—I'll ever meet, one would think you would be almost impossible to catch off guard. Yet you were taken by Blackstone's ham-handed handlers."

"Yes." Nova kicked back in the chair, propping his feet up lazily. It took a moment to realize he had propped them on absolutely nothing, even a bit longer to realize the chair was resting on the back two legs—yet it was as stable as could be. "And they *are* quite ham-handed, I gotta say. A bull in a china shop would catch less attention. As to why they grabbed me and how…" Nova jerked a shoulder in a shrug. "I let them."

I spun my head around so fast, it was a miracle I didn't get whiplash. For a few seconds, I could only gape at him and then I shoved the confusion, fear, and more than a little residual anger aside. "I don't think I want to know. If I don't need to know to help Justin and Colleen, then I don't *want* to know."

"Whatever you say, Kit." Nova crooked a grin at me. "What you *should* know is that they experiment on people—just like Justin feared. They have had some successful experiments. And..."

His gaze slid away.

"And *what*?" I pushed.

"Chaundry, Kit."

A muscle pulsed in my eyelid. "What?"

"Fuck, Kit." Nova drilled the heels of his hands into his eyes. "Think it through, Kit. I've already been to Red Branch—the salamander is probably going to die. It's traumatized by what happened with Chaundry. They weren't meant to be used like that, and it knows it killed its handler. And Chaundry—*she* wasn't like that. They had her and they broke her."

Memories of the way Justin had said her name, how he'd stared down at her, like he couldn't quite believe what he was seeing.

"How?" I barely managed to force the question out as the staggering knowledge of what he was telling me drove home.

They could *remake* us—control us.

"They're mind-wiping the NHs they take in. Manipulating them and turning them into the puppets they'd planned Banner to be." Disgust dripped from Nova's words. "This isn't *brainwashing* we're talking about. The NHs they've successfully…reprogrammed, for lack of a better word, have minds that are essentially a blank slate. They then send that one out to help hunt down their problem children."

Shaken, I sank back down into my seat.

"How do you know this?"

"Like I said. I let them take me." Nova looked tired now, exhausted really. He turned away and braced his hands on the window that faced out over the small courtyard. I realized he'd lost weight.

"They had you for two months?"

"Maybe a little less, maybe a little longer."

"And why weren't you...wiped?"

A mean smile curled Nova's lips. "They couldn't *get* to me. They open a door, I slam it shut. They try to wait until I'm asleep, I wake myself up. They decide they won't feed me, I steal food from them—while they are *eating*. Trust me...I pissed them *off*. You know how testing goes with psychics—they can't get a decent grasp on what psychic ability is, how it works, because every single psychic ability works on a different level. Once I had what I needed...I left. Actually, I left because of Chaundry. They were done *programming* her and I wasn't going to let her go down like that. It took me a while to get out, though." The look on his face darkened ominously. "I didn't catch up with her in time. You know how that went down. Getting in was a lot easier."

"Why did you do it?" Damon asked, speaking for the first time in quite a while.

"Because it's what I'm supposed to do. There are a couple of...people there," he said. "Some guys I've been hunting for a while. I went in to start laying the groundwork and realized there was a lot more going on than I'd expected."

I sucked in a breath, unable to stop it.

Nova glanced at me over his shoulder and our eyes locked. "Don't look at me like that, Kit. I told you the time was coming. It cometh right soon."

I got up and moved away as fast as I could, pacing over to the corner and staring blindly at a wall. "It's...this is what does it?"

"*I'm* what does it."

A hard knot settled inside me, a miserable ache and I turned to face him.

The smile on his face was gentle, almost like he was trying to tell me it was okay.

The hell with that. He shouldn't be consoling me right now—not about this. And it wasn't *okay*.

As if he could sense my line of thought—and maybe he could—Nova just lifted a brow. "Yeah. This is it, Kit. I'm kinda glad. I'm tired, ya know? Besides, Blackstone...you have to admit, it's a good cause."

"What are you two talking about?" Damon demanded bluntly.

When there wasn't any answer from Nova, I turned to look at

91

him. He was still looking outside but he shrugged, as if to tell me he didn't care if I said anything or not. But this…it wasn't my place to say anything.

Nova's sigh escaped him and he turned, leaning back against the window, his head falling to rest on it as he stared upright. "Ever wonder what it might be like knowing when you'd die? And how?" Now he straightened his head, pinning Damon with a sardonic look. "The one really shitty thing was never knowing *why*. But I got that now. Mostly. It's a decent enough reason."

An empty, hollow pang resonated through me and I tipped my head back, staring up at the ceiling until I'd convinced myself there was nothing to cry over.

"Now, not to be so flippant about my much-anticipated and likely to be under-appreciated demise, but none of that's not why I'm here." Nova braced his hands on the table. "Once I figured out just who they'd send Chaundry after, I tried to close the distance, but I had to make sure she didn't pick up on me—and that made it dicey. I couldn't get in touch with you by phone—makes sense after hearing you'd destroyed it." He grimaced.

The quick shift in topic had my head spinning, but I knew I needed to pay attention. "I'll make sure to give you the new number. Next time, if you…" I just tapped my head, my gut too knotted to say what I was thinking.

"I'm still recuperating from my…escape, Kit. Had to blow a lot of power to do it." He crooked a tired smile. "Otherwise I would have. Don't worry, I'll be right as rain in time for the big day."

I wanted to slap him for being cavalier about his death, but nobody better understood than I did how caustic humor could help a person cope. "Yeah. You'll have to explain that, in detail. Soon."

"Sure. In detail." He wagged his brows at me. "It included me being naked."

Damon didn't move at all, but the predatory interest in him sharpened down to a knife's edge.

"I should also mention it included a body bag and more blood and guts than you normally see outside of butchering day." Nova's smile went ugly. "They'll be more careful about who they toss in a body bag in the future. They were running on a light crew that day because it was the same day they sent Chaundry out for the first time and they had as many people in the field with her as they could spare for risk *containment*. They make it sound so clinical. *Risk containment*. Like she was some sort of mutated rat. Anyway, I pulled a headfuck on them, because I needed them watching me less so I could watch her more. A shrink came in, told me life would be easier, better, if I'd cooperate. I'd get freedom, fewer restrictions if I'd stop resisting, blah, blah, blah…So for about a week, I'd been eating the food, then I started taking the pills—or so they thought. I was really just pulverizing them and that day, they switched the meds. It was perfect. I faked an allergic reaction, slowed my breathing, made my heart slow to nothing—"

"You can do that?"

He looked at Chang, brows arched as if to say, *Can't you*? "Yeah. I can manipulate anything—your heart included. Want a demonstration?"

Damon snapped, "No."

"Yes." Chang came forward. "A demonstration—I don't want it *stopped*. I assume you can do it without killing me."

Nova looked at Chang as if he suddenly found him a lot more interesting.

"Chang…" Damon's voice was a low warning.

But the slim man turned to look at Damon, one straight black brow arched. "I'm of a mind to trust him, believe everything he says. If he's serious, then we have a lot of problems and we need to be ready to put the weight of the Clan behind him. And we owe Justin and Colleen debts that likely can never be paid. *I* owe Justin—I owe him for you. But I want proof that this man is everything he's claiming. And I need proof—not Kit's word that I can trust him. Her word means a great deal to me, but for this…I need more."

Damon closed his eyes.

A taut moment later, he nodded.

When Chang looked back at Nova, he asked, "Well?"

"I can speed it up, I can slow it down. If I really wanted to, I could rip it out of your chest and slam it into his—but that would kill you and we've established you don't want to die for this little…demonstration." Nova crossed his arms over his chest. "What do you want me to do?"

"If you speed it up too much, my body will want to change. Best not to tempt it."

"I'll control that."

Chang's mouth tightened. Then he nodded.

The only sign I had that anything was changing at first was the increase in Chang's breathing.

Damon sensed something else, though.

He came out of the chair, pacing closer to us. His nostrils flared and he stopped a few feet away from me, his eyes flicking to mine for the briefest moment then he gave a slow shake of his head and stopped.

I looked at Chang, arms wrapped tight around myself. The tension in the air started to gather and it sent goosebumps crawling up and down my spine. Shifter energy has a feel all its own. When a shifter is going to change, that energy spikes and grows, until it's like there's a storm just waiting to explode.

That storm was here now and it hovered.

And hovered.

Seconds passed into a minute and then a minute became five.

Chang's face was covered in sweat, his eyes a brilliant burning gold.

Damon said, "That's enough."

Chang almost went to his knees. I saw him sway, start to bend. Then his body steadied and through damp hair, he stared at Nova. "You...I think you just might be one of the most dangerous creatures I've ever met."

Nova's mouth twisted. "The first time I heard that I was five. Then my mother gave me a kiss and hugged me."

"How sweet." Damon's voice was pure acid.

"The sweet part came after. The man she'd been shacking up with came up behind me and slammed a metal pipe into my head. They threw me into the river next. Of course, that wasn't the first time she'd tried to kill me—nor was it the last."

Instead of looking at Nova, I moved over to Chang, grabbing a towel from the small bar set up near the table. "Here."

He swiped it over his face, his eyes coming to meet mine for a brief moment. "How many times did his mother try to kill him?"

"You don't want to know," I said quietly.

The door closed behind Chang and Nova with utter silence.

To me, it felt like it dropped with the force of an atomic bomb.

Damon was still on the far side of the room from me, near the table, while I was closer to the floor-to-ceiling bookshelves and the gas fireplace. A shiver raced down my spine when he remained quiet, his gray eyes on the table instead of moving in my direction.

Arms crossed over my chest, I watched as he took a step closer to the table and reached out, nudged one of the casings of the rounds I'd shot earlier. He did it again, sent it spinning. It spun and spun in dizzying circles and then, abruptly, he scooped it up and started to toss it up in the air, catching it before deftly tossing it in the air again.

"You sure as hell know how to make sure I'm paying attention when you got something to say, don't you, Kit?" he asked, voice as soft and smooth as silk.

"Can you think of anything else I could have done to make sure you actually *were* paying attention?" I knew this was going to get heated and fast. I'd known it the minute I'd taken the actions that put us where we were now. And if I had to do it all over? I'd probably do the same damn thing.

"Well, you kind of got me there." He nodded slowly, eyes still on the casing he was tossing so lazily up in the air. Up. Down. Up. Down. "Man comes into the place I swore I'd protect—with my life, if I had to. And he's standing next to the woman I'd give my soul to protect…and I'd do that willingly. A dozen times over. My brain's locked on one thing, and one thing only. You know that."

A few taut seconds of silence passed, broken only by the ever-so-faint sound of the casing striking his palm, then being thrown back up into the air. I think I could hear the subtle sound of his breathing. It was steady and easy. I could hear his heart beating. That was *anything* but easy. Anything but steady.

My palms grew slick with sweat as he turned his eyes my way.

"I think you were put on this earth for one reason only, baby girl. You know what that is?"

I didn't even have the air to offer some smart-ass quip at this point. I had the strangest feeling that I needed to brace myself, but for what?

"You were put here to drive me to the breaking point."

He threw the casing up.

By the time it came down, he was already all the way across the room, merely a breath away from me.

"Guess what?" he whispered, his lips so close, I could already feel them on mine. "I think I just went over."

CHAPTER THIRTEEN

Shoving my hands up, I braced them against his chest, which rose rapidly under my hands. He was hot, burning like a furnace. Burning like the fires that had chased Justin and me through what felt like half the south.

I wouldn't escape this inferno, though.

I didn't want to, but at the same time, I was more than a little terrified.

"In two hours, I'm supposed to meet Nova so we can start tracking down Justin and Colleen." My voice came out a lot steadier than I would have thought.

Damon reached up, closing his hands around my wrists and dragging them up. The room spun around us and I ended up with my back against the nearest wall, with him wedged between my thighs.

"Don't worry. I know what you have to do," he whispered against my ear. "But do you really think you can do something like…" My shirt ripped. No…*shredded* was more like it, and I felt the grazing of his claws against my skin—there one moment, gone the next. His fingers slid down, tugged at my belt, freeing the holster that had held the Glock in place. "Put a fucking *gun* to your chin and squeeze the trigger in front of me and then walk away so easily? I'm not some tame house cat, baby girl."

His mouth closed over mine and I shuddered, lost under a wave of sensation and the sheer, overwhelming *possession*. Not just in his kiss. Not just in his hands as he went about stripping me naked—removing every blade, every weapon, every stitch of clothing.

It was everything.

All my clothes were gone and he stood fully dressed in front of me, one knee pressed between my thighs. Damon pulled away, his eyes holding mine. One hand slid up from my waist, along my torso, lingering on the ache there. No bruises remained, no sign of the busted ribs that had pained me for days. But he knew. Somehow he knew.

He continued on his path, straight up to my throat and then he rubbed his thumb over where I'd pointed the gun. I hadn't touched the muzzle to my skin—I wasn't *stupid*—and Nova had needed time and room to maneuver.

"If you *ever* do something like that again, Kit…" He raked his teeth along my neck. "So help me God. Just put the bullet in me. I'd sooner die than feel that kind of fear."

"I'm sorry."

He boosted me up, one arm holding me steady while he reached between us and tore open his jeans.

He came into me hard and fast and I cried out, unprepared.

"Swear to me," he said, fisting one hand in my hair and forcing my eyes to meet his. He withdrew, thrust deeper.

Impaled on him while the gray of his eyes was slowly replaced by the intent burning green-gold of the cat inside him, I stared. I couldn't breathe, couldn't think. This was how prey felt, I realized. When a big cat is stalking some cute, harmless little thing and looks up, realizing the predator is about to strike and it just freezes…this is why.

Damon had me in his sights and I was done for.

"Swear it," he said again, lunging deeper.

Whimpering, I strained closer, my nails clawing at his shoulders. I opened my mouth to answer, but no words came out.

Damon swore and pulled away.

I would have protested, except I couldn't make my mouth form the words.

Everything turned into a blur of heat and motion as he picked me up and carried me over to the bed. He didn't lay me down, though. He bent me over me the side of it and drove into me from behind, pulling me upright so I was pressed against him. His teeth sank into my shoulder and I gasped at the feel of his teeth invading me, the same way his cock did.

He swelled inside me and I felt his desperation, the fear.

Ragged breaths and moans fell from my lips as he drove us straight over the edge, but that desperation still didn't let up.

My shoulder was throbbing when he lifted his head. Wicked, teasing fingers slid between my thighs, seeking out my clitoris as he pressed his lips to my ear. "Swear to me, Kit," Damon demanded, his voice caught between a purr and a growl. "Tell me you'll never do that me again."

"I won't." The words tripped out of me this time, shaky and broken, rising on a sharp note as he rubbed me harder and sent me shuddering into orgasm.

It was hard and intense and he followed, his hips pumping against mine while one hand gripped me with bruising force. I sagged against him, too drained to even move.

When he let me go, I might have collapsed right there if he hadn't caught me.

He did, though.

He caught me, boosted me onto the bed and turned me around, spreading me out onto the thick, downy mattress.

Then he crawled up my body, cupped my face and pushed inside me.

"Again."

The shower pounded down on my body. Hands against the wall, face downcast, I tried not to shudder at the pelting spray. Every nerve in my body felt scraped raw and exposed. Even the water felt like it was too much.

When the door opened, I closed my eyes, barely suppressing the urge to jolt at the sound.

Over the water, I could hear him undressing and when the shower doors opened, I let my lashes lift, holding still as he stepped inside.

His hands moved to my hips and he tugged me back against him.

"Do I need to apologize?" His lips barely moved as he pressed them to the still throbbing bite mark on my shoulder.

"Did I sound like I wasn't enjoying myself?" Really, though, *enjoying* was such a tame word for what had taken place over the past hour.

I *enjoyed* sundaes and chocolate and tea and a good book.

He'd pretty much just consumed me. I don't think *enjoy* was the proper term for what had happened.

There might not *be* a proper word.

Damon rested a hand on my belly and curved his other arm

around me, tucking me tight against him. "I think you could have shot *me* and had less impact, Kit."

"I wasn't going for less impact, you hardheaded son of a bitch." Sighing, I turned in the circle of his arms. Needing some space, I eased back and rested against the wall of the shower. "You can't possibly understand the damage you would have done—not just to yourself or the clan—but to a lot of things—if you had kept pushing it."

His jaw tightened.

"You know why Nova goes by that name?"

"I'm taking his mother didn't name him that." He flicked a damp strand of hair back from my face.

"No. He actually doesn't remember what his birth name is. She called him her little monster until it stopped being amusing for her." As much as I hated my grandmother, at least she hadn't *made* me into a monster. Nova's mother had done her best to try. It was a miracle she hadn't succeeded. "She tortured him, did her best to try and make him into her little pet and when that didn't work, she tried to kill him over and over again."

Damon's jaw went tight but he said nothing.

"He goes by *Nova* because of something he started to figure out when he was fifteen or sixteen—he's always had dreams, premonitions, really. It's about how he's going to die, and there's no doubt, no mistake in his mind. He's going to die in a big, fiery spectacle—like a sun exploding…a supernova. He explained it to Justin once that he'd be going out in a blaze of glory, and taking a few fine fuckers who just needed to die."

"Is that supposed to scare me?" Damon asked, his voice sardonic.

"No. But maybe the fact that anybody who *tries* to kill Nova and gets even close to it ends up dead, no matter what Nova does to avoid it. I've seen it happen." The skepticism on his face made me want to shove him. "Again, I've seen it happen. We were sitting at a bar one night after a job. Group comes in to hold the place up and somebody pulls a gun on Nova, holds it at the back of his head. Jumpiest thing ever. Nova told him he'd be wise to point it elsewhere and the kid tells him he's lucky he doesn't it shove it up Nova's ass. Nova just sighed and shook his head and was ignoring him, never even *looked* at him. When they start making everybody empty their pockets, we were still just sitting there—we weren't going to give our money to some idiot human hoodlums. Nova laughed at the guy who came to our table and the kid behind us started screaming. Nova went to take a drink of his beer and the kid panicked, squeezed the trigger. Nova didn't plan on doing *anything*—he knew it was a kid. But his power— it works subconsciously to protect him and it kicked in, reversed the bullet. He was only fifteen. It tore Nova apart."

I shoved him now, angry. "And you were going to send *Doyle* in there as a distraction? You want to know why in the hell I felt it was necessary to do something crazy?"

I shoved him again and he let me. But I went to do it again, he just caught me up against him and held me.

"You stupid son of a bitch. Why didn't anybody tell me he was looking for me?" I demanded, my face pressed against his chest.

"Scott's finding that answer out, kitten." Damon sounded tired now and we both just stood there under the water.

"You all don't understand what you're dealing with. He could have killed whoever was at the door and a hundred others without blinking."

Damon stroked a hand up my back, not responding.

Pushing back, I stared up at him, still torn inside over the fury and the fear. And heaven help me...*resentment*. "Is this my home?"

"It is." Water caught on his eyebrows, beaded there before rolling down the hard, square lines of his cheekbones.

"Then your people need to understand that *I* deserve the same respect they get—when I have somebody come looking for me, *I* get to decide if they get turned away. *Not* some shifter I don't know from Adam."

"Consider it done, Kit." He cupped my face, staring into my eyes, a grim promise written in his own.

As it turned out, his name *was* Adam.

The shifter who'd been assigned to stand guard at the Lair's entrance stood in front of us, looking insolently at me as I finished strapping my weapons into place.

I already wanted to punch him.

That wouldn't do much good—it would just break my hand and amuse him, or piss him off. Okay, then I'd cut him with something silver and sharp. He was only a midlevel shifter. His power wasn't anything to write home about. He was just a grunt. Grunts, I could handle.

Damon wasn't here yet.

I wondered if that was by design.

I had fifteen minutes left before Nova was going to arrive. He'd called to change plans, and so I'd spent the last thirty minutes packing up gear and making calls.

There was a knock at the door and Adam turned to answer it.

"Are these your rooms?" I asked quietly.

He frowned at me.

"Are these *your* rooms?"

"No. But the Alpha—"

"These *are* my rooms." Saying nothing else, I called out, "Enter."

Doyle came striding in. He flicked a look at Adam, looked bored, and then came over to me. His hands came up, gripped my shoulders. "Are you okay?"

"I'm pissed."

"We'll find them, Kit." He hugged me tightly and I squeezed his waist, eyes closing for a minute at that simple reassurance. Nobody else had offered it. Sometimes, it helped to just have somebody say something like that.

"They're my family, Doyle. We have to."

"I know." He sounded so mature—so grown up. He was almost nineteen now, far more mature than the skinny kid we'd saved from a pit. His blue eyes held mine for a moment before he looked over at Adam. "You got a problem, Coombs?"

"No, Enforcer."

"Then maybe you can quit staring at Ms. Colbana." Doyle's voice went hard, softening to a dangerous gentleness as he stepped around me, taking a few steps closer to Adam.

"Yes, Enforcer. I..."

"You what?" Doyle crossed his arms over his chest.

"I'm just wanting to know why I'm here. I was told to come here and talk to her, but all she's doing is fluttering around and talking to you."

"Fluttering?" I snorted.

Doyle looked at me. "Kit, you flutter? Can you show me?"

"Sure. Let me go find my wings." Moving to stand next to Doyle,

I cocked my head. "So you were told to come and talk to *me*?"

The door opened before he had a chance to answer and Damon entered. Damon didn't *walk* into a room—it was almost like he just…took *over* a room. His presence filled it and blotted everything else out. In a black shirt that gloved the hard planes of his body and worn, faded jeans, he looked like danger personified.

Doyle gave him a deferential nod, eyes falling to the floor for a moment.

Adam on the other hand looked at the floor and kept his eyes there. Such a good little soldier.

Damon nodded at Doyle and then focused on me. He didn't even glance at Adam.

"You deal with him?" Damon asked me.

"Me?" I cocked my head, studying Adam. "Am I allowed to?"

"You're the one he disrespected, Kit. Not my place." Damon stood on the other side of me, his eyes narrowed.

"What? Alpha, I did *not*—"

Damon cut him off. "Kit's guest is here, wasn't far behind me, Doyle. Why don't you go see if he remembers the way?" He continued to stare at Adam. As Doyle moved to the door, he finally decided to address him. "Word went out a while back that Kit was mine—she was moving in and was to be accorded all respects given to anybody else living inside the Lair. Did you not *get* that message, Coombs?"

"I…yes, Alpha." His gaze slid to my face.

Nova was indeed here. I gave him a casual glance as he came strolling in behind Doyle less than a minute after Damon had sent him out.

Nova gave Adam a look of mock surprise that was so obviously feigned, I almost rolled my eyes. "Oh, hey…it's you again. Am I allowed to talk to Kit now?"

Adam's lips peeled back from his teeth.

"Perhaps you'd like to call my friend *meat* again," I said, stepping forward and drawing Adam's attention to me. "While you're at it, maybe you'll call me the same thing. I'm half-human after all. Or didn't you know?"

Adam's lids flickered.

Oh, he knew.

"If he'd been here at the Alpha's request, would you have

insulted him?"

"You're not the Alpha." Adam's voice was stiff.

"True." I shrugged. "Okay, what about Doyle? Or Scott? The people on rotation who come in and clean the public rooms here at the Lair?"

He looked away now and I felt the tension rising in the man beside me.

"I guess I have to earn your respect." Nodding, I stepped even closer, one hand moving to the sword at my side. "I'll tell you what. If you can shift and draw *my* blood before I can draw *your* blood using my blade, then I figure we're square and you're right. You don't owe me anything. No respect, no nothing and I won't make you apologize to my friend for the rudeness you showed him."

Adam started to laugh.

When nobody else did, the sound died in his throat and he asked, "Are you serious? If I harm one hair on your pretty little head, the Alpha will gut me."

"No, he won't." I shot him a look. He stood there, impassive, arms crossed over his chest as he looked on. "He told me to handle it and that's what I'm doing."

"Hell, no." Adam backed away. "I am *not*—"

"You can do it," Damon said. "Or you can apologize to him in front of the entire clan. Take your choice."

I gave Adam a sunny smile. Issuing a public apology like that would go down real well.

A growl rumbled in his throat and he stood there, hands clenched. "Fine." He glanced around. "In here?"

In response, Damon nodded at the couch. "Doyle?"

Before Doyle had a chance, though, it lifted in the air, floating back, gentle as a feather. It was followed by the table.

"Allow me, Alpha," Nova said.

Adam's eyes tracked the movement before they slid to the psychic's face.

"Even *meat* likes to be helpful."

Adam said nothing. He just backed away, cracking his neck one way, then the other.

Hands loose at my sides, I waited.

I felt the energy gathering while behind me, Doyle said to Damon, "Is it wrong to bet money on this?"

"You're welcome to, but if you think I'd bet against her, you're nuts."

"Shit." Doyle rubbed at his jaw, sounding disgusted. "Oughta do it in front of everybody. I bet there are a few suckers stupid enough."

A muscle twitched near Adam's eye while the energy gathered and gathered. Right as it culminated, I whipped my blade out. Pain slashed through the back of my head, catching me off guard but I shoved it down and moved, tucking my body tight and darting forward.

Adam had no half-form, it would seem. He went straight into a medium-sized cougar and I brought my blade up, dragging it down his belly. Hot blood splattered as I came up out of the shoulder roll and turned, staring at his downed body.

Low whines came out of his throat as he melted from cat back to man, nude now.

Walking over, I bent over him, the tip of my blade on the ground.

He looked up at me, eyes dazed from shock. "You can wait until you're healed up before you offer that apology. But do us all a favor and be sure to let people know...if somebody comes asking for me, *I* decide if they are welcome or not. You could have cost lives with this bullshit of yours. And if my friends *do* die..." I pressed the tip of the sword against the underside of his chin. "So will you."

I turned and met Damon's eyes.

The corner of his mouth tilted up faintly before he looked at Doyle. "Get him out of here."

CHAPTER FOURTEEN

"Kit."

Chang stood in the doorway.

He'd changed into a fresh suit, had combed his hair—likely showered, too. I nodded at him. "You look steadier."

His mouth twisted in something too...dour to be considered a smile. "That was unsettling. In the future, if I ever seem to doubt you again, smack me—or *shoot* me—sooner."

"I think I'll avoid using the shooting thing in the future."

"For Damon's sanity, that might be wise." He came inside and shut the door. He handed me a slip of paper. "More of the missing. I'm sorry."

I looked at it, felt something inside me clench in denial and I had to shut it down. *Missing...they are missing. You need to help find them.* "Thanks."

"Of course." He flicked at some imaginary speck of lint on his sleeve. "I need to ask you something about these...jobs you've been doing."

"Ask me what?" Uneasy, I checked the time. I didn't have much, and I still had to call Whitmore. Technically, for another few hours, I was still in his employ and I owed him a follow-up for what had happened with Chaundry.

"Damon told me that Justin had some valid concerns about your client."

Heaving out a sigh, I turned to look out the window. "Valid. You could say that."

"Is it possible the man you're working with is an imposter?"

"Anything is possible, Chang," I said quietly. "I could always sit around go over video of him from the time he started—in my copious free time."

"I'm already having one of my best men tackle that." Chang

folded his hands in front of him, staring at the floor, his brow creased with some heavy, dark thought. When he looked back at me, the intensity of his dark eyes made me even more nervous. "You mentioned something about caves…in Alabama."

"Yeah. So?"

"What about these caves?"

Nerves had my hands going slick and I turned away before swiping my palms against my thighs. "Why?"

"Please, just answer."

"He insisted there was something important inside a series of privately owned caves and he wanted me to check them out, see if anybody might have been squatting. Said he'd give me more detail after I'd been out there." I hitched a shoulder, remembering the malevolence that all but dripped from those caves, like water had dripped from the mouth of the limestone opening.

"And?"

He had one hand clenched into a fist. A tight one.

Yeah…something wasn't good.

"Something was in there. I wasn't going to check it out without backup and I didn't want *his* backup. I wanted people I knew and trusted with me." I lifted one shoulder. "If Justin had made it clear he was ready to work, I would have looked him up regardless. But I didn't think he was ready to work and Wh—my *client* shot down the option of letting me reach out to other contacts."

I don't know what it was that kept me from saying his name, but instinct was screaming at me. *Don't do it…don't do it…* "Anyway, long story short, I didn't go in. Just gave him my general impression of the place and four hours later, I was given the information for the next job."

"Which was…?"

"The one that almost ended up turning me and Justin into toast," I said sourly. "My turn to ask questions—what's going on?"

He reached inside his coat and handed me his tablet.

I flicked the screen—he'd deactivated the password and the images flared to life.

Freak wildfire—

I took in the headline, saw the date. Right before Justin and I had left East Orlando.

Nobody had arrived at the house we were asked to watch twelve hours after us…and we'd been late getting there. Three days late, thanks to getting sidetracked by Colleen.

The media article speculated about the *arcane nature* of a fire that had swept through an isolated patch of private property, possibly started by a fire set by non-human vagrants who had been using a privately owned cave. Five bodies had been taken from the deepest section of the cave, but the damage had pretty much made identifying them impossible. However, the bones were *not* human.

"I have police photos of the bodies."

I handed him the miniature computer and a moment later, I was staring at long, thin skeletons, hands that were more claws than anything else. Oversized heads. Photos had been taken of the teeth and I grimaced, pushing it back to him.

"There were bones hanging in the trees," I said. "When I approached, I saw bones. The smell…"

"Do you know what they were?"

"If I had to make a guess? Black Annis. Lots of Scotsmen settled in Alabama a few hundred years ago." I slid him a look. "I don't know much about history in general, but when it might be associated with monsters…" I shrugged. "When you move a lot of people around, their monsters tend to follow."

"Yes," he murmured. "We do."

I handed him the tablet, shuddering at the thought of possibly having to face the ghoulish things.

"If he sent you there to die…" Chang let his words trail off.

"They weren't always deadly." I shrugged and turned away, shooting one more look at the clock. "If he had Chaundry wipe them out first, then I assume it was because he *did* want something in that cave found. The question is, why not tell me what it was?"

"He's leading you around on a string, Kit. Be cautious with him. I don't trust this man."

"Yeah." I met Chang's eyes. "Me, neither."

After Chang left, I placed the call I'd been putting off.

This wasn't going to be fun.

Jaw tight, I braced my hands on the surface of the table and waited, counting off each ring of the phone.

One.

Two.

Three.

Four.

Five.

It didn't go to voicemail which made me think he'd been waiting on my call and was now sitting there, staring at the phone and making *me* wait. Tension knotted between my shoulders and I thought of Justin and Colleen, dread so heavy in my gut, I could practically taste the sourness of it creeping up my throat.

Just when I was about to hang up, the phone was answered.

There was no change on the video feedback and silence greeted me on the other end of the line, but I knew he was there.

Going to try and play cat and mouse? Irritated, I stayed quiet, waiting. Damon played the game a little too well for me to be thrown by some prick not speaking on the other end of the line.

"Hello, Kit," Whitmore finally said, breaking that interminable silence.

"Hello, sir."

There was a humming pause before he spoke again. "You rarely use my name. Is there a reason for that?"

Don't say his name, don't say it, don't say it…

I blinked at the question, a little surprised. But he was right. I'd only grown conscious of my aversion within the past few hours. However, I'd avoided it for quite some time. Whenever I *thought* about saying it, there was just some sort of…reluctance.

"While I've got a reasonable expectation of privacy where I am, I prefer to take utter caution," I said, thinking of that deliberately just so it would ring true. I *did* have a reasonable expectation of privacy here but if I were ever overheard, questions might be asked. Thus, a good reason to *not* use his name. I knew a hundred ways to circumvent telling a falsehood. I'd been doing it for most of my life.

"I appreciate your dedication, Kit. Truly. I am…concerned, though, for how things have been going of late. That display earlier, your apparent lack of concern in reaching out to me…"

I kept my gaze on the blankness of the monitor and resisted the urge to flip it off. "I had an urgent matter arise, sir. That's why I ended the call. A…security breach here in the Lair, as matter of fact." Chang and I had discussed what I'd tell him and he'd decided there was no harm in letting Whitmore think Damon's protections might be…weak.

Let him send his goons in if he feels the need to test us. We'll peel the skin from their bones and send him the remains. Gift-wrapped.

I wasn't entirely certain he'd been joking.

"Oh?" Something that might have been interest stirred in Whitmore's voice. "I hope nobody was hurt."

"No. No, of course not. But in the aftermath, I received disturbing news about Justin, as well as another friend of mine. Which leads to why I'm calling. I want to finish detailing what happened with the final job and then I'll be unavailable for some time. As our business concludes this afternoon, I imagine there will be little concern, but I wanted you aware." There was still no life on the monitor yet I had the strangest feeling that while *my* video feed was inactive, his wasn't. Slowly straightening, I took the phone and went to audio only, tucking the phone in my hip pocket.

"You wanted me…aware." Cool displeasure filled those three words.

"Of course."

"Kit, you failed me in several of the jobs—you can't believe I'm really going to let our business be *concluded.*"

"It *is* concluded. You asked me to find a dryad—I did. You gave no specifics beyond that. You wanted me to pursue information about a possible Green Man—I did. I found no sign that a Green Man was *ever* in Alabama, and I even continued researching it after you put me on another assignment. You sent me on several information runs pertaining to Blackstone and each of those was quite…illuminating. Several people have already been questioned by their respective Alphas. You asked me to observe a witch who *should* have been harmless enough and she almost fried my ass. I don't believe you can call it a failure that we had to defend ourselves against her."

"There should have been no *we.*" The angry pulse in his voice slammed into me.

Clenching my fist, I refused to acknowledge it. "As I wouldn't be here without having that back-up, I'm finding it hard to be sorry I took a partner along."

As I paced over to the window, I heard a faint clicking, like nails tapping against a hard surface. *Tap, tap, tap, tap…tap, tap, tap, tap…*

It was enough to put my teeth on edge.

"I'm not satisfied you fulfilled your end of the bargain, Kit."

"I'm afraid you'll have to be unsatisfied then. I've got two friends who are missing and they need me more than you do. I can give you the names of others who could be of use to you."

There was a faint pause. "Missing. Who is missing, Kit?"

"Justin Greaves and Colleen Antrim," I said coolly. "It would appear somebody within Blackstone might have them. And I'm going to get them back."

"Oh, Kit." A heavy sigh filled the line. "This…this very thing, it's what I was trying to prevent."

"Yeah. It sure seemed like we were getting a lot done on that front." The words escaped me before I thought about the insult, but I didn't try to grab them back, nor did I apologize. Instead, I went to the table and looked at the list of names Chang had given me earlier.

"Do you think it's an easy undertaking I have? I have little support among the Senate, the Congress *and* my contacts within Banner are resistant to the idea that a subtle strike against Blackstone is the best way to handle this." He paused a moment before continuing. "Every *day* those within Banner become more resistant. I need allies who will work *with* me, not *against* me."

I bet you do. Staring at the names, I touched my finger to the first one, then moved down the list.

Seven more in Florida.

Twelve in Georgia. Nine in Alabama.

These were just the names reported.

How many had gone unreported?

"Personally, I don't care if you want to go subtle or use a micro-bomb to incinerate the place," I said. "Want to know what I care about?"

"By all means, Kit. Tell me what you care about."

"Edith Banks. Orin Fuller. Wes and Jen Li, plus their four-year-old daughter. Gayla Tremayne. Jason Nolan." I stopped after I'd finished reciting the names of the missing from Florida. "Know who they are?"

"I'm a smart man, Kit, but I'm afraid I can't account for every shifter in the country."

"Huh. Odd that you know they are shifters." My hand tightened on the phone as a sickening suspicion began to form inside my mind. "Just how did you know that?"

"You're more caught up in the lives of shifters than anybody else. It's called taking a stab in the dark." His response came on the heels of mine, flippant and hard. I sensed no nervousness or anything else in his words.

But—

That *but* was there.

"Uh-huh."

I didn't believe him. I might as well just skywrite it for all the doubt apparent in my voice. Instead of lingering on it, though, I forged ahead. "I have to head out shortly. I'll be checking in with Damon regularly, so if you decide you want a name to take this job on, leave word with him."

"I'm afraid I'm going to have to insist you continue this job, Kit. Don't make me use the weight of my office."

"You want to force me to do a job that requires stealth, a minimum of fuss, and me being somewhat…discreet." I smirked. "Sure. That's going to go over *really* well when my gut is telling me that I have another priority, sir. You got any idea what my kind are known for?"

"Don't push your *luck*, Kitasa."

"I'm not the one pushing it, sir. *You* are." I disconnected the phone and shoved shaking hands through my hair. "This is going to go straight to hell."

A handbasket wouldn't suffice, either.

I'd need something more along the lines of a wheelbarrow. Or maybe a dump truck.

"I never figured it would be a party, Kit."

"And here I was thinking you were the all-seeing, all-knowing Nova." I scraped the toe of my boot across the tire tracks, wishing *I* was all-seeing and all-knowing.

There were five others with us and while that wasn't a surprise to me, it was a few more people than I'd like to have. The good news was that all of them knew how to be quiet. I was probably going to be considered the loud one of the bunch, followed closely by Nova.

It had been decided that this *issue* was a threat that needed to be taken seriously by both Clan and Pack. As such, the group hunting for the witches known as Colleen Antrim and Justin Greaves would include shifters trusted by each group's Alpha.

That had been suggested by Chang.

Colleen's house, while not exactly isolated, was set apart from the others around it and while I was going to ask, I already knew nobody would have seen anything.

Nova had been very rude and done a mind-scan, pulling impressions from surface thoughts. He'd told me he didn't *see* it as rude since those surface thoughts were no more than white noise to him—nobody had seen anything out of place. If they had, it would still be lingering close enough for him to pick up on, and there was nothing there.

One woman had seen a black car and Nova suspected it was government issue. She hadn't thought much of it because one of Colleen's neighbors actually *did* work for the government—drug enforcement. He had no problems having a witch close by, and actually came by from time to time when he was going to be pulling some long hours.

And strangely enough, the DEA agent wasn't home—hadn't been for a few days—so it wasn't his car the woman had seen.

But there was nothing more helpful than a vague time of day.

I wasn't getting much of anything useful myself as I paced around the house, but I continued to do it, because sooner or later, I'd find something. Widening my perimeter check, I moved into the trees. A familiar, overly strong scent caught my nose. Lemongrass.

Colleen used it, but it seemed out of place here—and way too strong. Following the scent, I let my gaze skim up and down, my thoughts drifting. I didn't want to guide them. I'd tune in on things faster if I let my instincts take over.

When I saw it, everything inside me tensed.

"Doyle."

Although he was on the far side of the property, he heard me and was at my side in under a minute. Others followed after, the two cats from the Clan, one a tall, thin man who'd told me to call him Roper and a svelte woman who was so pretty and delicate, she looked like a fairy. Her vivid red hair was cut short and her eyes, blue as the summer sky, twinkled and laughed. Her name, incongruously, was Mo. When I'd asked her about it, she'd said it was short for Maureen and nobody ever called her that. Of course, I'd asked why.

She'd stopped smiling. "It was my mom's name."

There was pain in the answer. I didn't ask any more questions.

While I didn't know Roper at all, I'd seen Mo around off and on and I knew she was a wicked fighter. That they were here meant Damon trusted them.

They both stopped some distance away and Mo crossed her arms under her breasts, while Roper muttered, "Well, ain't that some shit."

The wolves were slower to arrive, but they'd been checking things out around the small subdivision.

"It's a hide," I said softly.

Nobody responded. It was obvious what it was, and the smell in the air made it even more obvious why it hadn't immediately been obvious to anybody. Somebody had crushed lemongrass, and the pungent odor was masking the subtler scent that I could only barely pick out.

"Somebody's been watching," I said.

"Yes." It was one of the wolves who spoke. Pilar's dark eyes were hard, deepening the lines around her eyes. She'd been in her mid-forties when she changed—a handsome woman, strong-featured and strong-willed and she looked unimpressed with the world, this assignment...me. "Question is, was this person watching your friend, the same one who grabbed her?"

"Who else would it be?" Mo asked.

"Seems to me that whoever has been here was here for quite a while. The lemongrass is strong in the air. It's been being used regularly, for days even."

"They could have been waiting for both of them." Roper popped a piece of gum into his mouth and started to chomp on it in a way that made me wonder if he used to have a smoking habit. The way he looked at Pilar made me think he wasn't disagreeing with her, simply offering another option.

"How likely is that?" Pilar directed the question my way. "Did your friend Greaves make a habit of coming out here with the other witch?"

"No." Crouching in the grass, I studied it. It wasn't crushed flat, the way you'd expect if somebody had been tramping around here—somebody who could come and go without leaving a trace. "Nova?"

He'd been quiet for the most part, but now he pushed his way through the others to crouch at my side.

"The people who took them. Were they human?"

He grunted his assent. "Went for Colleen first. Tranqed her, then him." He paused, eyes just slits in his face. "I see it, clear as a movie in my head, Kit. Fuck me for not being here."

"You're not all-powerful, Nova." I rested a hand on his shoulder, felt the muscles tensing under my hand, his whip-lean body taut as a bowstring.

"The hell I'm not." There wasn't arrogance in his voice, just a calm assurance of his own abilities, as though he *knew*, without a doubt that he could have stopped this, if he'd only known in time.

I had little doubt of it. If he'd been here, he *would* have. Pushing it aside, I said softly, "Tranqs. How did they catch Justin off guard with *tranqs*?" But I answered my own question a moment later. "He was still injured, moving slow. That damage to his lungs would have killed him if he wasn't a witch. Plus, he was still on the mend from the last injury. Once they had Colleen, his focus would have splintered. It was the perfect storm of badness, just waiting."

"He's running low on power, strength…they couldn't have timed it better and if they knew he was injured, knew how to handle witches?" Nova suggested.

"They would if it was Blackstone." I tipped my head back, staring up at the tree, seeking out the branch where somebody had perched—regularly—until recently. "This person—our watcher—wasn't human. Humans can't do this, no matter how patient, how well trained. So who was watching…and where is he now?"

"She."

I looked over at the male wolf who hadn't spoken until now. Michael Grimm rubbed his nose when I looked at him and glanced away. "Whoever was here, ma'am, we're dealing with a woman. I can tell that much, even under the stink of all that lemongrass. Can't make out much more and couldn't track it if my life depended on it, but it was a woman."

I sketched a glance around at the others, but nobody offered an agreement or dissent. After remaining quiet a moment, Michael said, "My Alpha sent me along for a reason, see. My nose is…better than most. Or worse, depending on how you look at it. See, I've got what they have determined is—"

"Don't mess with the scientific explanation, Grimm," Pilar said. "Keep it short."

He grumbled under his breath, but hitched his shoulders in what was likely an acquiescent shrug as I'd already determined her to be the dominant of the two. "We'll go with the fact that my nose is fucked up, ma'am. A mutation of sorts, thanks to twice as many olfactory cells in my nose than most people. I can smell twice as good as the typical wolf—if something dies five miles from here, I can tell you where it is. And there's a lot of dead things. If we get close enough to your people, I'll be able to track them. That tree right there…there was a woman up in it. Not a man."

Slowly, I turned my head and stared back up at the tree.

For some reason, I found myself thinking of the rough, gravelly voice that had pulled me out of a sleep not all that long ago.

You need to move. Four simple words.

I reached into my pocket and pulled out the piece of shit cell phone, dialed a number.

I hoped I had it right.

I'd only seen it twice.

It rang.

Once.

Twice.

Three times.

The fourth, there was a dead air, then a beep.

I left a message and hung up.

Let's see if my instincts were as good as I thought they were—as I *hoped* they were.

CHAPTER FIFTEEN

It was another four hours before we stopped.

I'd had three calls, but none were the ones I'd been waiting on.

Chang had been sending me leads on what he thought were possible sites to check out. I marked two off the list just by looking at a map and told him so.

"It would make this easier if you gave me a general idea of just where you're going."

"North," I said.

"North. Lovely."

"I'm going to Georgia. I know that much." Brooding over the map, I shoved my hair out of my face and tried to think of anything but Justin and Colleen. Especially Colleen. Justin, even injured, could handle a whole lot of torture and misery. Colleen, though, she'd never had to. She was a healer. She was an empath. She'd been through the loss of her daughter, and that had all but shattered her. I didn't want to think of the kind of hell this might be bringing on her.

"Nova—he said he escaped Blackstone. Are you heading in that direction?"

"No," I murmured, unsure why that was, but something was steering me away from there just yet. "Gimme a minute."

Bent over the map, I made a few more marks on it and then took a picture, sending it to Chang. "Focus on that area." After I disconnected, I called Nova over and he looked at the map, his mouth tightening when he did.

"Chang is tracking down the facility," he said.

"What?"

Nova glanced up at me and tapped the wide circle I put on the map, located between three of my Xs.

"I don't know how long I walked, but when I busted loose, yeah. It was around there. Big ass place, a private facility, hospital or something at one point. It had been fortified, turned into a veritable fortress. It was all underground. The surface of the place was just ruins, or it looked like it. But they'd reinforced *everything*. I practically needed wings to get out." He shrugged. "I guess I could have blasted the walls, but like I said, some of those people can't get out. Others…well, they shouldn't. Blackstone's destroyed them. If Chang didn't track it down…" His eyes slide to me. "Oh."

"It's called logic and reason. Three missing persons that we know of, but nothing *in* that spot. Just around it." Scowling, I tapped out how the *Xs* I used for each missing person formed a vague path, pointing that direction, save for the final two, one maybe thirty miles east, one maybe thirty miles west. "They stay out of that immediate area. I figured it was for a reason."

"Well, their spot in somewhere…" He waved a hand at the map. "Yeah, you're on the right track. Tell you what—that whole place? It's dead there. There's people but the place is…it's dead. It's like the life of the earth is dying. Any witch in that vicinity, you'd think she'd go insane. That…emptiness. I've felt it before. In the war," he said absently, scraping at the beard growth on his face and frowning.

"The war?"

The frown on his face deepened and he turned away. "We should get something to eat before they devour everything in there."

We'd stopped at a roadside dive advertising BBQ, along with a sign that read, *Your money is good here*. It was a subtle way for the owner to make it clear he didn't care about the type of customers, just the color of the money. Green was what mattered to him.

But as empty as my belly was, that little bomb Nova had just dropped made my head feel like the world had shifted around on its axis.

The war—

The last *war* that had been fought had been forty years ago. At least the last major war that America had been caught up in. And it had been one that had involved pretty much the entire world. When it was done, the face of humanity had been altered forever. That *us* vs. *them* mentality that was supposedly settled by the treaties hadn't been settled at all—and the marks left, the prejudices left, we were still dealing with them.

The war. Forty years ago.

Nova couldn't be *that* old. Could he?

"Were you in the war, Nova?"

I didn't raise my voice when I asked him.

But I didn't have to.

He stopped in his tracks and looked back at me, his face remote. "Which one?"

Then he kept on walking.

The phone finally did ring.

Somehow, even before I looked, I knew who it was.

So I didn't look.

I just swiped the screen and pressed it to my ear and waited.

"It took you long enough to make the connection. Where are you?" Her voice, raspy as ever, came out as it had the first time we'd talked. Blunt and to the point.

"Interesting question. And really, it didn't take that long. I called you hours ago. Before I tell you where I am, I'd like some information myself. Why were you watching my friends and who the hell are you?"

"Perhaps we should consider exchanging some information on both sides, Kitasa."

My skin went tight at the sound of my real name and I closed one hand into a fist. Looking around, I debated on whether or not to share anything with her.

We'd stopped to reconnoiter and let me think; I couldn't help but marvel over the timing of the call. It almost had me thinking I needed to ditch the phone, but even as I considered it, I brushed the idea aside. I needed to talk to this woman. I wasn't entirely sure why, but I wasn't severing this connection. Pacing over to the window, long since emptied of the glass, I stared outside at the vastness of the forest.

It grew around us in almost feverish desperation, as if determined to reclaim the earth. The house we were in was one Justin and I had used before. Two hundred years ago, it had been a lush, elegant mansion—a plantation, I'd learned they'd called them—used back when humans enslaved humans. The first civil war.

The brutality of people in general—human and NH alike—never ceased to amaze me. Even now, the air around this place was thick

119

with sadness and despair, as though it had been worked into the soil, along with the tears, blood, and sweat that had dripped from the bodies of so many slaves.

Finally, I said, "I'm standing on the grounds of an old hell. And I go by Kit. Now where are you?"

"I'm witnessing the making of a new one. How interesting...Kit."

She rolled my name around on her tongue as though learning the taste of it.

"Interesting." Eyes narrowed, I shifted my gaze to the skeletal remains of what I'd learned had been the slave quarters. Back when this place had thrived, they wouldn't have been so easily visible, but time had a way of undoing what man tried to do. "Just what do you find interesting about witnessing hell in the making?"

As I'd gone through my own hell under the eyes of witnesses, I wasn't so keen on somebody finding anything interesting about another's *hell*.

"Oh, it's not the making of it that interests me. It's just the fact that both of us find ourselves on the edge of hell, old and new." She sighed softly. "I often find myself on the sidelines of such."

I didn't want to deliberate over that too long.

"Why were you watching Colleen?" I demanded.

"I was waiting for you."

That wasn't what I expected. Rubbing the back of my neck, I turned away from the window and stared around. Doyle had slipped into the room. Part of me had realized that, but I was so used to him, so attuned to him, I hadn't thought much of it and now, seeing him standing there in the doorframe caught me off guard.

"Why were you waiting for me?"

"I needed to speak with you and your home, your office, they are not particularly...private." She spoke slowly as if choosing her words with care. "And the cats with whom you have allied yourself have made it clear they are not particularly welcoming to outsiders."

My jaw went tight at the reminder, but didn't let anything show as I said, "If you were that determined to meet me, you could have called, left a message at my office or at my house."

"And you're the trusting type. Would have willingly agreed to approach me at a place of my choosing, alone." She laughed drolly and the amusement in her voice sounded real.

"There a reason why I have to talk to you alone? Because generally people who don't have any ulterior motives aren't all that worried about that kind of thing."

Again, another laugh. "But I do have ulterior motives. You might trust your cats, Kit—"

She stopped so abruptly, I wondered what else she'd been about to say. When she didn't continue, I forged on. "Yes. I do trust the cats—or at least most of them." There were still a number of them who didn't like me, and who believed I had no place there as I wasn't Clan—and never would be.

Whether there would be a reckoning over that, I didn't know but it didn't change the fact that I had placed my faith in the Clan—Damon, in Doyle, Chang, Scott. Even in Shanelle, although I knew she would have to make a hard choice on where *she* placed her faith soon.

Pushing all of that aside, I said, "So if this is about the cats..."

"It's not. It's about...well, I was there because I wanted to talk to you about things that are of no concern to them, and I wanted to make sure I had your undivided attention. They seem to think what concerns you concerns them and I don't share that idea. And none of that has anything to do with the fact that I'm now trailing your two friends."

She couldn't have shocked me anymore if she reached through the phone and punched me. I'd been trying to get a gauge on whether or not I could trust her, trying to decide if she'd lie or mislead me when I pushed for information about what she'd seen—but she was *trailing* them?

"Where are you?" I demanded.

"The signs I passed tell me I'm in Georgia. There were other signs—road signs, all numbers that blur together. Then a few names for towns. We're in a small one now. It's dead. Decayed. A war ran it over."

"A war..." I stopped, shaking my head because I understood what she meant. There were a number of small towns that were just gone, more victims of the war. "Where is it? What's the name?"

"I haven't seen it. There are houses, all empty. People died here. Nobody comes here. I think that's why they chose this place. It's abandoned and save for me, nobody hears the screams."

Screams.

"Who has them?" I demanded, fury starting to pump inside me, so hot and potent, I could feel flesh giving way under my blade. Heat gathered in my hand and I rubbed it against my leg repeatedly, trying to ease the ache there. "Tell me."

"Humans." She sounded bored, as though she weren't describing anything more interesting than a dead cockroach. "Meaner, more resourceful than I would give them credit for, but they are just human. If your witch wasn't so injured, he would have turned them to ash by now. They have him drugged, and her. But they watch her less. She isn't one of their fighters. They seem to understand witches."

"They would." Drilling the heel of my hand against my head, I stared at the map. "Are you..." I blew out a breath. "Are you closer to the east or west?" I needed to go *north.*

"North. Then east. We crossed the border to another state—they've begun to build walls," she said, her tone dry. "People always think *walls* will keep them safe."

Walls.

South Carolina.

I strode over to the map and bent over it. They'd started the construction, just as promised, claiming they would focus on the more rural zones because that's where the feral vampire menace had raged out of control. Strangely enough, the government was subsidizing it. At first, they'd demanded that the vampire houses cover the cost as they'd been the ones responsible for getting the feral population under control, but then things had changed.

"Where?" I demanded again. "How far north?"

"You are very demanding. There are falls. A lot of water. Use your brain, girl." The line went dead.

Furious, I spun around and threw the phone.

Doyle snatched it out of the air as he came my way.

I was already bent back over the map when he reached me. If I looked at it much harder, I might go blind, but that didn't stop me. The roads, names of towns, the very lines on it seemed to waver and dance in front of me. *Use your head, girl.*

Those words echoed in my brain, mocking me.

"Who was that?" Doyle asked quietly.

"I don't know." I gripped the edge of the table so hard, the splintering edges of it cut into my fingers. I ignored the minor stings and focused harder. North. North. North.

If Justin was here, he'd tell me to focus.

He'd tell me to breathe, to think.

Doyle rested a hand on my shoulder.

"Kit."

"It was the woman who was in the hide, Doyle. She's following them. But she can't tell me where she is. What kind of fucking idiot describes a place by a mess of trees and a waterfall and…" Ready to scream, I shoved my hands through my hair and then went back to trying to squeeze the table edges into nothingness.

"If this was me right now, you'd be telling me to take a breath. Breathe. Focus. Do all the shit you're always telling me to do."

It startled a sharp laugh out of me. "Fine…I'll shut the hell up and listen."

"That's the idea."

Somebody came into the room and he turned to deal with it. I stared at the map, bent over closer. The walls.

They had already started on them, working in the least populated areas.

A waterfall.

Grabbing my knife, I started to toss it from hand to hand. So many lakes and rivers around here. Almost like my own personal hell—my *home*, I thought sourly. Not that it was home.

It was just…hell.

Use your head, girl...

The knife slipped from my hand.

The point went straight down on the map.

Head cocked, I bent closer.

Calhoun Falls.

And I knew.

"Here," I said to Doyle. "We're going here."

CHAPTER SIXTEEN

"If you are going to toward the South Carolina border, why am I digging up information on this area around..." Chang paused. "Milledgeville?"

"Because they don't have Justin and Colleen there."

Mo was driving while I split my time between talking to Chang, trying to convince him that he didn't need to update Damon about our destination all while I was trying to dig up my own information about Calhoun Falls.

So far, I was having luck with at least one of my goals.

I could tell a whole lot of nothing had happened with Calhoun Falls since the end of the war. A couple of weres had tried to make it their stronghold, refusing to toe the new line drawn by the Assembly. The small, troublesome faction of weres no longer existed. Not just for refusing to toe the line, of course. They'd drawn their *own* line by slaughtering nearly thirty people while reinforcing what they'd thought would be a solid fortress.

They'd been one of the first cases for the newly formed Bureau of American Non-Human Affairs. The earliest Banner units hadn't been quite as neat and they'd cut an ugly swath through more than a dozen others, including innocent shifters before they took out the bastards involved. Most humans had left smaller places like that, taking up refuge in larger cities or the camps that had popped up by the dozens—all clearly marked by the National Guard or other military units—*humans only, all others will be exterminated*. Not executed. *Exterminated.*

It had turned into just another one of the ghost towns, a sad, silent victim of a war that hadn't needed to happen.

Tracing a finger over the line that marked the border, I said, "Nova knows the general area of the hospital—he has it narrowed down to a few hundred square miles. I'm guessing Milledgeville—it's almost dead between the two northernmost disappearances, and then there's nothing. The incidences were like a trail leading north, then it stops, right there. My gut tells me we've got something going on there."

"So why aren't *you* going there?"

"Because that's not where Justin and Colleen are." I didn't tell him about the call or my odd helper. It would come with questions I couldn't answer and I knew anything I said to Chang would be relayed to Damon in some way, shape, or form.

There was a pause that lasted forever and when it finally ended, Chang said, "Would you switch to video?"

"Can't right now. Need my attention on something else." I was still eying the map, but that wasn't exactly what held my focus. I just wasn't going to look at Chang and risk him seeing something in my face that he didn't need to see. "But I need that info and I can't do what I need to do here and dig up info on that area, too. Besides, you're better at it then I am."

"Nice snow job, Kit. Very nice. I almost believe that's entirely why you called. Almost." After an exaggerated, pained sigh, he continued. "I assume that whatever you are up to is something that would cause Damon great concern. I'm going to go with past experience and assume you can handle this. Don't make me regret it."

"Never." Rubbing my thumb over the hilt of my sword, I considered the roads leading toward our destination and I mentally compared them to the roads presented by the computer's GPS mapping system. Some of the roads on my map no longer showed on the GPS, but that just meant they weren't actively used or kept up.

The roads themselves, or parts of them would still be there.

"Go in that way," I murmured.

"Kit..."

Chang's voice drew me back to the conversation. "Stop worrying. You're like a mother hen."

"I'd be insulted except that sometimes you *require* a mother hen. Keep your neck safe, if you would." He disconnected and I went back to brooding over the map.

"Eat." Doyle shoved some food in front of me. It was a sandwich wrapped in wilted paper and I suspected it would be about as tasty as the paper itself, but I took it and unwrapped it, shoving a quarter of it into my mouth. It was like sawdust.

Doyle nudged me over and settled in next to me, studying the map.

He'd figured out the general area of our destination. It had taken him longer. but he was younger and he had only received what miserable training I could offer. Mine had never been as thorough as it could be. It had been ended rather abruptly after I killed a cousin who raped me, then two of the royal guards and fled, knowing I'd be dead if I was caught.

He was coming along well, though. Shifters were instinctive creatures anyway and he'd never been taught to shy from those instincts.

I continued to eat the tasteless sandwich while he studied the two maps.

"We'll never make it there in the cars, not without drawing attention," he said finally.

"Nope."

Slanting me a narrow look, he asked, "Have you figured out what we'll do next?"

In response, I used the tip of a pen to point out the nearest small town on the Georgia side that still had through-traffic. "It's ten miles out. We can cover that distance on foot in no time. There are hotels. I'll get rooms. We'll leave the cars."

Doyle grunted in disgust. "Rooms in Georgia for us?"

"Nova and I will handle it." Sighing, I pulled a hand through my hair and then looked down at my clothes. "I can pass for human as long as nobody there is anything *but* human. If Nova wears shades and doesn't act too crazy, nobody will think anything of him. You all...well..."

"Let us out a few miles outside of town." Doyle tugged absently on his left ear. "Whole place has coverage. We'll stay to the trees. Nobody will see or hear us unless we want them to. We'll find you. Maybe you'll luck out and they'll have those separate units and we can all meet up in one of them."

"Maybe." I grimaced, doubting the kind of luck I had was going to stretch *that* far. "So we leave the cars there, wait until nightfall, and head in."

"Best bet." He turned then, facing me. We were at a small, rundown gas station, another place that had a sign out in front. *Your money is good here.* I caught the scent of weres all over the places.

126

Seemed there were more than a few people who weren't all too keen on the idea of shutting people out, although for the most part, Nova and I did most of the interactions while the shifters kept to themselves.

I didn't blame them.

Earlier somebody had seen Pilar and pegged her in an instant. He'd spat on the ground at her feet, as if waiting to see what she'd do.

She hadn't done anything.

But Nova had given him a nudge to move it along, in the form of his car starting to roll its way out of the parking spot.

He had given me a look of pure innocence, but I'd seen the amusement in his eyes as the jerk screamed obscenities and ran the car down.

As if he'd sensed my thoughts—and maybe he had—Nova came strolling up, the remains of a sandwich similar to mine in his hand, the paper crumpled into a ball. "Are we ready, fearless leader?" he asked, drawling so hard on the *r*, it came out more like *lead-uh*. "I assume y'all have worked out your plan of attack."

Doyle cocked his head, curiosity in his gaze. "Just what are you?"

"Crazy." Nova flashed a grin. "Haven't you figured that out yet?"

When Doyle went to press further, I bumped him with my elbow. "Let it go. If he decides to elaborate, he will. Otherwise, you'll figure it out on your own soon enough." As Nova shifted his attention my way, I nodded. "We've got an idea. You want to hear it?"

"No. Like I said, you're the fearless leader." Restless, his gaze roamed all over and I could tell there was something on his mind.

"Doyle, why don't you go round everybody up?" I looked over at him.

He recognized the ruse for what it was—giving Nova and I the pretense of privacy. Unless Nova decided he really, really wanted to be private. If he decided he wanted to have a one-to-one chat, it would happen inside my skull where only the two of us were privy to it.

"Everything okay?" I asked as he took up the spot where Doyle had been just a moment earlier.

"Yeah. Maybe. Yeah. Just something weird in the air. Unexpected." He hitched a shoulder. "What happened with your sword, Kit?"

Now *that* was unexpected. Shoving away from the car, I paced a few steps away as tension turned my spine into a steel pipe. "Not something I wanted to talk about, Nova."

"Somebody had their hands in your head. I can see that. She do it?"

Gnashing my teeth together, I pivoted, a hundred ugly things on my tongue, but the expression on his face shut them all down. He looked worried...and a little sad. I couldn't think of any time when I'd seen him sad. Even knowing he was looking down the gauntlet to his own death hadn't made him sad.

"Why haven't you just looked for yourself?"

"Because you asked me not to go poking in your head." Those white, eerie eyes moved away. "I try to respect it when a friend asks. I'd only do it if I felt I had to. Just like I'm only asking now because I feel like I need to know. I can tell it hurts to talk about it. It's all over you, the pain of what happened. It's stinging my head, so trust me, I'm not doing this because I want to."

Oxygen had gotten trapped up in my lungs, and I forced myself to breathe out. Then to breathe in. As long as I was focusing on breathing, it was easier to stay somewhat distant.

"Jude Whittier," I said, and I was surprised at how calm I sounded.

Nova's lids drooped lower. "He's a piece of scum. Haven't heard much about him lately."

"That's because he kidnapped me almost a year ago. Hauled me up to someplace in the Canadian Rockies. He had a witch—one of the warriors who doesn't really give a fuck who he fucks over as long as he gets the money he's owed. The guy was able to go in and snap the bond with my sword. I can't call her anymore."

A slow sighing sort of breath escaped Nova, and he lifted his head to the sky.

"The witch?"

"Dead. That's one ounce of flesh I got back at least."

"And Whittier?"

"Locked in a silver casket for another forty-nine years." My gut crawled thinking about it because as long as Jude was *alive*, I don't know if I'd ever feel safe again—and I *hated* that, hated that fear. Hated it.

"Huh." Nova ran his tongue along his teeth. "I should have asked back in Orlando. I could have turned his insides into his outsides and when they exhumed him, it would be a *real* exhumation—nothing but a true corpse."

It was enough to make me smile.

Nova shoved off the car and came closer, his eyes on mine. "And the woman—the one who stuck her hands inside your head?"

"Her hands…" Hissing a little, I pushed that image away. I know he didn't mean it literally, but I'd been too busy screaming, then being unconscious to know just what had happened. "I don't know. She was trying to…I think she tried to fix it. But it can't be *fixed*. It's not like putting a car in a repair shop. This is more like shattering a blade."

For a second, Nova's eyes started to glow and again, I had the feeling he wanted to say something.

But he just stopped and shook his head.

"We should get going. We've got friends to save, I've got people to kill, myself included."

He turned away.

"Don't."

"Don't what?"

"For fuck's sake, would you quit talking about it like you're just crushing a palmetto bug under your boot heel or something?" I snapped, circling around and glaring at him. He was a few inches taller than me so I had to tip my head back to do it, but I was so *tired* of hearing it. He talked about his death like it was…nothing. Like his life meant nothing.

To my surprise, he reached up and touched my cheek.

Shifters had gathered around us.

In their eyes, he was committing a cardinal sin. He wasn't part of their clan and he was touching the Alpha's mate. Man, I hated that word, but that was how they'd view it.

But he was my friend.

I closed my hand around his wrist, his skin cold under my skin. He was always cold, like the very energy inside him sapped all his body heat.

"Why do you have to do it? It's like you think the only purpose you serve is dying, by finishing whatever it is you saw yourself doing all those years ago. But there are people who don't like hearing about it, Nova." *I'm one of them.*

"It's nice," he said, smiling a little. "Realizing there are people who are going to miss me. I didn't think that would happen."

Then he turned and headed toward the second car.

"Asshole," I muttered.

As I climbed into mine, I tried to pretend there wasn't an ache inside.

I tried.

I failed.

We'd left the hotel behind more than two hours ago.

It had only taken us thirty minutes or so to reach the road I'd intended to use to take us the rest of the way to Calhoun Falls. The remainder of the time was spent moving through the woods, because the road that I'd *expected* to be little more than ruins had been surprisingly well-maintained—and in use.

Government vehicles traversed along that well-maintained road, which was why we'd retreated into the woods. There were several paths we could have followed, as pointed out by Pilar and Mo, but I wasn't following a path. Paths were there because they were *used*. Night or not, I wasn't going to walk along something that other people used regularly enough to leave a trail.

Besides, there was more coverage in the trees and after looking for a short time, I'd found a game trail. *That*, I would use.

Mike had asked me if I ever went hunting.

I'd laughed and told him not the way he thought.

He was in the lead. He'd said earlier that he could smell humans—and something else. He was having a hard time nailing down that something else, but his nose had impressed me, so he was taking point, following my general guidance about what direction to take.

"Something's not right about this," Doyle muttered as Pilar signaled for everybody to freeze yet again. Another vehicle. Nearly a half mile off, but if they were scanning the area with any sort of electronics, motion would tip them off quicker than anything.

"Yeah. I figured that out from the get-go," I said as we pressed our backs to the closest trees.

"If they're constructing walls to help with a so-called vampire threat in the rural areas, where are the vampires? I haven't caught scent of even one. And ferals, aren't they pretty…noticeable?"

I nodded. Feral vamps retreated to a state so animalistic, they might as well *be* animals. Very rabid, very dangerous animals. They stank of rotting blood and rotting meat, thanks to their lack of intelligence—they forgot they weren't meant to *eat* their prey and very often, they did and that meat just collected inside them, going fetid and eventually it sickened the vampire and it collapsed, dying from true starvation. Nobody is meant to carry food in their gut forever.

Their bodies couldn't process solids anymore, but they didn't understand that and while that…meat stayed inside them with no way to come out, well, it wasn't pretty.

"So what's the deal?" Doyle asked.

Shaking my head, I continued to work the puzzle in silence.

The last time I'd been to South Carolina had been following up on a job…hell, well over a year. No. Right around a year ago, I realized. Delivering severed heads.

We'd had to cut through South Carolina to do it, and then again on the way back.

I'd caught the scent of a few ferals on my way out, south of our general location. But nothing out of hand, really. It had been worse, actually, on my last trip in.

Worse.

And yet they had insisted...

"Cover up," I muttered. They were doing a cover up. Most humans had *left* South Carolina anyway, leaving the population under half a million at the last census and more were being offered various incentives if they, too, would leave. *Civil security is our highest concern. We don't understand why this land is so appealing to the ferals who have nested here, but many were changed here and we know that vampires are territorial. We feel that they will not spread beyond the borders. You will be safer elsewhere and we will help you find new homes.*

That had been part of the lip service offered to those who would voluntarily just go.

There was another puzzle there, but I'd have to figure it out later.

Pilar sounded the all clear and we continued on, moving maybe another two miles before Mike send back word that the scents were getting stronger.

Humans. Maybe your friend—the woman. Hard to say. Something harsh in the air, messing with my nose.

Something harsh. I couldn't smell anything, but my nose wasn't as good as a shifter.

"You smelling anything yet?" I asked Doyle.

"Maybe. I—"

He never really had a chance to finish that thought.

Up ahead, I heard somebody, Mike, I think, call out a warning.

"Hold up, guys…this…whatever it is, it's getting stronger."

"Unless it's life or death, you can figure it out while we move," Pilar said and as I looked up to tell her to stop, it happened.

Time shifted and spun away on me.

It was like I'd been flung straight into the past.

Spikes sprung up, out, from the sides, while something swung down from the air. More of them, mounted on what might have passed for an oversized child's swing, save for those thick, deadly spikes.

All of the shifters reacted with fluid, easy grace, moving out of the way. But in the time it took them to *not* be where there was a spike, more of them came up and arrows started to rain down.

Fast…so fast.

I'd only ever once seen somebody who could shoot like that.

Fear began to burn in my throat, my breaths coming in harsh, ugly bursts. Denial turned me into something so useless, the only thought I was even capable of for a few seconds was…*run.*

My brain kept shrieking that warning, over and *over* and over…

"Kit."

Doyle's voice, harsh and heavy, reached my ears, dragging me slowly out of the past.

Shaking with terror, I looked over at him.

He was pinned between one of the traps that had swung down out of the tree and another. An arrow pinned his sleeve to the tree, while one hand gripped the rope that had been used to rig the tree-trap. It was, unsurprisingly, wrapped in silver wire so his hand smoked.

He wasn't the only one trapped up in silver, so smoke was a steady stream in the air, mixing with the smell of cooked meat.

"Told you dumb fucks I smelled something," Mike said, sounding so completely disgusted. "Something on these spikes. Don't let them touch your skin."

"We can't be poisoned," Pilar said.

"It's not poison," I said.

I wasn't the only one who said it.

She emerged from the shadows just as Nova moved up to stand at my side, his hand resting on my shoulder.

At first, I couldn't see her at all, her clothes blending so seamlessly with the dappled moonlight, she looked like she belonged to the shadows.

Recognition hit.

"You," I whispered as a fist reached up and grabbed my throat.

It was the woman who had called me and warned me.

It was the woman who had shown up just as Justin and I finished dealing with Chaundry.

The woman with the raspy voice.

As I watched, she straightened, rising to her full height and reached up to pull down the mask covering her face.

The sight of her was a punch to my gut, hard and brutal.

"Hello, niece."

CHAPTER SEVENTEEN

I had my bow up, an arrow nocked in the next few seconds, leveled straight at her.

She stood on the far side of the clearing—such a perfect place for an ambush and I'd led my team right into it.

Stupid, stupid Kit.

"I'm not going back," I said quietly. "If that's what this whole set up is for, you just might as well kill me now. I will *never* go back."

Rana cocked her head, studying me with curiosity. "You're even faster than you were. Impressive. You didn't call your weapon, though. Curious."

Then she looked away from me and picked her way through the trap of spikes to stand near Pilar who was at the perimeter. "I should tell you that your packmate is correct. If you even scratch yourself on one of the spikes, you'll be…" Rana's lips curved in a cool smile. "Quite useless for quite some time. Not dead, however. It's rude to kill for no reason and I'm not here on business. I hope you appreciate the warning—and heed it."

"Rude." I bit back a laugh that probably would have been tinged with hysteria if I let it out. Watching her with trepidation as she edged closer, I eased back a little more. Nova. He could… I tried to gather my thoughts to reach out to him. If he could just do something about the spike trap, then...

Fuck.

"Trying to puzzle your way through this, I can tell. Would it make it easier if I tell you I have no interest in bringing harm to your friends?" Rana had fully circled them now and was standing close to Doyle—very close. "You're the boy."

A low growl rumbled in his chest as he stared at her, blue eyes glowing brilliantly.

"That's probably because you're too smart to pick a fight with two shifter factions." I felt like I was going to puke. My heart was pounding in my ears, so hard and fast and loud, it was making thought all but impossible. I had to think, had to figure something out.

But *what*?

"There is that. And you haven't answered. Why didn't you call the bow? You've got a bond with her. I hear the music. It's…sad. Your weapons are lonely, Kitasa."

"Fuck you." I spat the words out at her, thinking of all the times she'd stood over me while I lay bleeding in the dirt. Thinking of how often she'd stood by Fanis' side.

Her right eyebrow winged up and something very close to amusement danced in her bright eyes. "You have claws now, don't you? I always suspected you'd grow them."

She took another step toward me.

"Come any closer and you'll get an up-close and personal look at my claws, *Auntie Dearest*," I said.

I heard Doyle's swift intake of breath and I could have kicked myself for my stupidity. It was too late to take it back. His anger flooded the air, the rush of it rolling across my skin.

Rana felt it, too.

"Ah…you've got yourself a protector there, don't you?" She angled her head, one of her long braids falling over her shoulder as she looked back at him. "What would he do if I tried to attack? Risk the injury he knows he'll get?"

"I'll kill you," Doyle said, his voice no longer human. Stripes were ghosting in and out of his skin as he struggled with the beast inside him. "Be smart, bitch, and just walk away. This is trouble you don't want."

"You're quite right there…boy," she said, shaking her head. "If I'd had my way, it wouldn't have come to this. But if it wasn't me, it would be another."

Then she looked at me. "Kit, you want it to be me."

"I'm *not* going back."

"Why didn't you call your bow, Kit?" she asked again, her voice hard.

The sound of it almost made me flinch, too close to the way she would speak out on the training fields. *Don't lower that guard, fledgling. Are you a warrior or not?*

"I can't." I bit it off angrily, hating to make that admission to her, more than anybody else.

"Haven't you learned how to call other weapons?" Her gaze flicked to the sword at my hip. "You have your mother's sword—my *sister's* sword. It last sat in the chambers of my mother. Your *queen*. You've been charged with theft, Kitasa. If you cannot prove you *mastered* that weapon, you know what the penalty is."

"It's *my* sword." Heat gathered in my hand.

"Prove it." She lunged for me.

Oh, hell.

Terror rose inside my head, a scream that came from the very depths of my nightmares. I swallowed it down and tried to channel that fear into fuel as I flung my bow down and dove to the side.

I came up in a crouch, sword in hand.

"That's drawing it." Rana eyed me steadily. "Very fast. But you still drew it. If you don't want to face death at the hands of the Tribunal, *call your sword.*"

"It's in my fucking hands—"

She came at me hard and fast, a blur of silver and steel and speed that had me backing up.

Somewhere off to my side, I heard a growl, followed by a scream that ended far too soon.

"They think to get free and interfere. To save you," Rana said, her voice as calm and steady as her eyes. She slashed down, forcing me to evade or risk evisceration since I hadn't gotten my guard up.

I was off balance and off rhythm.

"What I will do is simply kill you if you cannot show me what I need to know. Then I will kill each of them. None of them are fast enough to stop me—"

Enraged, I ducked under the next strike and swung out.

"You're letting your temper control you. You were taught better than that."

Bitch. Fucking bitch. I hated her and I hated that she was right. Needing a few seconds to breathe, to level out, I darted into the slim, scraggly trees. I was smaller and—

Faster.

That caught me off guard, but it was the truth. Using the trees to my advantage, I managed to come up behind her. *Finally*—

A form moving off in the shadows distracted me for the slightest second, costing me what would have been my one advantage. Rana heard me and spun around, bringing the blade in a wide arc.

I went backward, avoiding the blow that could have taken my head.

"Very good. It seems you've continued your training. You shouldn't concern yourself with your friends, however. If you do...well, there won't be anything left of you. Prove yourself and end this, Kitasa."

"How do I do that? Kill you?" I asked, my breaths coming in harsh pants.

We'd moved back out into the clearing and a stray ray of moonlight fell across her blue eyes. She looked like she wanted to laugh. "Do you think you can?"

I sure as hell wanted to try.

I took a chance and moved in close, trapping her longer arms and legs up. It almost worked.

She knocked me back and I ended up on my ass, leaping up a split second before she would have been on top of me.

Something glittered out of the corner of my eye.

"You're getting distracted again, Kitasa."

Something pulsed at the back of my head.

"So far, I haven't seen *anything* that proves to me that you can *call that blasted sword*." Rana's jaw went tight as she began another frontal assault that had me scrambling to evade her.

My foot caught on something.

I heard somebody snarl—a howl.

Growling.

That glittering...

"Ah...you see it, don't you?"

I tore my gaze from the shield, a simple bolster-style that really shouldn't seem so lovely. But I knew it. It had lain under a delicately etched cover of glass, next to my sword.

It, too, had been my mother's.

Each breath burned as I managed to catch myself before I would have gone down. Rana swung her blade lazily. Sweat gleamed on her face but her breaths were only the slightest bit accelerated.

"You know that shield, don't you?"

I didn't answer her.

"It's a pity that you're not a *true* warrior," she said with a sad smile. "It might have saved you."

She lunged once more. I got my sword up, but it did little good.

She had me disarmed in a move I should have seen coming—she'd used it on me so many times.

As the blade went flying, she kicked me in the stomach. I went flying, too. In a different direction.

Unable to move or breathe now, hearing nothing but the pounding in my head, panic swelling inside me, I tried to make my body move. That glittering shield looked so terribly bright—

"I'm sorry for this, Kitasa."

I closed my eyes and screamed.

Pain exploded through the back of my head.

There were growls.

Metal swung down.

CHAPTER EIGHTEEN

Her blade, swift and true, came down and struck.

The shield, burning hot in my hands, vibrated as they connected and a sound, clear as a bell, echoed throughout the clearing.

Dumbstruck, I lay there.

I just lay there.

Rana acted first.

Instinct told me to move, to get up, get away.

She crouched by my side and as I stared at her, a faint smile appeared on her implacable, emotionless face. "That took long enough. You have a head like your mother's, I think."

"...what?"

She rose and held out a hand.

Suspicious, I scooted backward and rose on my own. My legs were shaking under me as the adrenaline drained away. The shield. It felt unbelievably heavy. When I went to adjust it, my fingers brushed the metal and again, I heard bells.

I heard *him*.

The shield.

And a dozen other weapons, clamoring to be heard.

Most of all, I heard the soft, patient music of my blade from where she lay on the ground some twenty yards.

Twenty yards.

I could walk it in seconds.

Taking a deep breath, I closed my eyes.

My palms heated.

I heard her—

The solid weight of her was in my hand in the next instant.

I heard a harsh intake of breath from the clearing and Doyle said my name, but I didn't look at him. I had eyes only for my aunt.

"How did you do that?" I demanded, looking at Rana.

"I did nothing." She lifted a shoulder negligently. "It would appear somebody *else* did something. I could feel the…rift. But it was mended. However, the first time you call your weapon tends to come with a surge of adrenaline. Fear. The bond had been damaged, then rebuilt. Crudely, but it was done. You had to reestablish that bond…again, with fear. Adrenaline." Her eyes went sharp and hot. "Were you afraid the first time you called the blade, Kit?"

"I…" My mouth was dry. I so didn't want to answer that.

The first time I'd called it had been when I killed one of my cousins. One of *her* charges.

As if sensing what was in my head, she studiously turned her attention to her own blade, giving it a thorough inspection. "A body was found outside the pit where you were held. There was a struggle. Nobody knows what happened and it was declared non-criminal."

"By whom?"

Rana inclined her head. "As I was the chief marshal at the time…by me. There were no charges for that death. I can say nothing for…similar deaths however. But you can call the blade and the shield. They are your weapons."

"Be still." I smacked Doyle on the shoulder before turning my attention back to his hand. There were shredded bits of silver wire in his hand. We could leave them alone and they'd work themselves out, but he'd heal slower as long as there was silver in his system so I wanted all of it gone

He was still staring at Rana, though, his eyes glittering, full of rage.

"Damon will want her dead. *I* want her dead," he said.

She glanced toward us.

"She hears you," I pointed out.

"Do you think I care?"

My head was pounding. The music of every weapon I had was jumbled up inside there. I'd forgotten how to tune them out and part of me was so happy to hear them, I didn't *want* to.

He did spare a look at me, finally. "You called that shield. Your sword."

"I know." I kept my focus on his hand, pulled another sliver out.

"How?"

Before I could figure out how to answer, Nova dropped down next to us.

Smalls bits of silver, all of them shreds, fell like miniature tinsel on the rock I'd been using to collect my shrapnel. "That's all of it," he said.

"Who's left?" Doyle asked. All of them had gotten silver in them as they tried to work past the traps without brushing up against the spikes.

Nova looked at him. "You."

"Show-off," I muttered. But I didn't let go of Doyle's hand. I needed the distraction.

"You realize there's a reason she did it the way she did," Nova said, bracing his elbows on his knees and staring Doyle down.

"You should learn to mind your own," Rana said from her position by the small, smokeless fire she'd built.

She was the only one who had one, and everybody had raised hell when she'd gone to build it. Then it had blazed to life without smoke and they'd sulked into silence, although a couple had grumbled how the light was a hazard.

"Nobody who could see it can get close without one us hearing," she'd pointed out. "You heard every last car. Have you another objection?"

I would have made a similar fire. I knew how. But I wasn't about to do it and show that weakness.

Since those few comments, she'd lapsed into silence and looked at nobody and at nothing until now.

Nova looked unconcerned, not even looking at her. "If I minded my own, you'd be dead. It was pretty hard standing there and watching all that play out. If I mind my own now...well..." He gave a one-sided shrug.

"Watching it all play out," Doyle said slowly.

Then his hand shot across the inches separating him from Nova, too fast for me to stop him. He yanked the psychic across those inches.

Nova let him, and I tried to wrest Doyle's hand away before Nova got it in his head to *rip* it away—literally.

"Let him go, Doyle. *Now.*"

"You *watched* it all play out. That sounds to me like you knew it was coming. *Did* you?"

"Psychic, kid." Nova touched Doyle's wrist.

Doyle made a pained grunt and I heard bones crack, watched his skin cave in.

From the corner of my eye, I saw that Rana had risen. She was on her feet, eying us all a little too closely.

Doyle snarled in his throat, but I was between them before he could do anything else. "No," I said. "No."

"Kit..."

"*No.*" Disgusted, I shoved his shoulder and sat down on the log next to him, glaring at Nova while I did so. "Sometimes I feel like I'm around a bunch of school kids. No, no, no..."

There was a wet, sickening crack that I knew was bone, realigning itself as Doyle's hand set. He made no noise, although his eyes tightened with the pain.

"You knew," he said, the accusation in his eyes clear.

"That something was going to happen with Kit and her sword?" Nova nodded. "Yeah. I admit it. I did. Okay, lock me up and throw away the key."

"She was going to kill her!"

"No," I said, my voice rusty. "I'd come to acknowledge that, myself, over the past hour. "No, she wasn't."

Out of all of them, there had always been *one* person in my family who had *tried* to care for me, in the best way she knew how—and that was the woman still watching with dispassionate eyes. Perhaps she'd never outright stood up to my grandmother, but she'd always made sure I was fed, made sure I had clothes. She'd sent Rathi to get me out of the pit—yeah, that hadn't gone over so well, but she couldn't be blamed for the actions of some sick little son of a bitch.

And she was the one who'd kept training me after the others had stopped trying.

"Did you not see what I saw?"

"She was pushing me." The pulsing at the back of my head had finally stopped. It had been there in some way, shape or form ever since I'd woken up after the fiasco with Frankie. "When you were fighting the vamp, your adrenaline was up, you were fighting for your life. That's what does it. Apparently..." I hesitated, because I still hadn't explained what had happened in Tallahassee, wasn't sure *how* to explain. "Apparently, I've done some healing up, but that initial

142

bond can't be made without adrenaline pushing through."

"Basically, you had to be scared shitless," Nova said.

I made a face at him. Asshole.

He gave me a winning smile and I didn't even realize I was smiling back until the woman sitting beyond us began to stare at me. She looked like she'd seen a ghost.

"What?" I asked warily, the smile fading. I wasn't even sure how to talk to her, this woman. This...*stranger*.

"You." Rana lowered herself back down to the stump she'd claimed as her own. "You look very like your mother."

Then she pulled the edge of that dappled cloak around her. Although I knew she was there, if I hadn't seen *exactly* where she had been when she'd covered herself, I wouldn't have been able to pick her out.

Shaken, I looked around at the others.

They were all looking at me.

Waiting.

I checked the time.

One in the morning.

"Let's take a thirty-minute rest. No more. Then we move. We need to be done and gone before anybody knows we're here."

Sliding down to rest my back against the log, I braced my elbows on my knees. Doyle moved to join me. "You sleep," he said. "You need a little more than we do. I'll stay up."

I didn't bother arguing.

Not that I'd likely sleep anyway.

Not with her so close by.

But to my surprise, I did.

"Where do you think you're going?" Pilar stood in front of Rana, her solid body like the Rock of Gibraltar.

Rana took her time looking Pilar over from her head to her feet. "Twenty-two years," she pronounced.

"Huh?"

"You're a wolf. You were bitten and changed twenty-two years ago. You're strong, but not alpha and you never will be. You think *bossiness*—or surliness—makes up for that, and I assure you, it doesn't. I could have you dead in under two minutes and helpless before you could shift. I'm going and you're not stopping me."

Pilar barked out a laugh—but when nobody joined in, the laugh faded.

Mike Grimm looked at me. "Ma'am?"

One by one, they all looked at me. Rana was the last to do so, and the slight smile came and went on her face once more.

"You do not know where they are holding them. I do. You do not know where to find the traps they have set. I do—and I've disabled quite a few. You do not know where their recording devices are. I do. You do—"

"I get it." Holding up a hand to stop the recital of just why she could be useful, I looked at Doyle. His jaw clenched tight. "You'd work with the devil for Damon."

He let out a hiss from between his teeth, then gave the cats a short nod.

Grimm stepped up to Pilar and said something in a low voice. I caught bits and pieces of it, including the words *orders* and *the Alpha*.

When Pilar gave both Rana and me a disgusted look, I decided there was another reason Mike Grimm had been sent along. He was the smarter of the two.

It wasn't long before I realized just how…useful my aunt could be.

I'd never want her at my back, nor did she attempt to place herself there, but she pointed out the traps that started not far from where she'd chosen to draw her line in the sand.

That had been by design, I had no doubt.

The first problem was a camera.

She stopped us with a lifted hand and pointed it out. "Recording device. I've left these alone. I do not know how to manipulate these without destroying them."

"Then why don't we just destroy them?" That came from Roper.

"We do that, people start getting suspicious." Mo rolled her eyes at him.

"I can handle electronics." Nova smiled serenely and focused on the camera. It was so small, all I could see was the lens, small as my thumbnail. Embedded in the tree, it had likely been there for some time, because there was no human scent around it.

Electricity gathered in the air around him, cutting off abruptly.

"Are you done?"

"Not…quite," he murmured softly, lids drooping. "Dealing with the rest. They'll assume some issues with the connections and look inside for the problem first. Technology, so nice when it works…there we go."

"You can do that. All from here?" Mike looked intrigued. "What do you do, like hack into their system?"

"No. I've got a brain in my head, not a computer. But I can manipulate anything with electricity." He tapped his brow and then nodded. "We should go. This won't last forever."

The cameras were easy.

Some of the traps…weren't.

Two of them weren't man-made, either.

Witch-made—and if I hadn't dealt with the likes of them before, I would have had serious doubts about forging onward. Even more doubts than I had with one of my kin leading the way.

It was knee-jerk, that reaction, and I knew it because if she had really posed a threat, I'd feel it. But being there with her went against everything I knew.

If it weren't for the fact that I could *feel* that tugging inside of me, I would have turned back at the first magical ward.

Two of the shifters were already trying to.

"Bad shit up there," Roper said, his mouth twisting. His sentiments were echoed by Mike, who kept rubbing at his nose.

"Dead things. People. Like a cemetery—but they didn't bother embalming anybody. Ain't nothing here but death," he insisted.

The others were quieter, but I felt their aversion all the same— and it echoed mine.

"No-seeums," Nova said softly, leaning down so he could say it directly into my ear.

I jabbed at him with my elbow, vaguely aware that he had started to radiate cold the same way others radiated heat

He gestured around us. "What you're feeling. You know this magic. Justin's used it in your place. This is just on a much…wider scale."

"He doesn't call them *no-seeums*."

Nova gave me a sly grin. "But that's what they are. They make people want to look away, go away, stay away. I'm sure he has some clever witch term to describe them, but I don't know what it is. But that's what you're dealing with. Other than Colleen and Justin, there are no witches here. If you can find the power source..."

"Are you *nuts*?" If he was right, then this was a charm-based ward. And...well, it did *feel* like that. Just a lot bigger and stronger than anything I'd ever felt. "Are you implying that we should *find* the source and destroy it? That would be like throwing a match inside someplace with a gas leak."

"Then it's a good thing you've got me here." His white eyes flicked my way. "Can you track it or not? You're better at locating magic than I am."

"And here I thought you were all-powerful," I muttered. I wasn't going to do this. It was insane. I turned away and my gaze collided with Rana's. She had been listening.

"You've learned to track magic, then."

I bared my teeth at her.

She took that as an invitation to approach. Behind me, I could feel the shifters drawing closer. As a rule, none of us traveled close together, in case we missed one of the traps, but they seemed more concerned about her than anything human-made.

If I hadn't been so thrown off by her presence, I might have appreciated that.

"I don't think I've mentioned it, but you made wise allies, Kitasa. Very wise," Rana said, looking amused.

"Kit." I gritted the name I'd taken for myself out through clenched teeth. "I don't answer to *Kitasa*, anymore."

"You should." Rana's eyes looked almost...gentle. "It was the name your mother gave you. She did nothing but love you. It wasn't her fault that she died, wasn't her fault that you were...not cared for."

I wanted to hurt her then. So bad. My hand clenched into a fist so tight, my knuckles cracked. She heard, too, glancing down. The emotion in her eyes cleared, fading away into nothingness. "The magic—if you are any good at tracking, then that would be the best option. These wards are very powerful, but they cover a large area. Have you a map?"

"I don't *like* the idea."

"Because I do or because it's not wise?" The expression in her eyes challenged me. Not by being outright defiant, but simply...*questioning*.

Stalking away, I moved until I had a good ten feet of space and sucked in a deep breath. It wasn't enough, but I couldn't *run* far enough away right now. I didn't even know if Orlando would give me the distance I needed. I turned back and saw Doyle had moved, subtly placing himself between me and everybody else.

Damn, I loved that kid. The youngest of all of them, and he was the one offering himself as a shield.

A shield who could probably break one or two of them, but still.

Looking at Nova, I asked calmly, "Can you *contain* it? Whatever we find, are you sure you can contain it?"

"When have you ever known me to be *not* sure?"

CHAPTER NINETEEN

Rana found it.

She'd taken Nova with her—I didn't trust any of the shapeshifters not to try and kill her and for now, I was going to assume she had reasons for either not trying to kill *me*—or worse…take me back.

I wasn't going to go so far as to say I trusted her, but I didn't want her dead.

If she died, Fanis would know and she'd send somebody else.

I'd much rather have the devil I knew.

When the charm-ward died, I felt it, like somebody had reached inside me and ripped my guts out. I sagged and went to my knees only to be hauled up by Doyle while the rest gathered around me. His mouth was tight around the edges, but other than that, there was no sign he'd felt anything.

The other shifters looked vaguely puzzled, but that was it.

Magic didn't hit them quite the same way. Considering how they kept eying me, none of them had exactly expected my reaction. Yeah, well, I hadn't been expecting something to drop down on me like a lead weight, either.

And that had been *contained*?

Nudging Doyle aside, I nodded. "I'm good."

The tight lines remained around his eyes, though. We'd need to have a talk at some point. I needed to figure out just how sensitive to magic he was, and we'd have to figure out just what we could do to help him—although I'd suck at it. I couldn't do much to help *me*.

Nova and Rana rejoined us not long after. I'd recovered but if she had been affected by whatever Nova had contained when he destroyed the charm-ward, I couldn't tell.

She looked from me to Doyle and then gestured north.

"We're not far. You'll see the final barrier." That weird amusement glinted her eyes as we started forward. The path began to climb, a slow, easy climb at first that quickly became steeper. A light sweat broke out across my forehead, but the walk wasn't particularly challenging. This couldn't be the final barrier. The terrain was rugged enough to pose a threat to a human who didn't experience much physical exertion, but even one who occasionally went for a run wouldn't have too much trouble here.

I was about to question Rana when we reached an abrupt crest—so abrupt, if we'd been moving at full speed, it would have been easy to fall off balance.

They had picked the perfect spot for this, almost too perfect.

The dense coverage provided by coniferous trees made it harder to pick out the tiny, pin-point streams of light. Harder, but not impossible. Particularly when one had eyes that could easily penetrate the darkness.

"What in the hell...?" I breathed out.

"This has made it somewhat problematic to stay close." Rana delivered the words in a flat voice, one hand moving to the short sword that was her preferred weapon. She stroked it idly, staring at the series of small, squat buildings that lay tucked inside the cage of lights.

"Motion detectors. They'll pick up anything starting about twenty yards out from where we are, if I had to make a guess," Roper said, looking disgusted. "I'd imagine it's got a size range, so they don't have every forest critter activating it, but that there is a right mess."

Pilar eased forward, head cocked. "Noise coming from...there." She gestured to the east. "Faint hum, but some pretty solid power centralized there. Power source?"

Roper nodded, rubbing at his jaw. "I'd reckon. You know tech?"

"A bit. Did security before the bite." She hitched up a shoulder. "Not so much use for it now, but the Alpha calls me for consults from time to time. The technology has changed, but I keep current. You?"

"About the same. I did a tour or two before the war—then it was discovered that I was...well. Take a guess. I specialized in this sort of thing." The two of them skimmed the area, talking in low voices while I studied the perimeter.

"There's something up there," Rana said during a lull of their

149

conversation, gesturing up toward something all but buried in a small burl in one of the massive trees. It took me some time to make it out, but Roper saw it immediately.

"That'd be it." He nodded pensively. "If we can destroy that and take out the power source at the same time?" He shot Pilar a look.

"Have to. That unit will have a back-up system so if you take out the power source but not that, it will send an alert to the main security system. Take out that? Same thing."

"You're forgetting something," Nova said. "You have ten people inside those buildings."

Everybody swung their head toward him.

"What? I can count." His brows shot up. He singled out the buildings, calling off the numbers. "And then the witches, in the most central building. If you take out their security system and not them? They'll be looking for back-up in a flash. Have to take all of them out."

"We're not worried about *human* back-up," Pilar said dismissively.

"You should be." Nova's eyes gleamed in the darkness. "These humans managed to incapacitate a warrior witch. Who here has experience in dealing with one of them?"

Roper spat on the ground. "I fought with a few in the war. I'll take one I trust at my back any time. Would rather not have one I don't trust around me—ever." Then he slanted his eyes over to Pilar. "Listen to the kid, wolf. If they've worked up tricks to take down that Greaves witch, then they are some pieces of work. You don't want to go in there thinking you can just snarl and they'll fall over in fear."

Pilar looked skeptical but before she could offer another argument, I asked, "So what do you suggest, Nova?"

"Me." He cracked his knuckles and rotated his head. "I'll deal with the humans, but I'm not going to be much good after that and they've got dogs on the loose. Four of them, mean pieces of shit."

"Just how are you coming up with all this?" Mike asked, his nostrils flared wide. "I got the dogs and I got the scents of people, but they've had more than thirty people circulating in and out, all of them regular. How do you know *ten* people are in there now? Ten and not more or less?"

"Haven't none of you figured that out?" Nova almost looked affronted, which was befuddling, as I knew he'd probably excise the parts that made him so powerful—if he could do it without killing himself.

Before he could make a display of it, I cut him off. "He's psychic, Mike. He can probably tell us what those people ate for breakfast and if he wanted to, he could crush their bodies from a hundred yards out. If he says he can handle the humans, then he can handle the humans."

"Problem." Doyle's voice was soft. "We're more than a hundred yards out."

"Don't be so technical." Nova eased closer to those pin-prick lights.

"Careful…" Roper advised.

My heart leaped up into my throat, my hands going slick with sweat.

"Relax. I can see the lines." Nova's voice had gone soft, almost hypnotic.

"It's electrical?" I asked when a few of them looked confused.

Roper shrugged. "It's powered. Doesn't run on air."

"Then he can see it. However far the range, he can see it. It's just…what he does," I said.

"I can get them from here," Nova said a moment later. His voice had gone dead.

The sound of it sent a shiver down my spine. "If they move?"

"Won't matter. I'm already inside them."

"Okay." I turned to Rana. "Can you get the one in the tree?"

She just blinked at me. I guess she thought it was a request. Or maybe she was insulted.

Turning to Roper and Pilar, I said, "I need you to show me where the power source is."

That took a little more time, and each second had the tension inside me ratcheting higher and higher. The power source didn't provide line-of-sight to the others. Roper and I moved back to the others and I went to Doyle. "I need my pack."

"The suitcase?" With a smirk, he unstrapped a slim case he'd insisted on carrying. He knelt on the ground with me and watched as I opened it, going for the arrows I'd thought would be overkill. Ever since a little trip down to the Everglades, I'd decided overkill was *good*.

When I'd seen the explosive arrowheads, I'd never thought to need them, then remembered how I'd mused about a rocket launcher. I still hadn't found the rocket launcher, but one of these buried in the chest of Jude would leave him in pieces so small, he'd never been able to put himself back together.

They could pierce a tank.

It would work well enough to destroy the power source for the motion sensors.

"I need five minutes to get back there. Another five just to be safe."

Nova and Rana nodded their agreement. Nova asked, "Who is wrangling the dogs?"

"I'll handle them," Mike said.

"I'll stand by in case," Mo added. "And I'm watching the gate. We were running it through while you were taking your walk in the woods."

"You have to grab Justin and Colleen fast," Nova said. "They'll be in bad shape. Who's on that?"

"I am. I'm taking Roper with me." Doyle's gaze slid my way.

"I'll be there." Shifting my gaze to Nova, I stared at him. "This is going to hit hard, right? You need hands after?"

He hitched a shoulder. "Might be. We'll see."

"I'll keep an eye on him." Rana continued to study the burl up in the tree, not looking at any of us.

"I don't think so," Doyle said tightly.

"I'm fine with that." Nova shot him a narrow look. "You worry about your end, cat."

Unease tugged at me, but I shook my head at Doyle. "We don't have time for it. Nova's the last person to put himself at risk—so if he's okay with it, don't argue."

We went through everything one more time.

My gut twisted as I turned to jog through the woods.

If this didn't work...

Don't, I told myself.

There's something imminently serene, peaceful about firing a bow.

I'd brought African blackwood bow that Damon had bought for

me on the job down in the Everglades. Hearing her slow, steady drumbeat echoing my heart was almost hypnotic. And even, especially after so much time with nothing but silence in my head.

Even though the urgency of the job propelled me, for those few seconds, as I drew the string back, everything in the world ceased to exist.

There was no hospital.

There was no crazy, cruel grandmother.

There was no aunt just a few hundred yards away who may or may not spell my downfall.

There was just me, the night air, and wind that teased my hair as I breathed in, breathed out.

Time—

The weighted arrow cut through the night, slicing at it like a blade.

I put myself behind the large, sturdy oak just as it made impact.

The blast rocked the peaceful silence and I gave myself only a few seconds to make sure nothing was going to pelt me before I sprinted back to the others.

The pin-point lights were gone.

For the briefest second, there was nothing but silence—

Then the baying of dogs rose in the air.

A howl joined in just as I drew abreast with Doyle.

"What took you so long?"

"Shut up."

Roper and he settled into what had to be an easy jog for them. I ran full out. It didn't take us long to get inside; even though I knew I was fast, I wished I were faster.

Nova stayed behind, Rana with her sword in hand.

We came upon the first body not even twenty feet inside the gate.

A gate that was tucked up against a very real, very *finished* wall, I realized.

They weren't supposed to have finished *any* of the wall.

I almost stumbled when I caught sight of it, but I steadied myself and pushed even harder. They had *walls*. Real ones. Partly built out of the stone of the mountain, much of it was freestanding and the very same design of the skeletal walls that were beginning to go up around the heavily forested *infested* zones in the state.

A state that was almost a dead zone now, a state that was moving to cede all governing authority to the feds, because there wasn't enough income from their citizens to provide for a working state government.

Shoving all of that into the back of my mind, I leaped up the steps to the building where Nova had said we'd find Justin and Colleen.

And we would.

I could feel them—him more than her. I didn't understand that— couldn't figure out why—and it scared the hell out of me.

There were three more people inside the house.

One of them was alive. The other two were little more than bone bags.

The one who still breathed looked at me, his face a mask of pain. "Take..." His eyes squeezed shut for a long moment. "Take me with you."

I fought the urge to drive my foot into his face. "No chance of that."

"Nova...says...you...take..." He gritted his teeth with each word. "*Getoutgetoutgetout—*"

Abruptly, his head was slammed against the wall and his eyes went foggy.

"Shit."

"Precisely," he said, his voice different now. "Kit, honey, just take the man. It's hard holding him like this after the work I just did."

"What the fuck?" Roper whispered.

"It's Nova."

They looked at me, confused.

"That's Nova talking now," I said, irritated. Gesturing to the man who now watched with calm, placid eyes, I continued. "That's Nova inside his head, talking to us. He wants us to take this bastard with us."

"He can..." Roper stopped, shook his head. "The witches."

"We'll manage it if Kit says we need to," Doyle said. "But he comes last."

We continued on, coming to a stop at the end of the hall. It was obvious where they were, because the smell of blood was so thick in the air, it choked us.

When we stepped inside, rage dropped over me so hot and thick, I thought it would smother me.

There was a form on the first bed that didn't even look human. Limp, with bits of loose flesh hanging from it, my brain didn't want to process what I was seeing.

A low, near animalistic growl came from the corner.

"If you touch him..."

That voice broke my heart.

"Coll..."

"Don't touch him."

I waved Doyle and Roper back. "Give me a minute."

"We might not have it," Doyle warned.

"We have it." I eased forward, going to the other...well, I couldn't call it a bed. It had been destroyed, twisted and malformed by something no human could do.

Colleen didn't look like herself. In just days, she'd lost weight, shrunk down in on herself. They'd cut her hair, hacked at it, leaving her with patches where it was practically bald.

"Leenie, it's me."

She flinched at the sound of my voice.

"Leenie."

She huddled down.

Reaching out, I went to touch her knee.

She struck out.

It shocked me so much, I couldn't move.

And she screamed, clutching her head as though she'd been struck—with something *sharp*.

She'd hit me.

Colleen, who'd never raised her hand to *anything* in her life.

She'd hit me.

What had they done to her?

As I sat there, horrified, she balled up her fist and swung out, but this time, she drove her fist into her temple, once, twice—

I caught her wrist before she could do it again.

That resulted in her swiping out with her other hand, fingers hooked as though she meant to claw my eyes out.

"If you need to bloody me to get this out of your system, Leenie, that's fine. I'm happy to let you," I said quietly. "But first...can you help me save Justin?"

Her body tensed at that. "Justin..."

"Yes. *Justin*. Colleen, it's *me*. It's Kit. I'm going to get you and

155

Justin out of here."

A harsh shudder wracked her body and she tried to twist away. I didn't let her.

"Come on. Look at me..."

She didn't want to. I'd take more time if I could, gentle her back to herself like she'd once done for me.

But while I'd take a minute, or several, to reach her, I didn't have time for more. We had to get out of there.

"Leenie..." I pleaded now, pleaded for her to hear me, for something to reach her.

"Kit." Her voice broke as she said it. But the clouds had started to clear. "Kit."

CHAPTER TWENTY

"How are they to travel?"

The question was delivered in a soft voice two hours later.

We'd lowered the seats in the back of the larger SUV, and Rana and I had piled in to do what we could for them.

Justin had been…brutalized.

His heartbeat was so faint, I could barely make it out.

Colleen had stopped speaking.

"We don't have a choice." I was calling in favors, though. Not that I planned on telling my aunt that. "You know, you can go. Like…any time now."

"Is that your way of telling me that I'm not welcome?" She wasn't looking at me. She remained bent over Justin. One of his legs had been shattered and run through with nails—iron nails. She was slowly and carefully removing each one.

Considering that I doubted I could do what she was doing—not with Justin—I decided not to respond. Instead, I turned my attention to Colleen and brushed her hair back from her face. "Colleen. You're safe. Do you hear me? You're safe."

She didn't respond, but I wasn't looking for a response.

"Why did the psychic insist you bring the human?"

She was going to *insist* on talking to me, wasn't she?

"I'll have to ask the psychic when he wakes up from his beauty sleep." I stroked Colleen's hair for a few more seconds and then fished out my phone from a cargo pocket. There were a dozen messages—from Chang, Damon, Alisdair. I'd texted all of them to let them know we were on the road, that we'd accomplished what we'd set out to do. Each had questions, Damon had a few demands…he was the bossy type. Chang had information. I'd read them all, responded to a few.

There were a few missed calls—some hadn't bothered to leave

messages, but others had.

One was recent and from a contact at Banner—not somebody I liked, either.

> *We've been advised that you might be involved in some illegal activities taking place in the South Carolina area. We need to verify your whereabouts, Ms. Colbana, promptly.*

I ran my tongue across my teeth and decided to forward the message to Chang.

He responded immediately.

> *I'll handle it, but you need to be back in the city by daybreak. All of you.*

I looked at Justin.

> *I'll do my best. Justin's in bad shape. Colleen won't even speak.*

Chang's response made me close my eyes.

> *Get them here. We'll take care of them.*

If only it was that simple.

"Get them there…" I muttered. And what if we ended up being stopped?

I needed help in the worst way.

"When you ask for help, you don't make small requests, do you?" The question was delivered in a stark, serious tone—no humor to it at all.

"I'm sorry. If there was any other option…"

"I understand, Kit. And we'll give you aid." The man on the phone sighed, so hard and loud that I heard the weariness in it. "Es was a friend of mine. You aided her house. Now mine will aid you and yours."

Hearing the name of a witch who'd died protecting me was

enough to make a knot settle in my throat. "Thank you, William."

He made a grunt deep in his throat.

I'd received a similar response when I'd put in a call to Allerton House.

Vampires.

I'd called *vampires*.

Granted, Abraham had proven himself to be useful and more than trustworthy, but I was putting my faith in a vampire.

He was already heading my way and Abraham, being what he was, had ways of traveling that didn't rely on *roads*.

He also knew ways in and out of Georgia that were less likely to be patrolled—he'd suggested one of the very same routes that had put me on the route to William's house—the Green Branch house where I was taking Justin and Colleen. He'd been the one to tell me about the place to begin with. *"There's a Green Branch house along that highway...did you know?"*

I'd known there was a Green Branch house in the area, but not right *there*.

Now, as I explained the troubles and what I needed, a quiet-spoken man on the other end of the line blew out a sigh. "We'll clear your way, Ms. Colbana and no, none of my house will admit to seeing you. But we can only provide an all-clear through the night. Anything else will draw...attention our way. That's dangerous these days."

"I understand."

"Wait in the front when you get here. I'll come out to meet you. Do *not* leave your vehicles, am I understood?"

"Yes." If he wanted me to stand on my head and spin around, I'd do it. Help from a Green Branch witch was no small thing.

We arrived less than thirty minutes after I made the call, and even once we were on their property and felt the safety of their wards close around us, I didn't breathe much easier.

The door opened and a man came up, his hand gripping the solid strap of a dog's harness. I saw why immediately.

William was blind. The members of his house trailed along behind him, although with far less grace. They couldn't see either. That was for mechanical reasons. They had blindfolded themselves.

None in my house will admit to seeing you...

"Speak, Colbana. It will help guide them."

A little bemused, I said, "Hello."

Like a magnet, they surged forward, surrounding us.

Magic swallowed us whole. It was quiet and delicate, settling inside my skin with barely a whisper.

It was fast work, too.

When it ended, William turned his head. "There are injured."

One of the witches reached up and tugged the blindfold, studiously not looking toward us. "I can walk you over, Father."

"It must be quick. The rest of you, back into the house."

Something that might have been relief burst inside me as the middle-aged man came closer. He wasn't as powerful as some witches I'd known, but there was a serious buzz to him. "Open the door to the one that bleeds. I'll stop that and deaden the pain. It will stabilize him. I can't do anything else."

His eyes came to my face. "I don't do this to be selfish. Great magic leaves an echo. If we do too much, they might sense it."

"Ah…yeah, that's fine. Anything you can do to help him."

"Of course."

Justin screamed when William put his hands on his head—a low, inhuman scream that made me want to cry—and kill.

It ended after five seconds and his mouth went slack.

His entire body did, really.

"He's not hurting so much now," I said softly.

"He will rest. His body needs it." William touched Justin's brow once more. "This is Justin Greaves…had I known…" But he stopped and shook his head. "Stay on this road. I have a contact who can make sure the roads stay clear of law enforcement who might wish to hassle you. Just don't stop for any reason. You have enough fuel?"

"Plenty." I touched his hand. "Thank you."

He gave a short nod. He went to draw back, but a sleepy voice stopped him.

"Will?"

The man frowned. "Well, damn. Nova? I should have…"

I glanced at Nova who was still sprawled, mostly boneless, in the front seat. He turned his head sleepily toward the witch. "Have you decided to see the light and get the hell out of Georgia?"

"Is it…" William pressed his lips together. "Have things changed, Nova?"

"Not for me. Not seeing anything too shiny on your horizon, but things are going to get ugly here for a while. You should protect your house, man." His vice got rougher, thicker. A moment later, he was asleep again.

William's jaw went tight.

"You know about his…" I hesitated, uncertain how well he knew Nova.

"I've known Nova since I was a boy." William passed a hand over his thinning hair. "Yes, I know."

"A…" I frowned, looking between the two men. William was probably in his sixties, easy.

"Things aren't what they seem with him, Kit. He's lived far longer than you would believe. Now go. I must think and you…need to be gone."

There was a car parked at the side of the road.

My heart sped up when somebody climbed out and stood there. Somebody—

Fuck.

"It's a state trooper," I said, fear boiling at the back of my throat.

"State line is five miles away." Doyle looked at me. "We run for it."

The man took a few steps and placed himself in the middle of the road, as though he'd read our thoughts.

"Pull over." I shot Doyle a look when he didn't slow. "We can't risk a chase with Justin in the shape he's in; and if he's a trooper out looking for NHs, then he's got firepower in that car."

He hissed out a breath but put his foot down on the brake.

"Just…stay inside," I said, shaking my head as I worked my way around them and climbed out.

The trooper was staring at the ground, hands on his hips, but as I started toward him, he lifted his head and weary blue eyes met mine. "I'm to understand that you folks need an escort to the border." He paused a moment, then added, "William says *hello*."

"You…" Reluctant just yet, I moved no closer. "You know William."

"He's my father." His jaw tightened. "That is something kept very, *very* quiet, ma'am, for understandable reasons. I would appreciate your discretion."

"Discretion on what?" I said, wide-eyed. "I don't know any William."

He managed a tired smile and then nodded to my vehicle. "If you'd return to your vehicle, I'll get in mine. I'm providing escort from here to the Florida/Georgia line, lights, no sirens. Several troopers do patrol this area as it's becoming increasingly popular for those who want to easily slip back and forth."

"And if you get questioned…?"

"That's easy. You're a family rushing to get back to Tallahassee because you got word that your sister was attacked by a stone cold killer werewolf." His mouth went tight. "I heard rumors of a shifter attack; girl thought she'd walk on the wild side and it didn't go well. Kid was just moving into his spike. He pushed her away when she tried to kiss him. He's already been *put down*."

He sounded so disgusted and pissed off, I wanted to hug him even as I wanted to howl.

"Come on, ma'am. Y'all need to go."

I nodded and retreated to my car. "Be careful," I said as I slid inside.

"He okay?" Doyle asked.

"That's Will's boy," Nova muttered, still half-asleep "David. He's good people. Let's go."

"He's fine," I said to Doyle when he continued to wait.

Lights went on. Doyle put the SUV into drive.

The last few miles sped by.

Once we crossed into Florida, I took what felt like my first free breath in months. It had only been a few short days, but it sure as hell didn't feel that way.

CHAPTER TWENTY-ONE

"You're not *doing* this." Damon had his hand around Chang's throat and the slimmer man was pressed against the wall.

"I am. She needs a solid reason that Banner will believe she wasn't anywhere *near* these...alleged events in South Carolina. This is one certain way to make that happen."

Sitting on the couch, head in my hands, I tried to think of another way to get around this. I had been trying for the past ten minutes. Because I really, *really* didn't want to take this route—it was going to *suck*. But I couldn't think of anything.

Justin and Colleen were safe.

They were tucked inside the safe room of the House of Witches, and those were sanctuaries. Even Banner wouldn't violate the safe rooms in the House of Witches. The bad news? You had to be in *bad, bad* shape to get inside there.

The witches guarding those rooms would say nothing of their wards, and most people wouldn't even think to ask about them—I hoped that meant Banner, but I wasn't going to bet on it.

However, that left me in a bad position.

As long as I could be accounted for, everybody else on my team didn't need to worry because *I* was the one they were after.

So, I had to be accounted for.

Chang had a way. I had to give it to him; he had come up with a hellishly diabolical way to make sure Banner believed I'd been nowhere near South Carolina.

He was one cagey bastard.

"Damon." I waited until he swung furious golden-green eyes my way and then I stood up. "Let him go. This is my choice. It's the only way."

"The hell it is. Banner wants you? They can try to come in and *take* you."

"We're not starting a war over this if there's another way!" I shouted.

"I'm not—"

"It's my choice." Taking one step toward him, I wished to hell that wasn't the case, but we didn't have time to think through other options. "You know as well as I do that this will work."

"I know it will *hurt*."

"I can take it." I moved closer and stared up at Chang. "Let him go."

Damon looked like he wanted to eat nails.

Or shove them down Chang's throat. But slowly, he lowered his second in command—and his best friend—to the floor. "There's got to be another option."

"They are already on their *way*," Chang said, getting impatient. "I convinced them to let her *recuperate* until morning."

"And just who was it that supposedly do this? Because everybody knows I'd kill anybody who tried this." Damon clenched his big hands into fists, so enraged, just being close to him was painful—the very air stung my skin.

"It's already been done." Chang offered a cool smile. "Adam proved to be very…reluctant in coming to terms with your relationship with Kit. After he called her a bitch several times, I decided I'd had enough and dealt with him. Quite messily, as you would. We'll simply make it clear that after the events that took place here the other day, he lay in wait for her and attacked her yesterday while you were out attending to Clan affairs. He was stopped by Scott and myself and detained. Upon your return, you killed him. You know how to sidestep the truth well enough to avoid an outright lie—so do it."

Damon's eyes narrowed to slits. "Why wasn't I informed about Adam?"

"You've been busy."

"Enough." I shoved Damon back. "We're doing this."

He said nothing else so I went to the dresser where I stored my clothes. "Who is doing the healing?"

"There's a man from Green Road who owes me a favor. He'll only be able to accelerate it by roughly twelve hours. You'll hurt for a while."

"Kit." Damon stared at me, his face twisting in a pained grimace.

"Don't. Banner can't take you *from* here. ANH law doesn't allow it, not without proof."

"But they can make things hard. We *need* Banner on our side, Damon." Ducking into the bathroom, I pulled on a loose pair of pants and a shirt that bared my belly. When I ducked back out, there was a third man in there and he looked about as miserable about this as I felt. Of course, in a few minutes, I'd feel worse.

I moved over to the bed.

"Could we get some towels?" The healer looked at Chang before meeting my eyes. He gave me a tight smile. "This is fun, right?"

"Yeah, sure."

Chang had several towels in his hand as he came back to us. "I'm not enjoying this either."

"I oughta fucking rip your head off," Damon said from across the room. "I can't believe I'm letting this..."

"Do it." I stared into Chang's eyes.

I felt the hot wash of blood first. The pain a second later. Then Damon's arms.

There was a crashing noise as well, but I was already shaking and shuddering, fighting not to cry out as the healer went to work on the four, gushing gashes—gut wound. Deep, ugly...so painful.

"Let me see if I can make this any clearer for you...she's *hurt*. She's *resting*. Now if you insist on asking your fucking questions, then you ask them. But if you upset her?"

I came awake to see Damon snarling down at the man clad in the familiar black and silver uniform of the Banner unit.

"Then *I'm* going to be upset—really upset."

"Alpha Lee." The calm voice from the woman next to her counterpart drew Damon's eyes.

She was a shifter of some sort. I hurt too much to think, but I could see the energy inside her. "We won't upset her. But it's...best if these questions are asked now so we can put this matter to rest."

"What questions?"

I only surprised the human.

He had been staring at Damon with a mix of disdain and dismay and he hadn't realized I was awake.

Now, stepping around Damon, he started toward me with such arrogance, I would have laughed. Except it would hurt too much.

His partner was the one to draw him back.

I bet she had to do that a lot.

"Timothy, remember what I said about courtesies," she said, smiling at him before offering Damon a nod.

He was looking at Timothy with contempt.

I cleared my throat.

Damon was at my side in a second. "How are you?"

"I hurt."

His mouth tightened.

"Help me sit up?"

He nodded and I bit my lip to keep from crying out at just how *much* it hurt. I really, really wanted to make somebody else suffer for this. Once I was no longer about ready to pass out from the pain, I focused on the two Banner cops. It took a few seconds. I had to blink hard a couple of times, because I kept seeing *four* of them.

Finally, my vision cleared and I managed to ask, "What does Banner want?"

"Why haven't you returned the calls from Detective Hargrave?" Timothy demanded imperiously.

"Calls…" I didn't even have to fake it. For a minute, I totally forgot that I'd been bombarded with calls from Banner. Sweat beaded on my brow and I reached up, swiped at it.

"You're running a fever," Damon said gruffly. "It's the virus."

"Excuse—"

"Timothy." This time, the female voice wasn't quite so polite. "How long ago was she attacked, Alpha Lee?"

"Don't worry, she won't change. She can't." Damon pressed a cool cloth to my brow. "Can you do this right now?"

The last question was directed at me and I took a moment let the cool chill of the rag seep into my skin before I answered. "I can do it. I've had worse."

The miserable fact was that I wasn't lying. The bitch of it was that I'd never had to do worse *on purpose*.

Nudging him back, I made myself focus on the irritating man next the shifter. "Calls." I'd remembered the calls, but I really couldn't let *him* know that, now could I?

"Yes. He called you no *less* than six times last night. You weren't at your legal residence."

"I've moved in with Damon." I pressed a hand to my belly and felt the heavy pad of bandages. "As to calls? Well, I was kind of, sort of otherwise engaged."

"I need details." He started to tap his foot.

"Hell, Okay." Damon had helped me get into a propped position, leaving the bandages where anybody could see them. If that idiot would *look*, he'd figure it out. Although…well, this was what we wanted him to see. "Damon? Would you?"

The look in his eyes made it clear he was still very, very pissed off but he carefully eased the edge of the bandage back, bit by bit until half the wound was bared. When I looked down, I could see the pink meat of my healing belly. Chang had gone all the way through and he'd been very, very neat.

It still hurt like a bitch.

The healer had closed up the internal damage, something that wouldn't be obvious without an exam, but that was the only good news.

"Is that detailed enough?" Damon asked, his voice scathing. "She's been pretty much flat on her back ever since some piece of shit decided to take a swipe at her."

And every last word rang true. He was so very furious with Chang.

Timothy was still staring, a fine sheen of sweat on his upper lip now.

His partner stepped forward, nudging him back. "Has a healer looked at you, Ms. Colbana?"

"My best friend normally provides my healing. She was kidnapped," I said, disgusted.

"I don't let witches in my Lair unless somebody I trust can vouch for them. With both Colleen and Justin missing, my options are decidedly limited," Damon said, sounding like the biggest asshole he knew how to be.

"So you're just letting her…suffer?" Timothy said, sputtering.

"She *was* sleeping until you pricks showed up." Damon came to his feet and moved closer. "She heals fast and the virus in her blood makes her heal faster. She would have slept until nightfall and woken up almost pain-free. But *you*…you had to come in here—"

"Alpha Lee, we apologize. But we have a job to do." Again, the shifter stepped in between them.

"Yes, Aretha. Exactly, yes." Timothy wagged his head up and down. "We...ah...we have questions."

"They aren't needed," Aretha said. "She was attacked by a shifter. Going by the healing and the progression rate of the virus I can smell in her blood, it was a good twelve or fifteen hours ago. Could I...is it possible to talk to the attacker?"

"Can you talk to ghosts?" Damon asked, sidestepping the question neatly.

Timothy paled.

But I saw the speculative gleam in Aretha's eyes. She'd noticed the non-answer, too.

But she didn't push.

"Very well. Unsurprising, I must say."

They were dismissed without another word from Damon. He simply turned his back on them and Aretha shot her partner a look that clearly said, *We're done.*

Damon sat down next to me and took my hand as we listened to the door close. For the longest time, neither of us spoke.

Finally, he stretched out and laid his head on my thigh. "I'm debating on whether or not to kill Chang or just go after Whit—"

"Don't say his name," I said, covering his mouth with my hand without fully understanding what drove me.

Damon gripped my wrist, his grasp almost painful. "This...fuck, Kit."

"I know." Closing my eyes, I tried to find something else to think about besides the pain, but that pain was so very intense, it tried to eat me alive.

There was a discreet knock at the door.

"Enter." Damon bit the word off.

Doyle slipped inside, soundless.

He held a mug in his hand and came to me, careful not to look at Damon.

Chang must have made sure everybody knew he'd gone and pissed off their Alpha.

Too bad.

I was probably going to piss him off more before long.

Wrinkling my nose, I stared at the mug. "Am I expected to drink that?"

"You probably want to," Doyle said, looking only at me. "You're hurting."

"Throwing up will make me hurt worse."

Damon lifted a hand and closed it over my thigh. "Drink it, Kit. Save what's left of my sanity."

I smoothed a hand down his short hair. "If I drink it, will you try to rein it in, Demon?"

"Demon..." He almost smiled. "I'll tell you what, little girl, if you'll drink that tea, I won't kill Chang the second I see him."

"You won't hit him or threaten to kill him or anything else." I still couldn't stop my lip from curling as I eyed the mug. That stuff was going to be horrible, I could tell from the smell. How was Doyle even holding it without gagging? And *why* couldn't they make any sort of healing brew that wasn't like death and piss all mixed together? "And you'll also owe me a favor."

The noise that left him was long and disgusted. "Leave the damn tea, Doyle. She's going to wring me dry."

"That's what you get for falling for somebody who isn't a shifter," I said, reminding him of a discussion we'd once had. I winked at Doyle as he slid back out. Sensing the storm was slowly passing, I picked up the tea. It was close enough that I could reach it without stretching, and as long as I didn't inhale...

"What's this favor?"

I drank the tea, burning my tongue in the process. "Too late. I drank it. You now owe me the favor, which I will collect upon my own convenience." Already, I was exhausted.

"Kit..." The edge of a growl crept into his voice and he flipped over onto his hands and knees, staring at me.

"No growling." I wasn't ready to tell him about my aunt. I'd already told the others I would inform him about our mysterious...helper. Pilar was too dense to get the undertones. but Mike had sensed that something strange was going on, and he'd said that the job had been completed. That both he and Pilar would remain quiet on the details, speaking about it only with me present. He was certain their Alpha would understand. Given the nature of said job, I was pretty sure that Alistair would rather know nothing about it.

Mo and Roper were a bigger issue, but Doyle had advised them that I should handle certain details. If they liked their throats as they were, they'd do best to just leave it alone.

I wasn't so certain I was helping anybody by not spilling everything right away, but there was something decidedly...odd about Rana's abrupt reappearance in my life.

Odd in a number of ways—I wasn't overcome by the urge to take off running. I could call my weapons. I could *hear* my weapons. She'd aided me.

When it came down to it, I couldn't find it in me to see her as a threat.

But Damon would want her blood.

Cupping his cheek, I asked, "Can you get news? I need to know how they are."

"That's how you're going to play it." Gray eyes studied mine and he curled his hand around my wrist. "I'm not going to like this favor, am I?"

"No. I'm sorry."

"Kit..." His teeth scored my lower lip, then he kissed my forehead. "You are forever tangling and twisting me up. You know that?"

"Yeah, well. Same goes."

"Another call."

Chang stood in the doorway.

Damon merely lifted his head and stared at him, eyes glittering.

"I've sent out an order that the Clan are to eliminate all unnecessary travel. Anybody lacking secured homes is welcome to come to the Lair," Chang continued as if unaware of the temper directed his way.

"Why?" I asked, frowning.

Chang slanted a look at me. "A...polite threat was issued against Scott last night. He was coming to the Lair when two government issued vehicles ran him off the road. He was told he wasn't watching where he was going. He apologized, shifted and made his own way home. I've shared the information with the MacDonald and he has decided to issue advisories to his own people as well."

"What is this?" I asked, dread creeping up the back of my throat.

Chang said nothing.

"You can go now," Damon said, his voice silky.

"I want to know what's going on." It had been well over a day since Chang had put his *let's give Kit an alibi* plan into action, and it had worked.

Banner had issued its formal statement that I couldn't have possibly been in South Carolina, due to a near fatal injury that I had taken. An investigation on a *private human compound* was being undertaken by the FBI—a possible NH terrorist attack was the word on the news, and they were putting their best people on it. President Whitmore, naturally, was quite concerned.

I'd spent the past day healing and sleeping and when I wasn't sleeping, I was eating and watching news reports roll across the media screen in Damon's—no, *our* quarters at the Lair. Damon had tried to get me to watch something else and I'd blithely ignored him.

I felt surprisingly strong. Chang was a powerful shifter, an *old* one. The virus in his blood would pack one hell of a punch and anybody he actually *did* infect would probably either die fast or change fast. Whether or not that translated to me healing much quicker... But, I didn't know.

What I did know was that the wounds were nearly gone. They were also going to scar. I didn't scar easily, but I'd care these five claw marks.

Damon wasn't going to be happy about that.

In another day, maybe less, I'd be back to my bitchy old self, with the new addition of some marks on my belly and back that shone like stripes.

Earlier, Damon had given me another update on Justin and Colleen—Colleen still wasn't talking and Justin was a healing sleep—*again.*

They would live, as long as they wanted to.

I didn't like that answer, and I wanted to see them. I needed to make sure they knew they were going to *live*, because I just couldn't deal with it otherwise. And I'd been so caught up in them, and the so-called *terrorist* attack on a so-called *private human compound*, I hadn't realized there was more going on.

But now, as I looked back and forth between Chang and Damon, I realized there was a *lot* more.

"What's going on?" I demanded.

"Chang, you are dismissed," Damon said, ignoring me.

Oh, no...

Climbing out of bed, I shoved my hair back and made my way over to the dresser. "Fine, I'll go with him and he can bring me up to date somewhere else."

"Chang is leaving the Lair. He's needed at the club," Damon said, his voice cold.

"Then I'll go with to the club. Or I'll find somebody else who will talk."

"Kit—"

Spinning around, I glared at him. "Yank the stick out of your ass before I do it and beat you with it!"

He jerked his head back as if I'd slapped him.

I was tempted. So tempted. "You're pissed. I get it. He gets it." Storming over to him, I jabbed him in the chest so hard, it hurt my damn finger. "But here's the deal. I have more reason to be pissed than you do, but I'm using my brain. He had a plan and it worked."

"You think I couldn't have protected you?" Damon's hand closed around the front of my shirt, dragging me closer.

"It's not about that!" Instead of trying to twist away, I grabbed his face between my palms and stared him dead in the eye. "It's about doing what's best for *all* of us—you, me, the Clan. He was trying to protect me *and* everybody else, including you."

"I'm not—"

I pressed my mouth to his. "Don't," I whispered as the door closed quietly. Chang had left. "I know you're not leading them because it's what you always wanted, but you *are* leading them. There's more at stake here than just protecting *me*."

"Kit..." The word was a growl against my lips. The hand fisted in my shirt came up and gripped the back of my neck, holding tight.

"I know you'd walk into hell for me, Damon—and probably stroll out, carrying the devil's head by the horns."

"Sometimes, baby girl, I think *you* are the devil. My devil, anyway." He shuddered, like a cat shaking water from his fur, but it was some of the rage he was shaking off, forcing it out of his soul, bit by bit.

His arms came around me, fast and tight and he held me.

I clutched him to me and tucked my face against his neck. "I'm *fine*, Damon. I'm fine. And maybe this was better—that arrogant son-of-a-bitch figured out that it's not easy to make a grab at me now—or any of us."

172

He said nothing for the longest time.

I could hear the seconds ticking by on the clock and they faded away into minutes.

Finally, Damon stirred. Pressing his lips to my neck, he lightly raked his teeth over a long-healed bite. This time, I shuddered.

He put me down and met my eyes, giving me a slow nod.

"Go get dressed, Kit. I'll get Chang. We'll talk."

CHAPTER TWENTY-TWO

Chang flew across the room just as I walked into it.

He crashed into the stone fireplace and I winced. *Ouch.*

He was immediately on his feet, blood dripping from his mouth and the lower part of his jaw was…wrong. Very wrong.

I heard bone crunch and he lifted his hands. Bone crunched again when he did something to his jaw.

Blood made an ugly mask on his mouth and chin.

Turning, I went to the bathroom and got a towel.

The bleeding had stopped by the time I returned, although it still gleamed wet on his skin. Damon leaned against the bar, looking as though the two of them were discussing what they might do that afternoon.

"Feel better?" I asked Damon.

"A bit. Yeah." His eyes were flat and hard.

Chang accepted the towel and wiped the blood from his face and hands. "Thank you, Kit." Inclining his head, he asked in polite, cool tones, "Might I use the facilities?"

"You might," I said, responding before Damon could. Knowing the man's mood, he might say no.

I turned and saw him watching me, eyes glittering.

"I'm not having a conversation with him while he's got blood on his hands."

"I didn't say a word, baby girl." There was a thread of amusement somewhere in those words, but I couldn't quite figure out why.

"You didn't have to. Your snarl says plenty."

Chang rejoined us, having shed the jacket to his suit as well. He'd probably shoved it into the recycle unit in the bathroom. The lovely gray fabric was trashed. Chances were he'd spent upward of a few grand on that suit—he did like his designer duds—but that piece was beyond repair now.

"So what's going on? Why is the Clan battening down the hatches and advising the Pack to do the same?" Arms folded over my chest, I looked back and forth from one man to the other.

"We're taking precautions." Chang adjusted the cuffs on his shirt sleeves. "I've also made the necessary calls to other leaders within the community, and Scott has done what he can to alert independent NHs. For the time being, we've offered accommodation to those who have no safe place, assuming they agree to abide by Clan rules. The Pack is doing the same. Hopefully, the independents will heed our advice and stay low."

"Oh, yeah. Great, that's just great...now what in the hell are we taking precautions *against*?" I demanded. "You're dancing around the issue and not telling me shit."

"Is that a fact?" He frowned, almost thoughtfully. "I thought you wanted to know what is going on, Kit."

A low growl rumbled out of Damon's throat.

Chang's eyes flashed gold as he turned his head and met the Alpha's eye.

"Whoa..." Cutting between them, I lifted my hands.

Damon wasn't the only one pissed off. Chang had just been hiding it better.

Damn it. If the two of them ever turned against each other, I wasn't sure anything would be left standing by the time they were done.

Chang blinked and as simple as that, the weight of his anger, the immense power I'd felt coming from him, was gone. "Apologies, Kit."

Damon said nothing. Stepping closer to him, I touched my hand to his chest. His heart was a hammer under my palm, skin hotter than a furnace. "Damon."

"We're good," he said softly.

I sure as hell hoped so. Looking at Chang, I asked, "Can you please just tell me what in the hell it is I'm missing?"

"Your former client isn't entirely happy you decided to end the business relationship," Chang said, moving into the small kitchenette. I watched as he put some water on for tea. "In the past forty-eight hours, I've fielded more than a dozen calls. He's had men at your place of business, at your legal residence—by the way, we need to handle changing the paperwork. You know the rules on that. If you're officially moving in here, all that tedious paperwork."

He flicked a hand in the air, like the forms I'd have to deal with were little more than a fly buzzing around our heads. I'd forgotten, though. "Shit."

"I've already gotten them started," Chang said. "They simply need to be signed by you. I've also taken the liberty of…addressing a few issues on your papers, Kit. They were good. Very good. Now they are flawless."

My heart lurched a little as he mentioned the forged documents that I'd used claiming dual citizenship.

Damon had dropped down on the couch as Chang spoke, feigning disinterest, but now he glanced over at his second. "What papers?"

Chang left me to answer while he got two teacups down. Two. Tea. Man, I needed some tea.

"Ah…well." Swiping my hands down my pants, I worked up a weak smile. "I'm not exactly what you could call a legal citizen…or legal anything, actually. I slid into the States illegally. Justin helped me get papers not long after we started working together."

"They were very good," Chang said, bringing me a cup of tea.

It smelled of jasmine and I breathed it in before taking a small sip. I gave him a smile of gratitude but he'd already turned away.

"However, we are about ready to come under some serious fire and I wanted to take no chances." The small twist to his lips couldn't really be called a smile. "It would serve his purposes quite well if you were to be found here illegally and he chose to have you arrested, wouldn't it?"

I felt a little sick. "Yeah. Probably. Thank you, Chang."

He stood at the bar, holding his own cup of tea. After a moment, he looked at me and gave a simple nod. "Of course, Kit. Back to those phone calls…at first, he was just very persistent. Then he became more…adamant. The last two calls were little more than threats. And not just against you, but the entire Clan."

The blood in my veins froze and I shot a look between him and Damon. "Are you…well, yeah. Of course you're serious."

"I've notified the Assembly," Chang said. He sounded so incredibly *calm*.

Damon's shoulders were tight.

"They had an informal meeting. Two of them were of a mind that you sign a formal contract and do whatever work he wished. It would, after all, end this nonsense and we wouldn't have to worry about any more *unpleasantness*."

"Wait a minute." I held up a hand, my heart starting to race. "You told the *Assembly* that I'm having some *work issues* with the fricking *president*?"

"Of course." Chang cocked his head. "I did ask that they fully respect the confidences under which you took that job. They…agreed it would be wise to remain quiet about it. Fortunately, only two of thirteen felt the best way to handle things would be to persuade you to continue working for him. I'd expected at least two or three others."

"Wow. Great. And you *still* approached them?"

"Of course." His black eyes narrowed. "I knew they wouldn't have seven view it as the lesser evil, Kit. There are thirteen members who act as Speakers. Of those thirteen, four are witches and two are with Green Road—their support for you is unwavering. Three are shifters and while not all are solid supporters of you in particular, shapeshifters, in general, back each other—you're also considered ours. Two are psychics and they already sense the unrest in the air. There are three vampires and one offshoot. The vampires tend to react in what one might consider the *logical* way—they support whoever has the strength behind them. The offshoot is Brett Hall and she also tends to follow a logical path."

He flicked at an imaginary speck of lint. "There were two vampires who felt it was prudent to turn you over. The third one was Amund. He was quite skeptical at first, but upon hearing about your troubles, he started to have doubts of his own. After seeing some proof I've gathered, he no longer had doubts. He knew without a doubt that he'd been well and truly fooled. He won't forget that." Chang looked decidedly smug, a cold smile lighting his face as he met my eyes. "He was the one who told the other two vampires that perhaps they might not mind reliving history, but he and his house wouldn't be doing it.

"We have an individual who is trying to strong-arm an independent NH into being his personal grunt. If we give in once…" Chang lifted a shoulder.

"The Assembly knows if we give in even once, then we might as well just roll over and give him our throats now." Damon finished for him, staring at Chang from across the room.

The tension between them was still thick and hot, enough to choke me.

"Precisely."

"What's this proof you were talking about?" I asked before that tension could turn into teeth and claws.

"That is something you will have to see to fully understand, Kit." Chang came out of the kitchen then and gestured for me to join Damon. "I'll be blunt. I never trusted the man, never liked him. I kept my counsel when he spoke with you and perhaps I shouldn't have. But he went from blatant hatred and subtle threats of genocide to approaching you for assistance and pointing us in the direction of people who have helped with the kidnappings. I knew something wasn't right."

"Genocide," I said, watching as he moved to the media screen and brought it to life with a touch.

"Yes. He ran on the platform that the only *safe* America was one without people like us." Chang retreated to the side again. "He was incredibly persuasive—people crying for our blood on the roadside. Now…watch. You'll want to see this."

This turned out to be a series of stills and some video, all put together on a disc. Side by side images of the president over the past couple of years, compared to him the first year he was in office, or his years serving in the Congress.

"He's become left handed," Chang pointed out. "Sometime in the last six months."

I'd already noticed. He'd made a few slip ups before that—going to do something with the hand that was naturally dominant before remembering.

"His wife has all but stopped appearing in public with him." Damon scraped his nails along the heavy growth of beard he hadn't gotten around to shaving off. "She's still alive, right?"

"Yes. She still does her normal things, but even when they are in public, she keeps a careful distance between them. And watch—" Chang moved forward and touched the screen, using the bar at the bottom to scroll to a certain point on the disk. We had a view of Whitmore spinning, gesticulating wildly, talking at a rapid-fire pace. Then it stopped as Chang found the point he wanted.

"Here we are…" he murmured, as much to himself as anything else. "This feed is from a member of the paparazzi. He sold it in a bit of a hurry for a fair amount of money—it was all an electronic exchange. The man who shot the footage disappeared a day after this was made. The original was already in the mail and made its destination while the electronic feed was posted to…well, multiple underground sources within an hour of being bought."

I heard what he was saying, but my mind was one hundred percent focused on the media screen.

"Replay it," I said when he paused. "I want to see it again."

"Of course."

Damon was now studying it as closely as I was.

It was Whitmore—or whoever…*whatever*—he was, walking down the sidewalk, surrounded by Secret Service personnel. His wife was by his side. He went to put a hand on her shoulder and she jerked away, stumbling into the agent next to her.

The agent had steadied her fast enough, but Whitmore had reached for her as well and she'd slapped at his hands, again backing away. This time, whoever had been shooting the film had panned in closer, and when the Secret Service personnel had drawn in around them to try and offer some privacy. It had narrowed her field of escape so that she ended up practically trapped between Whitmore and the large, plate-glass window of the building at her back.

And Whitmore's reflection was captured in it perfectly.

Or at least, it *should* have been captured perfectly.

For a span of seconds, only seconds, the reflection staring back at the woman had been…bizarre.

"Again."

It rewound.

"Freeze it."

It froze, the screen utterly smooth.

Rising, I moved from Damon's side to the media screen, oddly compelled by what I saw. Compelled. Repulsed. Intrigued. All of it, rolled into one. Placing a hand on the media screen, I focused in the one part of the image I wanted to see. The screen was part entertainment center and part computer, a much higher end model than I'd had at my old place. When I went to enlarge the image, it magnified until I couldn't even tell what I was looking at so I had shrink down more. "Computer, clean image."

Ten seconds later, I studied it again.

"What in the hell is that?" Damon asked, voicing what I'd been asking myself for the past few seconds.

"*Hell*," I murmured. That, to me, sounded oddly on base. Maybe that was what we were dealing with.

"Who bought the feed? How many people have seen it?" I asked softly.

"Outside the US? Millions—possibly billions. In the US?"

At Chang's pause, I looked at him, turning my back to the screen with some reluctance. It wasn't that I was worried about the *screen*.

But the thing I'd seen reflected in the window instead of Whitmore's face?

Yeah. *That* was unsettling.

"And in the US?" I asked, prompting Chang and trying to forget about the uneasiness induced by whatever it was staring back out at us from the reflection.

"Hard to say." Chang paced closer to the media screen. "You see, the original feed had what we'll call a…trace in it. Anytime a copy of that original feed comes up, an alert gets sent out, that feed is marked, and it gets shut down—even if it means shutting down the website."

"They can't just shut down a website." I tried to smile, but found that I couldn't.

"They do. They have." Chang was still staring at the screen. "Fortunately the buyers of the original were clever and knew to make copies from the original feed and they changed the names. They also aren't within the US and they make certain to keep that feed circulating."

He paused for a moment and I could tell he was now taking his time, choosing each word with care. "It would appear that there are many who have concerns about this man, Kit. Enough that there is actually an entire underground movement that watches him and they are very organized."

"Well." Puffing up my cheeks with air, I turned back to the disk. "Maybe they could prove useful."

"A few of them already have. I received a name and have forwarded the information I gathered on to what we shall call…fair eyes in the media. There is going to be a considerable shit storm dropping down on him shortly." He checked the time on his watch. "Very shortly."

SHADOWED BLADE

I'd been trying to think back over everything that had happened in South Carolina, wanting to make sure we hadn't done anything, left anything behind that could trip us up. There was a risk we might have been caught on camera, but Nova had mentioned he was blowing them en route, before they could even zero in on us.

Nova.

Cameras.

"Where's Nova?"

It struck me as weird that I had only just thought to ask, but even as that occurred to me, I realized why.

Nova—*he* was the reason why.

That was what triggered the memory onslaught and just like that, I felt like somebody had jerked a veil from a bank of memories. Him talking to me by the SUV as somebody carried Justin in on a litter, Colleen trailing along behind like a lost stray.

He'd hugged me, spoken softly to me.

I'd told him to wait.

He'd touched my cheek and smiled.

That was when the veil dropped down.

"Man, I'm going to hurt him," I muttered. I went to shove my hair back, irritated beyond all belief—I'd wanted to talk to him. Just…talk. And he was already gone.

"What's wrong?"

Damon had come up behind me and he rested a hand on my belly. His thumb rubbed across one of the mostly healed claw marks as I turned to him. An ache settled in my chest and without thinking about it, I wrapped my arms around his waist. Damon cupped a hand over the back of my neck and kissed the top of my head. "What's wrong, Kit?" he asked again, his voice softer now, gentle.

"Nova. He's gone." And he might as well be *gone*, gone. He'd left East Orlando and was probably out of Florida by now, on his way to the compound in Georgia where he'd do as he'd once told me he'd do—go out in a blaze of glory, taking out a bunch of bad people along the way.

"What are you talking about?"

Tipping my head back, I met his eyes. "He was with us when we met at the Green Road house here in Orlando, wasn't he?"

Damon's eyes clouded. I saw the instant he broke through

181

whatever haze Nova had put on his memories. "What the..."

"Nova. He can do that. I doubt he got in your head, so to speak. He just clouded your thoughts so he could slip away without anybody thinking much about it. He didn't want anybody mentioning him around *me*—that's the thing here. He wanted to leave without me knowing. Without Justin or Colleen knowing."

"Why?" Damon flexed his hand on the back of my neck and I caught the glint of anger in his eyes, but he was holding it in remarkably well.

"Because he's heading off to die." Easing away, I sniffed and tried to blink back the burn of tears. "Nova knows the exact day, hour, and minute of his death and he's figured out the where and the why, too. It's got something to do with Blackstone. He..."

A bit of more memory worked free.

I suck at good-byes, Kit. You've got things here still to do and Justin, Colleen, well they need you. I've got this deal handled.

You be good.

Nova, wait—

"He's gone." I set my jaw tight. "That bastard."

The tears spilled out.

Damon wrapped his arms around me. "Go ahead and cry, kitten."

CHAPTER TWENTY-THREE

I took the next call.

Damon didn't like it.

It didn't matter.

Chang had appeared as if summoned by magic, knocking politely while I stood in front of the screen, hands on my hips and staring down the man who called himself Whitmore.

I was *angry*.

I was *so* angry and just staring at the blue-eyed blond with the arrogant smile only made it worse.

My two best friends were tucked away in the healing hall of a powerful witch house. Another friend was on his way to die. The Clan and the Pack were hunkering down for who knows what, all because this smug, smirking piece of work had decided to use me as his personal pawn and I had no idea what his end game might be.

"Ah, so you finally arise from your sick bed," Whitmore said, the doubt all but dripping from his words.

His eyes flicked down to my belly, eying the scars just barely visible under the bottom of the shirt I'd put on. I'd chosen it deliberately, for that very reason. Not so much as *See? It couldn't have been me*, but more like a…*you can't prove anything*.

And he couldn't, otherwise he would have already sent the federal version of Banner to come and get me. He wasn't done, though. I was sure of that. He would make another try. Or perhaps that was what this phone call was about.

"Well, it hurt a little too much to get up and move around earlier. Gotta tell you, the were virus packs a punch." Chang moved across my field of vision and I glanced up, watched as he came to a stop in front of the media screen. He activated it manually and turned, catching my eye.

Damon was standing behind me and he came to ready alertness

almost immediately. He had been slumping against the counter, a bored expression on his face, but he wasn't bored now.

Although the media screen's sound was off, there was no question just what had started to go down.

"Kit, I must say, I've never had anybody seem quite so…bored with talking to me as you." The cold snap in Whitmore's voice had me offering a smile of mock sympathy before I looked at the TV.

Yeah. Things were about to get very, very interesting.

"Mr. President, are you familiar with Guerilla News?"

He pursed his lips. "A shoddy operation full of crazies and conspiracy theorists. Sadly, they're based outside this country and we can't do much to silence them."

"Well, technically, going by the US Constitution, you couldn't do much to silence them *here*, either." I looked at the screen again, wondering how much longer—

There was a *beep* that came across the line, briefly interrupting our conversation.

Whitmore's mouth went tight, his eyes flashing silver. "You're a naïve girl if you truly believe that. It's not *always* best for the public to know *everything*."

"True. I don't really think they need to know whether or not some celebrity put on weight or has her daughter in private school, and really, it's nobody's business if their next door neighbor is a shapeshifter. But those mortals love to natter on about it, don't they? That's not why I'm asking, though. You got any idea what GN is talking about right now?"

There was another *beep* that came right in the middle of his reply.

He leaned forward, ignoring me completely as he pushed a button. "I said I *wasn't* to be disturbed—"

Over another line, a man's voice came through. "Mr. President, this is urgent. You *will* want to know this."

I heard something else—a door. Whatever screen Whitmore was using for our conversation was averted and I saw nothing but darkness. The line remained open, though. Chang, Damon, and I had no trouble listening to the low, intense conversation as a man who had to be human spoke to the man we knew *wasn't*.

"It's a smear campaign, sir, of the worst sort, and it is bad. You need to be watching Guerilla News *right* now."

The man spoke in a babbling sort of rush and his heart rate was so erratic, even I could hear it. If he wasn't careful, he was going to have a heart attack.

"Very well, Robert. Tell me, just what sort of garbage have they concocted this time? Do I have an alien lover? Am I involved with a devil-worshipping cult somewhere down in Zimbabwe?" The snide derision in Whitmore's voice came off as a verbal slap and I had no doubt that the human, Robert, felt it.

Still, he carried on. "Sir, they are…they're claiming you're not *human*."

"Really." That single word carried more icy menace than I'd heard in my entire lifetime.

Goosebumps broke out over my flesh.

"Please, Robert. Might I use your computer?"

"Of…of course, sir." The words came out in a stammering rush and something clattered. "I'm so sorry. Here you go, sir. I'm sorry."

"Think nothing of it."

Listening to the conversation and being unable to see had become strangely nerve-wracking. Uneasy, I eased closer to Damon. He smoothed a hand up and down my spine as we continued to listen.

There was a tinny noise—the newscaster and though Chang still had the media screen on mute, when I glanced over, I had a weird sort of stereo effect.

"…long suspected by a number of individuals, but the proof now presented by an unknown source looks to be quite alarming. We're having it reviewed by several experts in the field. As you can see in these side-by-side comparisons, the president of our closest ally has undergone a number of strange, seemingly unremarkable changes. While taken separately—"

The sound cut off.

"Very effective, don't you think, Robert?"

"Yes. I've contacted the Canadian Prime Minister, however, you know their views when it comes to this sort of thing."

"Quite, Robert, You've been very helpful. Thank you."

Abruptly, the screen shifted and we were face to face with Whitmore once more.

Only, he wasn't Whitmore.

The face wasn't too dissimilar, really. Long, thin, aesthetically handsome. The eyes were larger, though. For too large to be human and the brow was very pronounced. He was oddly beautiful, but it was a satyrical, almost demonic sort of beauty and looking at him was enough to freeze my blood.

His hair had lengthened in the short moments since we'd seen him and I realized I'd been off—way off. He was a shapeshifter of sorts.

Absently, I recalled thinking that I'd heard rumors about NHs who could change their shape due to some sort of magic, rather than the virus. I'd never met one, hadn't ever really wanted to.

But I was looking at one now. I knew it in my gut.

"Well, well, well..."

He looked at me over the screen, his eyes still blue, although they were more vivid, more intense. And they glowed in the dim room with a fire borne of nothing but malice.

"That, dear girl, was quite clever. How did you pull it off? Will you tell me?" He no longer spoke with the flat accent of an American. I heard the music of Wales and England in his voice now.

When you move a lot of people around, their monsters tend to follow.

I'd said that earlier. Maybe I should have paid better attention to myself.

Now I just needed to figure out which monster I was dealing with.

"You're giving me too much credit," I said, shrugging with more carelessness than I felt. "What happened to your buddy Rob?"

Something flashed in his eyes but it disappeared fast. "Robert? Oh, he's here and there. Literally."

I guess he didn't think I'd take him seriously, so he decided to show me.

Robert was indeed *here* and *there*. To be precise, his head was sitting on the desk, as though on display, staring ghoulishly. Then I had the pleasure of viewing his body, slumped against the wall, hands in his lap while the palm-sized tablet computer that had borne witness to all this unpleasantness lay between his splayed thighs, the screen now splashed with blood.

There was no sign of the weapon that had been used.

"So. That's where *Robert* is, my dear Kit."

He smiled at me with maniacal glee.

"If you're expecting me to shiver with fear, then you really don't know much about me. I've severed a head or two myself." Still, some part of me felt an odd sort of pity for the now-headless Robert. He'd rushed in, completely clueless and harmless. "Tell me something, since you're clearly *not* the president, what am I to call you?"

"Master would suffice."

Damon bent forward, crowding in until it was only his face filling the viewfinder. "Dead man will work for me."

"Oh...the big, brooding beast can speak." He chuckled, not impressed. "Boy, I was rutting on your ancestors—before they could make the shift to *human*. You don't scare me."

"Wow. You fucked animals. That's really going to put the fear of God into us." Out of view of the screen, I reached down and closed my hand around Damon's wrist, squeezing lightly. Letting him goad us wasn't going to help anything.

"Kit, I've fucked everything...the good, upstanding citizens of this country, the lovely goddess you so indiscriminately killed with one of your paltry guns." His lip quivered in a sneer. "Your *head*."

I only barely kept from flinching. "Is this about Pandora?"

"Oh, bloody hell, no. She was a great deal of fun, but no. This has nothing to do with vengeance, precious." He looked amused even at the thought. "Isidora—and that is what you should call her, child—she was fun, but no bit of pussy is worth bothering myself over."

"Then what *are* you bothering yourself over?" Folding my arms over my chest, I angled my head to the side. *Give me something, give me something...* Any small bit he dropped, any loose thread that, and I could use to unravel this. I didn't need much. "Why did you send me after the Black Anni? You wanted something from them, didn't you? Didn't plan on them killing me. I don't know why I didn't see that sooner. You were betting on my luck getting me through it. So what did I mess up when I wouldn't go in?"

"Finally figured that out, did you, poppet?" He braced his chin on his fist, looking for all the world like a school boy. "Clever little bitch. Yes, you did muck things up a bit when you wouldn't go inside. I figured you'd catch a whiff of their nastiness and forge on in. You've got a valiant streak a mile wide and the Black Anni will hunt down a dog that pissed on the wrong tree. *You* would hunt down somebody who stepped on a dog's tail—on accident, mind you. But you steered clear of those foul bitches. Why is that?"

"I didn't want to get eaten by one of them. Call me crazy, but it just didn't seem like a fun way to spend the day."

"Silly girl. They wouldn't have eaten you." Absently, he stroked his fingers through his hair, circling around one area, over and over again.

My eyes flicked to it.

He stopped stroking.

"What am I to call you? You never did answer."

"Why didn't you go in after them, Kit?" He swayed closer, his movement so liquid, he barely seemed human. "Why didn't you do what you were told? What stopped you? Who aided you in South Carolina?"

We locked in a staring contest that might have lasted...forever.

Damon stepped between us.

"You're a stubborn bastard, aren't you? Did you hear the statement from Banner? She was recovering from an injury." He waited for a count of ten, holding the man's eyes before he straightened.

Chang gave him a polite nod and then moved to address the fake president. "You realize, of course, that the threats you've issued against my Alpha's territory, his people, his lady...all of them have put you in a somewhat tenuous position." Chang had his hands linked in front of him, his polite diplomat's smile on his face. He could have been discussing the weather or his favorite sort of tea.

"Tenuous. Tell me, do you know that I could come through your city and squash each one of you like *bugs*?"

"Each one of us? What about *all* of us? Have you faced a united front before?" Chang looked amused now. "Do you know that if you come through, you'll be facing over three thousand shifters and two thousand witches? Then there are the vampires you've pissed off. Amund...well, he isn't pleased."

Emotion rippled over the other's face like water over stone, and Chang tsked. "I take you didn't consider that. Yes, they've all been made aware. The House of Witches has been advised. When and *if* you make it within ten miles of East Orlando, you can you expect the going to be much rougher than you previously expected. Each vampire house within two hundred miles of here has declared you persona non grata. You made Amund feel the fool and he is something of a name among vampires. Practically royalty. None of them will aid you and quite a few will throw every blockade they have to stop you should they see you coming." Chang gestured to the media screen in general. "I appreciate your willingness to show your true face—both of them, naturally, will be shared and one of our contacts within the Wolf Pack was able to collect enough samples from Kit's office so that a scent profile can be shared—odd, sir, but it would seem as though you were in the area far more recently than we were led to believe."

Those bizarre, oversized blue eyes narrowed.

"As for the Clan and the Pack...well, you've been given a particular name. You likely don't want to know the name that has been given to you among the shifters." Chang adjusted the cuffs of his jacket—he must have a room here, because the jacket fit him too well to not be his. "It makes *meat* sound like a friendly nickname."

"Indeed." His gaze flicked to me. "All of this over you, Kit. You must be quite pleased."

"All of *this* over a man who attempted to manipulate a friend of the Clan, over a man who kidnapped two more friends of the Clan, a man who is behind numerous other disappearances and has connections to Blackstone," Chang said, correcting him. "Seriously, have you not paid *attention*?"

Connections—

I shifted my focus to Chang.

That was a new one.

Rage started to pulse and brew inside me as I looked back at the screen, at him. Blue eyes narrowed, locked on Chang, dismissing me entirely. What had he found? What had we missed?

Blackstone—was this all about Blackstone to begin with?

"You overstep yourself, *boy.*"

The angry, low growl sent a shiver through me.

"Perhaps." Chang studied his well-manicured hand and flicked at a speck of lint on the lapel of his suit. "But at least my sin is arrogance and not foolishness or stupidity. You, on the other hand, assumed you would never be noticed and you didn't hide your tracks well. Not well at all." He left the comment open-ended, smirking a bit before turning his attention to Damon. "Sir, do you require anything else?"

"I think we're done here." Damon leaned forward.

"Wait."

"I'm the Alpha. I don't listen to demands from *anybody*."

There was a heavy bang that emanated from somewhere close to the man masquerading as president, then another. It sounded like a series of knocks, pounding on a door.

The muffled *sir…, sir…* carried well enough.

"Sounds like you've got some people wanting to talk to you," Damon said, a familiar, cagey grin curling his lips.

"Yeah. I think you're being summoned." Waggling my fingers at him, I said, "If you kill too many on the way out, they'll stick their bulldogs on your ass. And the more you kill…well. The more they'll put after you. You might want to just disappear. *Vamonos.*"

"You and I, girl…we're not done." He leaned forward and in a low, heated whisper said, "I'll rip your throat out, precious. It's a pity, really. I said I'd deliver you alive and I meant to do just that. Tit for tat, as the saying goes. Of course, I was led to believe you might be somewhat *useful.* Since you've outlived your usefulness, I think I'll just take the rest of it out on your miserable ass. Enjoy your last days on earth."

He straightened and stared at Damon for a long moment and then slid his eyes to Chang. "Gentlemen."

There was a crash.

I heard wood buckle.

And the man the world had only recently been known as Mr. President straightened. He seemed to melt in on himself, then faded. Within seconds, we were staring at a vivid pair of blue eyes that flashed even brighter for a moment. The last thing I heard was his voice as he murmured, "I'll see you soon, Kitasa."

Then the line went dead.

CHAPTER TWENTY-FOUR

Guerilla News wasn't the only network running wild with speculation now.

Rumors ran rampant in the Capitol, but after twelve hours of no statement, somebody finally did speak.

He was understandably grave and somber-eyed as he addressed the nation, calling on people from all walks of life—human and non-human—to come forward in this time of tragedy. *Our president is missing. While there have been some concerning reports in the past twenty-four hours, we do not know the truth behind them and now, we cannot even begin to uncover the truths. Why? Because of a vile, violent attack here in the White House that left one of the president's most trusted friends dead...and now our president is missing...*

"Blah, blah, blah..."

Turning my back to the screen, I paced over to the window and stared outside.

The sun was setting.

It had been hours since everything seemed to have gone to hell in a handbasket. Nova had left for Georgia and I hadn't heard from him. There was no change with Justin or Colleen.

I'd tried contacting my long-lost aunt earlier. Long-lost probably wasn't the right word. *I* was the one who'd been long lost and quite happy with it. She hadn't returned the call.

That was a shoe waiting to drop.

The door opened and just that light noise had my hand moving to my sword.

Damon lifted a straight black brow as I stood there, squeezing the grip of my blade, heart pounding. "Jumpy," he noted.

"A bit."

He ran his tongue across his teeth as he stood there. "Doyle left the Lair earlier."

"What? He—"

"He's fine." Damon held up a hand, cutting me off. "He called me a few minutes ago. Said he's bringing somebody in who needs to speak with you, and told me that I should probably talk to you first."

Oh.

Heat kindled in my hand and I lowered my head to stare at the floor.

Although he didn't make a sound as he moved toward me, I could feel him coming. His boots stopped just a few inches from mine and he reached up, placing his hands on my shoulders. I sighed and swayed forward until my head bumped his chest.

"I get the feeling this has something to do with that favor you conned out of me."

"Yeah." Slowly, I lifted my head and met his eyes. At the same time, I reached up and gripped his wrists. "You're not going to like it."

"I'm already figuring that out." Tugging his wrists free, he caught my waist and boosted me up onto the nearest counter. "If you plan on telling me that you're heading out to go look for Mr. Pseudo-POTUS, you're out of your mind and I will keep you here if I have to sit on you."

Narrowing my eyes, I leaned in. I bit his lip but that just made him catch my chin in his hand and he kissed me, hard and fast.

"Relax, Tarzan. I'm still trying to figure out what he is." With a sardonic smile, I added, "Besides, I'm pretty sure he is going to come to *me*. You and Chang pretty much laughed in his face. He won't let that go ignored."

"Nice to know. We were afraid we were too subtle."

"You wouldn't know subtle if it bit you on the ass." Reaching up, I curled my hand in the faded front of his T-shirt. "I told you once— you'd walk into hell for me."

"And walk right back out, holding the devil's head. Are you bringing the devil into my Lair, Kit?" He hooked an arm around my neck, angling my head back so I couldn't look away.

The timing, really, couldn't have been more perfect.

Just as I was trying to figure out how to start, there was a knock at the door. Damon turned his head, opening his mouth.

Then he stopped, a frown appearing—a deep line formed a groove between his eyebrows. As he turned away, I slid off the bar.

Carefully, I took my sword from the sheath.

He glanced at me, watched as I put it down, that frown still darkening his features.

"Come on in, Doyle," he said, nostrils flaring wide as he scented the air.

Doyle came in. She was with him, clad once more in that dappled gray that seemed to blend into anything, everything and nothing.

Once more, my aunt Rana was slumped and stooped, making her seem slower, older. Under the concealing hood, I saw the glitter of her eyes as she looked at me for the briefest second.

Then she sidestepped, creating a wide space between her and Doyle.

Doyle started toward her, but she held up a hand, staying him.

I moved toward Damon, although he was already closing the distance, and fast.

Rana didn't back down, but then again, I don't think she'd ever backed down from anything in her life.

"Hello, Alpha Lee," she said, not bothering to disguise her voice.

"Do I know you?" he asked.

Rana glanced at me and then, in an oddly feline movement, she uncurled from that slump, reaching up to tug back her hood revealing her face, her hair.

"We have a common…bond, you might say."

Every muscle inside him tensed.

I barely got in front of him in time.

"Don't," I said, hating the plea that came into my voice as I reached for him, sinking my nails into his shoulders.

"Not this," he said, staring right through me. "I'll do a lot of things for you, be a lot of things. Ask me for anything else, Kit. But not this."

"We wouldn't have made it to Justin and Colleen without her." I caught his shirt again, wishing I could dig into his flesh somehow, force him to be still. "They are *alive* because she helped us. Helped *me*."

"And how many times did she hurt you? Which one is she, Kit? One of the cousins or aunts who stood by? Is she your fucking grandmother? The one who *beat* you?"

"My aunt. My aunt Rana. She never beat me."

"Child, step aside. I don't need your protection," Rana said from behind me.

I ignored her. "Damon, listen to me."

Instead, he picked me up and set me aside. "Doyle."

He shuffled his feet and moved closer. I darted around to Damon's other side, keeping his big body between us.

"Kit..." Doyle gave me a look that was both apology and commiseration.

"No!"

Damon had pushed past me.

Instinct screamed inside and I simply opened my mind to one of the songs, always so loud now.

It was the drumbeat that echoed in my blood, and I let the bow and arrow come.

I had the target picked out just before Damon would have reached Rana and I let go, listening to the music—the music of the bowstring, the music in my blood.

Rana saw it and she ducked, diving forward and tucking into a ball; the same move she'd taught to me, executed flawlessly.

The arrow went past Damon's shoulder and buried itself in the wall.

For a second, nobody moved.

Damon's shoulders heaved as he sucked in a breath.

"She did something else, too."

Slowly, he turned. His eyes slid to the bow in my hand. Then to the sword.

"She helped me save Colleen. She helped me save Justin." I panted, staring at him over the arrow now nocked. The bow was between us...but not a barrier. A *symbol*. "She gave me the music back. Damon...please."

There was a knock.

Polite, short, clipped.

Nobody moved or breathed.

The knock came again.

"Doyle. Answer the door," Damon said, each word low and tight, squeezed out as though through a vise.

"Yes, Alpha."

Rana turned her head, eyes lingering on Doyle as she remained there in her crouch, one hand braced on the floor in front of her.

"Get up," Damon said on a snarl.

Then he spun to me, his jaw set.

"This…this is what you want." His breaths came in ragged pants as he crossed to me and there was hell in his eyes.

Slowly, I lowered the bow I still held. It was the one he'd bought for me in the days, hours really, before we'd found Doyle. I'd known him maybe a week and he'd changed everything for me. It was stupid and foolish and wonderful, but I'd found someplace where I belonged—somebody who *wanted* me.

And now I was betting everything on the fact that he understood me.

I'd been *broken* inside for so long. Even before Jude kidnapped me, even before the bond with my weapons was shattered. I'd been broken from years of abuse at my grandmother's hands. Broken bones alone hadn't done it, but the hatred that came from her, the way others turned their back when she beat me.

Others…a memory flickered in my mind and I locked on it. I'd have to ask. But not now.

Over the past year, I'd been piecing myself together, learning who I was without the weapons and I'd finally figured things out—I was myself, whether I could call them or not.

I didn't *need* to be able to call a bow to master it, and I didn't need to hear a blade's song to wield it.

But I sure as hell wanted those things back.

Holding his eyes, I banished the bow he'd given me and called my sword to my hand.

His lids flickered.

"When I was in Tallahassee, Justin and I met up with a…very strange woman," I said thickly. "She was…strange. Scary. She healed people. She cured *cancer*, Damon. Justin saw it and you can't fool a witch, baby. Not like that. Then she put her hands on me, and for a minute…" I lifted a shoulder. "Well, I thought she might have fixed me. But nothing happened. I think it hurt Justin more than it hurt me. Then there we were in the woods, trying to move in on where Justin and Colleen were—and there was Rana. I thought she was there to kill me or worse…take me back."

Damon's eyes went straight to gold and the muscles in his face shifted, rippled. He battled the monster within, cracking his neck and popping his knuckles, but I could see the grip he had on control slipping. So tenuous.

"The first time I called my blade, I was terrified, afraid for my life...my sanity." I shifted her now, watched as the light danced on her surface. She murmured to me softly in the back of my mind, a gentle, soothing song. "Rana pushed me to that point again—on *purpose*."

I slid in front of him, keeping up with him far more easily than I would've thought possible. "On purpose, Damon. And it wasn't my sword I called. She brought something else."

I called the shield then and it settled on my arm, fitting there perfectly. "The last time I saw this shield was when I'd been called in front of my grandmother." Curling my lip, I met his eyes. "But the first time...I don't even remember. I was young, probably not much more than a baby. It was my mother's. Rana stole him and brought him *here*. For me. You are *not* going to fight her, Damon."

He reached up, shoving a hand into my hair.

He cranked my head back to an almost brutal angle.

Dimly, I was aware that Chang had come into the room and we were now the focus of three people.

"That breaking point is getting damn close again, Kit," he said, pressing his mouth close to my ear. "You can't keep pushing like this."

I sucked in a breath and when he stepped away, I had to lock my knees to keep from wilting.

I ended up having to slam a hand against the table to keep upright as Chang and Damon shared a telling look.

Doyle moved closer to me while Rana stood alone, unfazed.

"Well," Chang said softly. "What unusual company you've been keeping, Kit. Tell me, madam...are there more of your kind coming?"

"Hardly." Rana gave him a cool smile before dismissing him, looking around with patent curiosity. "So this is where a king of cats makes his home. Interesting."

Damon's jaw worked and I could hear his teeth grinding together but Chang moved toward him, drawing his attention. "As interesting as this all is, I received a message that I believe needs to be addressed."

"What is it?" Damon asked.

"It was directed at Kit, but it's clear we were all meant to hear it."

He hesitated, eying Rana.

"She stays where I can see her until I decide what to do about her," Damon said flatly.

"Of course." Chang's eyes narrowed and I got a feeling he had a suggestion or two.

Staring him straight in the eye, I banished the sword.

"As I said, Kit…interesting." He moved to the table and placed a phone down a docking device. "Replay message."

A moment later, the media screen came to life.

It was just text, though.

No audio or video. Just a few pointed words.

Just how many cats will I have to kill to get a kitten? Shall we play a game and find out or will you just save us all the trouble? Call me, precious. Don't make me wait too long. You won't like the results.

My nails tore neat little half-moons into my palms as I stared at the number that came up.

"Call it," Damon ordered.

Feeling sick, I turned to him. "Damon—"

"If you even suggest turning yourself over to him, Kit, I'll have you locked in here for the duration." Damon turned his head, his gray eyes half-wild. "Now, I know what that idea will probably do to you. And I know if I did it, it would spell the end of us. But I'll live with that. I *can't* live with the idea of you trying to sacrifice yourself. So don't ask me. Just don't."

The phone on the table rang.

"Nobody in the Clan would allow it, Kit," Chang said quietly. "Don't even think about it."

"I'd follow you." Doyle bumped his shoulder against mine. "You know I can."

I felt sick.

The phone rang two more times.

The screen flared to life.

"Well, hello, precious." The blue-eyed, devilish looking man smiled at me as he leaned forward. "I got the whole lot of you sorry creatures."

"Oh, just shove a knife in me." Rana's caustic voice echoed from the far side of the room.

The man on the screen stilled. His features did that odd, water over stone dance and he blinked, reaching up to rub at his scalp. I saw them then.

Small, almost delicate horns, curving up from his scalp.

"Shit," I whispered, hardly noticing as Rana strode forward.

Damon started to snarl.

Chang rested a hand on his arm, a quiet, subtle...*wait*...

"It's you." My aunt stared at the man on the screen with something that could only be described as complete and utter scorn. "I should have known."

"Well, if it isn't the sword-hand of the wicked bitch of the east." He leaned in, the surprise I'd seen on his face gone now. "What's the matter, love? Did Fanis lose faith in me?"

"That would mean she faith you to begin with." Rana flipped the heavy weight of her braids over her shoulder. "But really, I would be a bad person to ask since I've rather lost faith in her. The job I'm on now is proof of that. Only the truly deluded would think it wise."

"Hmmm...and are you on a job or hiding from her, then? Does she know where you are, dearest?" His gaze slid to me. "Cozying up to one cast out from the family?"

"Tut-tut. I don't discuss family matters with things like you." Rana gave him a scornful look. "I'm curious about something, Rob. What's a puck like yourself doing running errands for her anyway? I wouldn't have thought you to be an errand boy."

A muscle in his jaw worked. "Bad form, Rana. Very, very bad form."

"What...you *are* running an errand for her. Gone to fetch the wayward stray back home and all." Then Rana smiled, a sly one and she lifted a finger, pressed it to her chin. "Oh, wait...maybe you had a trick or two up your sleeve and she only *thinks* you're playing her game. You're still angry, though. What's the matter, Rob? Did I let the cat out of the bag? Had Kitasa not figured it out? Well, pity. If it makes you feel any better, I've found her to be quite clever and what with the horns showing..."

Rob...Puck...

My mind was whirling as his blue eyes clashed with mine.

Rob—

Robin!

The horns vanished even as the pieces fell together in my mind, precious few though they were.

"Robin Goodfellow. Huh." As his face went redder, I pursed my lips. "I didn't know you were real."

"Oh, I'm *very* real, Kitasa."

My name sounded like a snake's hiss on his lips and the unblinking way he stared at me was unnerving to say the least.

Something about that stare was jarring, penetrating. He was trying to see inside my soul—

Rana kicked my ankle. Hard.

Sucking in air, I looked over at her, but she was staring blithely at Rob, that faint, almost-smile on her lips.

My throat had gone tight and dry and my heart was racing. Falling on the old tricks Damon had been using to help me control it, I let Rana talk a moment.

Something cold touched my arm.

"You should drink something." Chang was studying me closely. He'd realized something wasn't right. "You're still healing up."

I accepted the water he offered and took a sip before looking back at the screen.

"Yes, Kit. Heal. I want you to fully appreciate the gutting I'm going to give you." He stroked the spot where one of the horns had previously been visible as he eyed me and I could feel that pull on my brain as he tried again, trying to do whatever he'd done. It didn't work though. I refused to let his eyes connect with mine for more than a second. It wasn't too much different from looking at a vampire. Some of them could pull you in with just a flick of their gaze. I'd just treat the puck here the same way.

"Does Fanis know you've decided to sidestep your agreement? You won't ever get that spear you covet so dearly." Rana looked bored. "You've failed to honor your word and you know how she dislikes that."

"Hmmm. Perhaps *you* could get it. After all, there is no love lost between you and your mother." He tapped his brow, leaning forward. "I see it. You know this."

"True enough." Rana shrugged. "But as little regard as I have for her, I have even less desire to put a Druidic spear of untold power in *your* hands. You want it too much. That's never a good thing with your kind, puck."

"Are you certain? A woman like you, I could make a fine trade. I've weapons the likes of which this world will never see again. Blades so beautiful, they'd make you weep. All I want is one paltry wooden spear."

"Don't you have enough Druid-made weapons?" Rana flicked her fingers, brushing the topic aside. Holding his eyes, she lifted her short sword and rotated it so it caught the light. "The weapons I need, I have. Of course, you don't *need* your weapons, do you? You just need them out of the reach of others."

"I'm merely a collector, Rana." He smiled sharp, shifting his attention to me. "Make your good-byes, precious. And your apologies. I'll leave a trail of blood in my wake."

CHAPTER TWENTY-FIVE

The second the line went dead, eyes locked in on Rana, save for Damon.

He came to me and one by one, everybody else turned to look at him.

"You have one, don't you, kitten?"

My heart had started to hammer again and this time, I didn't bother to control it. I could hear it whispering now. Blood, death and tears, a sad song underscored by the bittersweet wail of what might have been pipes.

"Ah…"

"One what?" Doyle asked.

"That's one of the weapons you had me lock up." He stopped in front of me, arms crossed over his wide chest, eyes gleaming.

"Well, well." Rana circled, a look of pensive interest on her face. It was the most emotion I had seen from her in probably my entire life. "Do you indeed?"

"She's *mine*." The whisper of her song became a little louder in my head.

"A Druid's weapon isn't like a knife you pick up at a market or some pretty bow," Rana said. "You might be able to wield it, but you can't master it unless it lets you. How did you come by it?"

"Why are you asking?" The challenge in my voice made her smile grow.

"Haven't you wondered why it matters to *him*? He killed the Black Anni. He hunted a dryad. He killed a Green Man."

"There was no Green Man."

"Not now. He killed him. The dead woods—nothing kills a forest like that except destroying the Green Man who cares for it." Rana pursed her lips as she studied me. "You should know these things."

"Yeah, well, my education was sort of lacking."

"Yes. It was." She came closer. When Damon tensed, she stilled. "They are all connected, Kit."

"I'm gathering that—now tell me why. And how did you know about the Black Anni, the dryad, the Green Man. How did you find *me* to begin with?"

"I've always known where you were." She delivered the statement with calm finality. "I knew you would come here years before you even ran. But *that* isn't what matters. What matters is dealing with Rob, before he causes too much trouble. If he mucks things up too much, Fanis will figure out where he is—and then she'll figure out where *you* are. I spent too much time concealing that fact. I'd rather it all not go to waste now."

I felt like she'd just hit me in the head with a sledgehammer.

"You knew."

She inclined her head. "Indeed. Now…let's discuss your weapon."

Chang stayed between us on the walk down to the basement.

More than a few emerged to look at Rana, but one look from Damon sent them back to wherever they'd come from.

The Lair practically hummed with life, with the energy that pulsed inside shifters.

It was large enough to house almost the entire Clan now, and I suspected he'd pulled in just about all of them.

He wouldn't take chances.

My mind kept spinning from odd little details like…is there enough food here to what's the deal with Druidic weapons to I never got around to drinking my tea.

"Jada."

Damon's voice snapped me back into focus and I caught sight of the tall, thin black woman standing at attention across from the room where I stored my more dangerous weapons. She nodded at Damon, her gaze glancing off Rana before coming to me. I also received one of those polite nods before she greeted Chang and Doyle.

There were tight lines around her eyes. "Are you okay?" I asked, remembering how being near the weapons had affected Shanelle.

"Oh, yeah. This is about as much fun as telling my mom I'd been bitten." Her mouth tugged in a humorless smile. "But I'm handling it."

Doyle's face was tight. "Man, what do you have in there, Kit?"

"Stuff. You don't get to mess with it," I said.

Moving to the warded door of my new weapons room, I swiped my hands down my pants, the power coming off the protection spells stinging my skin.

"Are you trying to tell the world something powerful is hiding inside?" Rana asked, the question almost clinical.

"I've already told him he needs to tone it down." Giving her a quelling look, I opened the door. "You need to stay out here. You're not…part of this place."

"I already guessed as much." She studied the door, the darkness of the room inside. "You hired a fool to do this."

Damon narrowed his eyes at her. "It will do enough harm if I shove you inside, I bet. Want to try it out?"

"I think I'll pass." She took one step back.

I withdrew the bow and nothing else. She hummed—the moment I touched her, she hummed, coming to life in my hand like never before.

"Wow." The jolt of power that went up my arm was unlike anything I'd ever known and her music was loud enough to drown out the insidious call from the blade, Death.

"What else do you have in there?" Rana asked, her mouth drawing down in a tight line. "Something foul. I can taste it."

"Something foul." I said nothing else as I left the room, striding out and shutting the door tight.

The moment the door closed, Death's demanding cry faded and the muscles in my shoulders relaxed.

But the bow…she continued to talk to me.

I couldn't understand the words, but the message was clear.

"Oh, what a love you have there," Rana murmured, coming closer.

I flicked a look to her face. There was none of the avarice I felt when I spied a weapon that I wanted, though. Just appreciation. She reached out, slowly, giving me time to back away. When I didn't, she stroked a finger down the carved wood. "Where did you find her?"

"I killed a man. He had her locked away in a safe."

"Hmmm." Her eyes gleamed. "Was she his?"

"I don't think so. He wasn't her maker and she wasn't…happy there. She was in bad shape and he hadn't cleaned her or used her. I had to restring her, fix her up. The only thing I've ever done is practice with her." It felt strange to be talking about this with Rana, strange to be doing it *here* with the cats stretching out around me in a half-circle while she faced me.

"She's made you her own. She'll let you master her. She'll answer to you if you try to call her. But you'll have to show care, Kit. Druids bond with their weapons almost like we do…and Druids sometimes carried madness in their blood." There was warning in her words, in her eyes. She let her hand fall away from the bow and she backed up.

"What is it with Druidic weapons and the puck?" I asked.

Now Rana smiled and it was one that sent shivers up my spine. "Well, that *is* a question, isn't it? I could say it's because pucks are greedy, covetous demons and they love the rare and unusual. It's true enough, and a Druid's bow like that is rare indeed."

"But…" She looked around. "Let's not discuss it here."

Back in our quarters, Damon, Rana and I sat at the table. Chang stood at Damon's shoulder, back in his preferred spot.

I guess they had decided they were good, or that they'd work things out after this was over.

Doyle had been dismissed, though.

Doyle had sputtered, acting like the kid he still was under all that muscle.

"There are more still coming in. Scott will need a hand keeping this many shifters under control. I don't have enough enforcers out there to contain the numbers we're going to have you." Damon narrowed his eyes. "Walk around and growl at them instead of trying to argue with me."

Doyle hadn't been happy, but he'd left.

The only reason the attitude hadn't gotten him in trouble was because he was just as much Damon's son as anything else, and Damon gave him a short amount of leeway—very short.

Now, three of us sat at the table, Chang a silent shadow at Damon's shoulder while the bow lay in front of us like some bizarre, arcane table decoration.

"You want to know why he killed the Anni, the Green Man...why he had you hunting the dryad." Rana looked up from the bow and met my eyes. "It's because they can sense things, locate them. Not unlike us. And the Black Anni hoarded things that created death. I imagine he found something with them. The Green Man and the dryad, they were attuned to things of nature and the Druids forged their weapons from nature. Stone, wood. Even their few rare steel weapons had as much of the earth in them as anything else. Their magic was earth magic and the Green Man and the dryad, they would have sensed such."

"So you think he killed the Anni, the Green Man, to keep them from locating more weapons?" I touched my hand to the bow.

"I think the Anni *had* more and he took them. The Green Man wouldn't help him. I've known Green Men before, Kitasa. They are as unyielding as an oak tree, their roots just as deep. One of them would die before helping a trickster like that puck."

"The dryad." I remembered the misery in her voice. "She mentioned somebody. His name was Albus."

"A lover, perhaps. Dryads often mated with Green Men." Rana stroked the bow again. "This weapon is a weakness to him, Kit. He doesn't know you have it?"

"I don't see how he could." A cold knot of fear settled in my gut. Haltingly, I forced myself to ask the question. "He's been hunting me...for Fanis?" At her nod, I pushed myself again. "For how long?"

"Oh, not long. A few months." She flicked a hand. "He's been playing this game of his—you were just some small part, likely an amusing game to him at first. I think manipulating Mother was the same. A game. She had something he wanted, another way that could weaken him and he needed it removed before he made his next big play. You didn't even come into the picture until she returned from the..."

She stopped.

Damon lifted his gaze from the bow to stare at her.

"The Dominari." My entire face felt stiff. I knew what time of year it was. We were moving into the first edges of fall here. They would be moving into the first edges of spring, but winter there had an iron grip. "How many died this time?"

"None. A few serious injuries. But fewer run every year." Rana stared at me stonily. "You never would have survived."

205

"That was the whole *point*."

Damon's eyes, the weight of his fury, slammed into me but I didn't dare look at him.

"It's all old history, though. The puck went there. Why?"

"He's gathering those he might call upon as…allies," Rana said, a sick smile twisting her face. "He's priming this country for another war, one that will leave few humans standing, niece. Once he is done here, he will move on to the next country—likely Mexico, because unrest is rampant there and your neighbors to the north seem more tolerant than others in the world. Once he has the numbers, he will turn on Canada. Then he will spread out, annihilating as many as he can."

Chilled to the bone, I searched her face for any sign that she might be exaggerating, might be lying. I saw none. "Please tell me that Fanis isn't that crazy yet."

"Oh, she's *crazy* enough. But unfortunately for the puck, she's not *stupid* enough. She remembers war, Kitasa. It never goes well for either side, and our race numbers only in the hundreds now. She's not going to send them off to die in a war for some demon as crazy as she is."

"He's a…" My jaw tightened. "Pucks are demons?"

Leaning in, Rana said, "Some people in England still call them hobgoblins. Yes, Kitasa. Pucks are minor demons. Of course, there are even *older* stories that ascribe them to the fallen."

"The fallen." I blinked at her, confused.

"Fallen angels," Chang murmured, speaking for the first time since we'd returned. "I've heard some of those stories. The war in heaven—angels fell. Some sided with Satan, but others were locked in battle and when it ended, they just didn't make it back in time. Those who sided with the devil became the minor demons, while those who didn't make it back became the fey."

"Those would be the stories." Rana's tone didn't indicate whether Chang was right or not. Her gaze came to mine. "You might be more familiar with the modern myths—the Seelie and Unseelie Courts were quite popular with human storytellers for a long while. But the true stories…they go much, much deeper. And they are much, much older. And nothing you'll find anywhere can prepare for anything like Robin, the puck king. He wants to rise to his former glory."

Judging by the grim set of her shoulders, that wasn't something we wanted. "How do we stop him?"

Rana put her hand on the bow and pushed it closer. "There is no *we*. It's going to have to be *you*. The bow has chosen you. If you hadn't bonded with her, I would do it." Her mouth tightened. "This will come with risk, you must know that. But if he isn't killed, he will hunt you. If he isn't killed, he will find a new way to start his war. This..."

She paused, her eyes darkening. "Hospital. I've heard you speak of it. I know there are disappearances. I've been in these lands long enough to know things aren't as they should be. And the witch you killed. She didn't act on her own—her mind wasn't even her own. She was *driven*."

I could see the wheels turning in her mind, realized she was making the connections I sometimes made; the little leaps from one thing to another. I could all but see the pieces as they fell together for her.

"Chang." Without looking away from the bow, I asked, "You said there were connections between him and the hospital?"

"I might have stretched it a bit." He smoothed his finger down his brow. "I was following a hunch, but his reaction confirmed it. Several of the men assigned to protect him early on weren't fully human. Each of them disappeared. I had a contact in the Capitol try to find their families. Save for one, all of them are gone as well."

"And the one who isn't gone?"

Chang's smile was cool. "Actually, you might not realize it, but you've already spoken to him—it was Mo's brother. When he disappeared, she came here. He was a carrier and the last one to vanish. He had suspicions that something weird was going on within the Capitol and shared them with her. Told her if anything happened to him, she needed to get the hell out. That's what she did. She was the one I contacted when I started needing to reach out and get more information about our odd, horned friend."

Connections...

My mind seized on it.

Mind-wipes. The hospital. "He would have sensed them right off, I bet...worried they'd figure him out, too. So he sends them away. Could have been a private assignment, or he's out on a trip..."

"Anything could have happened. We won't know." Damon's hard voice cut the air. "I don't give a damn. I want to know more about why *Kit* has to be the one to do him. He's old. He's a fucking *demon.*"

"The *bow* can kill him. She is the only one here the bow will bond with." Rana spoke patiently, the way she would if teaching a child how to use a weapon for the first time. Then she looked at me. "She answers to you. Only you. A Druidic weapon is one of the few things that can kill a minor demon like the puck. You don't want to try one of the other ways. It's not…fun."

"Try me," Damon demanded.

"Do you have any fairies handy?" Rana didn't blink or bat an eyelash. "Perhaps a few tucked away inside your pocket? You need a larger one, at least hip high, so I don't think that's likely. You are rather large, but not quite *that* large."

Damon worked his jaw and I could see the snarl all but forming, the air around him starting to burn hot.

"Fairies?" Chang said, politely clearly his throat.

"Yes." Rana didn't look away from Damon. "They are, essentially, a puck's Achilles heel. Find one, kill it, get the femur—it's the strongest bone in the body. Make sure you save some of the blood, but don't get it on you, because it's somewhat poisonous."

I choked at that. *Somewhat?* How about *lethally* poisonous?

She heard. I could tell by the way her lid twitched. But she didn't pause. "You'll need the blood. Sharpen the bone on one end, then let that end soak in the blood for twenty-four hours. Assuming you have that long. Once that is done, let it dry. Then you need to shove that bone into the puck, either the eye or the heart." She waited a beat. "Did you get all of that, Alpha Lee or should I write it down? You don't want to miss a step."

Every muscle in Damon's body went tight.

I put a hand on his shoulder. "Look, I get that the two of you don't like each other—"

"On the contrary, I have nothing but respect for your cat, Kitasa."

The words caught me off guard. I doubt they meant much to Damon, but I had a feeling they surprised Chang.

She continued, unfazed by my obvious surprise. "He took out a woman who was, at best, a psychotic bitch. At worst…well, I believe she and Fanis would have made great friends, if the *Nerai* hadn't loathed shifters, one and all."

I hadn't heard the term *Nerai* in years. *Nerai*—it meant *Queen.*

Rana spat it out as though it tasted and felt like acid on her tongue.

"There is a debt I owe him, one I can never repay." Now she looked at directly at Damon. "But he knows nothing about this creature. I do. I know how it can be killed and I know the puck's weaknesses and strengths."

"If he's that dangerous—" Damon started out.

"Can I kill him?"

Rana's lips curved. "If I thought you couldn't, I would have already left to procure my own Druidic weapon. I didn't know you had a bow, Kitasa, but the moment I saw the puck, I knew what had to be done—and I know where one Druidic weapon resides. After all, it's quite a public item, is it not?"

In an instant, I knew what she meant.

"You're insane if you think you can break into that museum and steal it."

"There is no place I can't break into, nothing I cannot steal." Rana lifted a shoulder. "But I would need time and I'd rather not leave you to this task alone, if I had any other way. I plan to be there with you when you go—I'll guard your back until you return—or until the end, whatever that may be."

"You mean the staff on display at the National History Museum," Chang said softly.

"Yes." She inclined her head. "I've known about it for…well, quite some time."

"Guard." Damon said the word slowly as though he didn't understand what it meant.

I was actually doing the same thing, only silently. I wasn't entirely sure I liked where her brain was going although logically I couldn't deny there was sense in it.

It was my emotions that were messing everything up. They did that a lot. Right now, my instincts and logic were sidling up and calmly laying things out and my emotions were going to get told to get fucked. That *would* happen because my instincts would win out. They always did.

"Just what do you mean *guard* her?" Damon said, lips barely moving.

"Do you truly want her going out there *alone*? A true warrior, the best of fighters, knows when she needs her back guarded. Kit is, without a doubt, a true warrior." Her mouth quirked up as she raked

Damon up and down with a look. "Do you think to guard her? This needs subtly. You have no subtly to you. Everything about you screams possessiveness and protectiveness. You all but *reek* of power and strength—it's a wonder Annette didn't order you to be assassinated the minute you stepped foot into her territory."

Damon's brows shot up.

"What...you seem surprised." Rana settled back more comfortably. "There hasn't been more than a month that has gone by when I haven't been...around. I watched her. I watched the politics here. I watched you and the Alpha of the Wolf Pack. I always knew you'd end up as the Alpha." She stroked the grip of her sword and glanced at Chang, her gaze lingering but a moment. "I'd even wager your man there knew as well. It's the only reason he remained. As much as he loves those children he watches over, he'd never stay under that bitch's heel if not for a reason. You were always the reason."

Chang hadn't moved, hadn't blinked.

"Have you started seeing into the future?" I asked softly.

"I don't need to. I see into the soul." Rana blinked, her lashes sweeping down to hide her eyes. "And I've been watching these two for a long, long while. Alpha Lee...you are a protector, a vengeful one, perhaps. But at your core? You wish to protect. That's all well and good—in its place. But out there? It would get her killed." Rana slanted a look at Chang. "Perhaps him. He is a protector as well, but he chooses those he protects more carefully. Children. And he's had a long time to refine his art...he's like a shadow. But nobody could watch her back as well as I could—not for this."

"You think I would trust *you* with her?"

My temper snapped. "It's not up to you." I jabbed Damon in the chest before firing Rana a dark look. "And why should *I* trust *you*? You both need to quit talking about me like I'm not here. Done with it, okay? Now...let's take a deep breath and talk. Logically."

Rana held up a hand, indicating her acquiescence.

Damon, however, planted his hands on his hips. "Sure, Kit. We can talk about this logically. It's not like you'd actually go with her. Right?"

"It makes sense," I said, forcing myself to keep my voice level and hoping I didn't reveal any of the nervousness I felt. "She trained me—I still *move* like her. She echoes my move and I echo hers.

Nobody could back me up on a mission like she could. And when it comes to…" I almost said Whitmore and had to bite it back at the last minute. "The puck, she knows more things about him than I do. There was training I would have had, if…"

Now I laughed and it was a hollow sound. "If I hadn't been *me*, they would have taught me more. I already know things that none of you know. I know how to kill things you don't even know exist. But she has knowledge of things *I* don't know about. If I'm the one who's going to have to use that bow, then I want all the best weapons I can have with me. One of them is knowledge—she has it. I don't."

Damon's shoulders were tight, and his eyes flashed green-gold. Anger stung my skin and I knew he was taking in every word—taking the words in and hating them.

"Explain to me the sense in you going off on some suicide mission with her," Damon said quietly. "The scars on you—the ones I can see and the ones I can't—they won't ever heal and she *stood* there while those beatings happened. She *stood* there while you were brutalized, time and again. You told me that."

His words were a slap, scraping against nerves that had been left raw ever since I'd seen my aunt's face. My throat went tight and for a minute, I wanted to hit him. Hit him hard and then just…run. Run hard and fast and lose myself. "Damn you," I said raggedly. "Do you think I don't *know* that? That I've forgotten? I was *there*. I remember every lash from the whip and every blow from their fists. I remember every broken bone, every boot I took to the gut. I won't *ever* forget."

"Then why are you even thinking about this?" he shouted. "You're her blood and she turned her back on you!"

"Because I know it's the only way!" Whirling on Rana, I met her eyes, the pale blue of her gaze as cold as winter ice. Frozen, even. "He's wrong, though. *They* turned their backs. Unless she ordered them to join in. I remember that, too. Aunt Reshi—Rathi's beloved mum…she was the oldest, next to you. She'd join in or turn and hide her face. The others, they could barely stand to look at me. But you…you would just *stand* there, staring at me, through every beating, every broken bone, every whipping. I want to know why."

I think I could have asked her almost anything and it wouldn't surprise her.

But that did. She backed up a step, her hand slipping to the grip of her short sword. "The *why* doesn't matter. We have a job that must be done. Are we going to discuss that—and keeping these people you seem to cherish alive?"

"We can. After I have my answer." Absently, I went to rest my hand on the hilt of my blade, only to remember I'd put my weapons away. I flexed my hand, but I didn't call her. I wouldn't. I didn't need her to *talk*. "I need to know why."

Something told me the answer to my question was vital.

I thought perhaps she would just turn and walk out. But in the end, she sighed, weary. Sitting, she drew her sword and placed it on the table, holding the grip for a moment as if in prayer—or for courage. For me, it was often both. When she let go, she looked at me. "How much do you remember of your mother?" The words came out softly, almost a whisper.

It wasn't what I had expected to hear. Not at all.

Uncertain, I glanced over at Damon. I don't even know why. I just needed…something. He touched the small of my back. He didn't like this—didn't like her. But he loved me and that light touch gave me what I needed. "I barely have any memories." Licking my lips, I closed my hands into fists, nails biting my palms and fought the urge to ask why she was asking, what my mother had to do with anything.

Because I already knew—*everything*.

That was clear by the look in Rana's eyes. Solemn and quiet, sad and full of memory. I wanted to tell her to forget it, that it didn't matter. I couldn't. I'd never been one to take the easy way out. Even when I wanted to.

"There are flashes, bits and pieces. I'll hear her voice, a few forgotten words or a line from a song." My voice tried to break but I didn't let it. "I'll see the two of you as you danced across the training fields in front of the Hall. Swords would flash and the metal sang. Not much."

"Your mother was my best friend." Rana stared off into the distance. It was the past she saw. I knew it, without even asking. "I am the oldest—four had died before you were even born. Your mother was the youngest—fifty years separated us. I all but raised her. When she died, it was almost like I had lost my own daughter, not just my sister. Something inside me died that day. I wasn't there with her…but I knew. I was the one who left to bring back her body, her blade and her shield. I left you with Reshi. She…she didn't know our sister was dead. She wouldn't dare lift a hand to you. Was fond of you, even. She still had a spine then."

Emotion, hot and powerful began to pulse inside her, lighting her eyes. Rage—*hate*—so hot and powerful, it was a wonder it hadn't eaten her alive.

"Trisera died on a suicide mission. She knew it would kill her." Rana paused and looked away. Her lashes swept low and in a voice so faint, I barely heard it, she added, "We both knew."

My heart was beating so hard, blood pounding so hot, I felt sick. *Trisera. Mum...* I wanted to weep. Wanted to hit something. Had she died for *nothing*? Damon smoothed a hand up my back. Sucking in a breath of air, I caught the metallic taste of blood on it, but didn't realize it was because I'd torn ragged gashes into my hands until Damon leaned against the table and forced my hands to unclench. Chang held something out to him and Damon took it, pressing a soft piece of cotton to the minor wounds as Rana continued to speak.

"Tris—your mother—had a choice to make. And so did I. And I've lived with the guilt ever since. Just as I have had to live with the guilt over what my mother did to you."

"Bullshit," I snarled. It came out of me in a torrent, like acidic vomit, too poisonous to contain but almost too poisonous to let it out. I almost lunged over the table for her, but Damon caught my arm, stayed me. Why? Why wasn't he letting me attack her *now*?

"Doubt it." Rana's words rang hollowly around us. "I don't blame you. Hate me. I do not blame you. I would hate me as well. However, there were actions that had to be carried out and choices that had to be made. Neither one of us saw any other out. The choice was simple and awful—your mother could go on the fool's errand the *Nerai* had sent her on, knowing she would die and leave you alone. Or stay at Aneris Hall and I would take up the job. I would die—and make no mistake, I was happy to do it. But we were both practical, Kitasa. I was older." She laughed bitterly. "I was supposed to be wiser and I was being...*trained* to take over in the *Nerai's* stead. Who would do better at protecting you? Watching over you? Fanis already despised you—you were Tris' weakness. Her mistake...she'd fallen in love with a human and you'd carry that weakness inside you."

"In the end, we knew the truth." Rana looked away. "I tried to hide from it, but Tris wouldn't let me. I was strong. Fanis weakens more every year—she held her reign too long and rules through fear rather than strength now. There will come a time when I can dispatch her, but your mother…it would've been ages, perhaps half a century before she could take our Queen on."

Rana rose and paced over to the window, speaking in a low voice, soft and steady now. "But she would have *tried*. Perhaps I could defy her now and survive, defeat her even, but she would have tried *then*—and she would have suffered for it. Suffered, then died. And you with her."

I flinched at that hard, harsh statement and when Rana turned to fix her icy eyes on me, I wanted to hide. "Tell me, child. What choice do you think she made? She would have crossed hell for you." Her lashes fell. "As would I. The two of you were…well. You were my world."

I wanted to deny those words, yell at her for them, tell her to take them back. But the truth in them was stark, plain. Because I couldn't walk away from them, I ignored them instead. "What are you talking about?" I demanded. "What's this so-called *choice*? You say you knew what she was going to do? What does *that* mean? How did you know?"

Each successive question sounded more panicked than the last, but I couldn't stop it and when she just stared at me, it only added to my panic. "And you *talk* like you've always known where I was and you act like you've known Damon half your life, but I *know* that's not true and…"

Rana inclined her head and gave me that appraising look—

I knew that look.

"What?" The whisper squeezed out of me. There was no other way to describe it.

"There hasn't been more than a few weeks when I haven't known where you were—from the time you killed the man in the truck…even then, I knew where you were," Rana said softly. "When you were stolen away from here, locked up high in the cold mountains? I was on my way. I spoke to you as best as I could—your mind was closed, but I think you heard. I spoke to you then. Your friends arrived before I did. But even then, I knew where you were, and I was coming." Her eyes flashed with a hatred so bright, it cut right through me. "There would be nothing but pieces had I arrived first."

I sagged, the shock so consuming, I couldn't breathe.

The days I *never* wanted to remember slammed into me and I was back inside those rooms, tucked into a small ball and hiding. Starving myself and wishing for death, praying that Jude would never come back, or that I would die before he did.

You're not eating.

How can you be strong enough to flee from him if you do not eat? He is vampire and will not think to notice that until you drop from exhaustion or somebody tells him and his slaves fear him too much to mention it. You have to eat, Kitasa—

"You." Too staggered to even stay upright, I started to slump downward. It was only Damon who kept me from sitting on the floor. He caught me and eased me into a chair. "I thought I'd imagined it—hearing your voice while I was trapped inside that room. But you..."

"We are connected, niece. Your mother's blood in my blood. You were in trouble and I knew. I came as quickly as I could, but..." She looked away. "The best I could do was watch as they dragged that soulless monster away."

How can you be strong enough...

"I heard you. It was *you* telling me to eat. To stay strong. Wasn't it?"

Her level stare told me everything.

"All this time," I said, my voice ragged. "You've been watching me all this time?"

"I made a promise."

I turned away, shoving the heels of my hands against my eyes. "What's this *promise*? How did you know? *Any* of this? *All* of this? How did you know where to find me? Where I would be? And what is this crazy shit about my mother?"

A heavy sigh escaped her. "We...we were told, Kitasa. That a day would come when she or I would have to take an assignment from the *Nerai*. That whichever one of us went wouldn't come back. We knew the *Nerai* would be cruel—she was never *kind*, but losing Tris broke something in her. Out of all the children, the only two of us she...cared for were us. Tris and I. And it was the two of us that she always chose for the hardest assignments—proving ourselves, she told us, because one day, one of us would become the next *Nerai*." Rana's voice was scathingly cold. "She knew that likely one of the assignments could end in our death, but still she did it. And to lose Tris...it broke her."

Rana lifted her gaze to mine. "We were told, Kitasa. All of this. I knew you would come here...not this exact place, but I knew the general area and once I started looking, it was easy enough to find you."

"Told." It was getting harder to breathe. "You were...*told.*"

"Yes." She said it so simply. But there was a message in her eyes, one that was anything but simple.

I understood it, though. Somehow, I understood.

Her eyes held a message for me and I knew.

"Nova," I whispered.

I sensed the surprise from Chang and Damon but I couldn't look away from Rana. "Did he tell you about Doyle, too? Is that why you kept giving him the side-eye?" I demanded. "Do you know who his mother is? Is he another promise..."

The words trailed off, thought simply dying.

A sickening sensation settled in my belly.

Rana was no longer looking at me. Or anybody else. She stared down at her hands, her shoulders a hard, straight line.

I needed to speak, to say something. But while I struggled to do so, the men behind me had no such problem. Chang muttered something in a language I didn't understand, while Damon rose to his feet and paced around the table, coming to a stop by Rana.

"You."

She flinched at the sound of his voice, although she had known he was there, standing so close.

"It's *you.*"

Slowly, she lifted her head. Then she rose to stand before him. "As I said, I owe you a debt that can never be repaid. His father...he...I cared for him. He was a good man. I would have stayed with him, if I'd had the chance. But my life wasn't my own." Rana's eyes moved to me.

She'd been pregnant. I hadn't known. How old would I have been? Seven? Eight?

"When I heard his father had died, I didn't know what I was going to do." Rana snarled. "I knew I couldn't leave him with her. Bringing him home was not an option. He couldn't come to the Hall. Fanis had grown crueler, more insane. While she tormented Kitasa, she would have killed any child with shifter blood. I was torn. I had promised I would watch over my niece but there was my boy. Alone."

Damon's eyes were glowing and he stared at Rana with a stone-like mask.

She studied him in return. "But there was you. I knew of you. You took him. You said you'd care for him. I'd been watching *you* for a long time. I knew you'd keep him safe. And you have."

I was still stunned and trying to wrap my head around it. I squeezed my eyes shut.

The boy who had stared up at me from out of that pit with the face of another boy—one who had tormented me, abused me, violated me—he looked so much like Rathi, the cousin I'd killed.

"Doyle."

As though summoned by his name, he knocked on the door only a heartbeat after I spoke.

Damon was caught off guard, so intent on Rana. Jerking his head up, he stared at the door before turning his attention to Chang.

They knew it was him.

They could likely tell by scent, but I just knew in my gut.

Rana did as well. I could see the way something about her softened imperceptibly. Her hand flexed, as though gripping her sword. It was a nervous habit—one I recognized, and one I would have thought she'd have lost a long time ago.

"Should I send him away?" Chang asked quietly. His eyes flicked to Rana. There was no question that they believed her. I could see that clearly.

Damon straightened, still staring at the door. I was beyond surprised when he thoughtfully shook his head. "No."

Rana lifted her head and stared at Damon.

"The kid would hate me if I kept this from him." Aggravation was stamped all over him and he closed one hand into a fist before jabbing a finger at Rana. "But you haven't answered her question." Then he turned to me, holding my eyes.

"Doyle," Chang called out. "Give us another moment."

"We will not tell him." She shook her head slowly. "Not today."

"You don't want him to know?" The idea struck a terrible chord inside me. It came from losing my mother so young. Doyle had never known his mother—*Rana*—of all people. But better her than so many others.

"It's not that. Although whether or not he wants to know…" Rana shook her head and her eyes took on a distant look. "Because of…Nova, the past thirty years have been somewhat clear. I didn't

217

know everything, but I had some idea of what might come to pass—certain actions I knew I must take, certain roads I must avoid. But all of that stopped once I returned to Orlando this last time. He told me if I chose to come, I'd have to do it blindly and he could offer no aid."

Her mouth tightened and again, I knew the emotion.

It was grief.

Whatever the relationship she had with Nova, they'd been friends, of a sort.

"He won't survive this," she said quietly. "He has never confirmed it, but I know the truth, nonetheless. He won't survive it and I...I do not know what becomes of me once we leave here." Then she glanced at Damon. "But Kit does survive. He saw that."

Rana turned and stared at the door. "If I do not live through this, then I'd rather not leave him with nothing more than what we have here. A few hurried questions and the anger I know he has inside him."

"It's better than nothing," I said, only now realizing how angry I was.

"If I don't survive it...Kit...then you may give him whatever explanation you want." She looked at me then, her gaze solemn, steady. And sad. Then she slid her sword home and moved away from the table, taking a few steps toward me. "You asked why I watched. Tris and I...we talked, for weeks, months...it turned into years and there was no baby and we thought perhaps the half-crazed boy who'd approached us on an assignment had been wrong. She had no baby. I'd met no shifter. Then she came back from a journey—a long one. Gone almost six months...and she was expecting a babe. She clung to me, crying. We both knew. We had a choice to make. Did she go on the mission that would come before you were even five? Or did I?"

Rana looked away. "Since I was fifteen, I've been lauded as one of the strongest our race has seen in decades, perhaps centuries. Tris was the lovely one, the agile one, the charmer. She was a fine warrior...but she was hot-headed and rash. She would never be one to lead. She was easy to love, your mother." Rana wiped away a tear. "I think even Fanis loved her, as much as she was able. But Tris...no, she'd never lead. Her heart ruled her every action. And she knew it. She told me she would go. I argued with her, but in the end...we both knew who would have the best chance of keeping you alive. If I kept *you* alive—"

She stopped abruptly and I watched as her jaw clenched, teeth grinding together. "If *you* lived, then part of her did, too. If *you* lived, then Fanis lost. Some part of Tris would live on. So…she went. I stayed. And I swore I'd protect you as best as I was able. But we both knew there would be times when I couldn't."

"So *every time* you took a beating, I watched." Rana stared at me. "I had no right to look away. I couldn't stop it, not without making her come down on you harder, not without risking her sending me away and leaving you even more vulnerable. Every time, she lifted a hand, I watched. And if I could have taken every blow, every beating, I would have."

Tears blurred my eyes. I staggered, feeling like I had to do something, say something.

Damon steadied me and when I looked up, it was to find him staring at me, willing me his strength.

"We need to let him in. We've plans to make," Rana said curtly.

Chapter Twenty-Six

Doyle sensed the tension in the air. I wonder how much he had heard through the door. Chang had raised his voice when he called out earlier—and while the rooms were mostly soundproofed, if voices were loud enough, it was possible to pick up bits and pieces.

He may have heard something and I could tell by the suspicion in his eyes that he knew something was going on, but he didn't know the bones of it. That was obvious by the look he gave Rana.

"I have news." He stood in front of Damon, his face worried. "It's about…him."

Damon started to jerk his head toward the table. But he stopped and headed over to the sitting area, settling on the wide couch. "Come on over here, Doyle." He looked up and met my eyes, held them for a long moment. "The rest of you, too."

Rana lingered, trailing after the rest of us while Doyle dropped into the chair across from Damon. I sat down next to my lover, feeling the tension that radiated off him like the sun radiated warmth. Absently, he rested his hand on my back, his hand settling in that familiar up and down pattern.

He was staring at Doyle, his gaze so intense, so penetrating that it began to unnerve Doyle. After several long, taut moments had passed, Doyle managed a tense smile. "Do I have something on my face, Alpha?"

The *Alpha* managed to convey a whole world with just a single word.

"Nah, kid. I taught you better than that, didn't I?" Damon crooked a tired smile at him.

Just like that, some of the strain in the air eased.

Doyle glanced toward Rana, picking up on the shift that was taking place but before he could ask anything, Damon pinned him with a look.

"What is it you know, Doyle?"

"I've got a message—it's for Kit, I think it's pretty clear it was directed at the Clan, too." Doyle rubbed at his jaw, his eyes flicking around the room. "There was a cat who came through about a year ago...Anderson?"

Damon shook his head—then stopped and looked at Chang. "Wait, was that the wildcat? Black guy. Tall beanpole kind of guy?"

"We did have a man who fit that description." Chang came closer, eyes locking on Doyle. "He was an independent."

"Sounds right." Damon started to lightly beat his fist on the arm of the couch. "We never did bring him in. I'd remember."

"No. He...left." Yes. Chang frowned thoughtfully, dark eyes narrowing as he slipped through some mental file. "It's been over eighteen months. He approached us not long after you took the old Alpha out. We were going to accept him. Strong, solid man. Quick thinker. Had left the clan when Annette was leading it. We would have been happy to take him in. Then he just disappeared. I thought perhaps he had change his mind. Some of the people remaining from the old guard where the sort he'd bumped heads with."

"Yeah. I don't think he left, Chang." Doyle pulled out a cell phone and passed it across the table to Damon. "At least not voluntarily."

From the corner of my eye, I could see the way Damon's jaw went tight, the minute way his lashes stayed low, for just a fraction of a second too long. Then he looked at the phone.

His hand tightened on it. The casing made a tiny sound and Damon loosened his grip before he passed it to Chang.

"Where?" His voice was low, lethal.

"Ah...Georgia." He ran his tongue around his teeth and then glanced at me. "Over near a small town that pretty much died thanks to the war. Milledgeville. Most of him anyway."

Anger rose in the air like angry hornets, buzzing and stabbing needles at my skin.

"Most?" Chang asked as Damon fell silent.

"Yes." He kept his eyes on Damon, though. "The message came from Nova, Alpha. He sent it a little while ago. Said the message looked to be for Kit. He also added that he'd be happy to handle it all himself but he's picking up on some people who'll be caught in the crossfire and he'd just as soon n0t take anybody out if he didn't have to."

"I think we're still waiting for you to expand on that *most* part," I said. Turning to Chang, I held out my hand for the phone.

His mouth tightened in distaste but he turned it over and moved around closer to Doyle. "Nova called you?"

"Emailed. I've already forwarded the message onto you, but you won't get much. When I tried to contact him back, the message went bouncing to hell and back. He's already shut the account down."

"I'll look into it," Chang said, reaching into his coat pocket.

"No." Damon's voice was pure, deadly menace. "Suit up, Chang. You're going to Georgia."

After a brief pause, Chang gave a small nod. "Of course, Alpha."

Doyle surged upright. "I'm going, too."

"No." Both Rana and Damon said it at the same time, although Rana's voice was sharper, louder—practically a shout for her. Damon lifted a brow, staring her down and for once, she gave in and looked away.

Doyle had his mouth open, the scorn in his eyes so hot it threatened to burn. But before he could say even a single word, Damon cut him off. "You're not going, kid."

"What the hell?"

"Watch your tone," Damon said softly. "You've got more leeway with me than anybody else in the Clan ever has or ever will. But no matter how much I love you, kid, you're an adult and you asked to take a position here. That means..." Damon leaned forward. "*You follow orders.*"

Doyle's eyes flashed hot blue. He could shift into a white tiger and unlike most of the cats, his irises didn't make much of a color change with his shift, but the glowing was an indicator of anger.

But he sucked it under control.

"Are you sending *her*?" He didn't look at Rana, but there was no question who he was referring to.

Rana's expression didn't change.

"I'm sending the best team I can. And what I do, who I send, doesn't concern you." Damon nodded to the door. "You should get back to Scott. We've got planning to do."

"But—"

Chang intercepted, stepping up to clap Doyle on the shoulder. "Come on." He walked him to the door, talking in a low voice.

Doyle's spine was rigid and we all knew that whatever Chang was saying fell on deaf years.

I stared at him over the phone, the images of what had once been a man burnt forever into my head.

Feeling Damon's eyes on me, I slowly looked up.

"You think I should let him go?"

"I think you have to handle your people, Damon." I shook my head and focused back on the phone. "Doyle's one of yours until he decides he isn't—and I don't see that happening."

The first image showed a man's arm, from just below the shoulder, stretched out with the finger pointing to something off in the distance. It wasn't immediately obvious that the arm had been removed with near surgical neatness from the rest of the body.

It had, though.

I tapped the picture and watched as a message came up next to it.

This was the first part of him found. Note the rest of the images. We've got ourselves a sick piece of shit.

A sick piece of shit.

Yeah. The hand had forced into a fist, index finger extended.

It was pointing in the vague direction of Milledgeville. Fifty miles down the road was the next piece of Anderson, although how they knew it was him, I had yet to figure that out.

This time, it was the torso and one leg. And one of those little toy shopping carts that children liked to play with. There was a doll, too, tucked inside the ruin of Anderson's body—and her poseable hand pointed in the same direction.

Come and play, the message was telling us.

I got the message, loud and clear.

The body parts came closer together after that and the messages more violent. There was a set of eyes, ripped out of the rightful owner and shoved into the open mouth of a teenaged girl. I don't know if she was human, shifter or witch, but she sat tucked up against a tree like a broken doll, her head tied to the trunk and her mouth grotesquely open.

The eyes were stabbed through the middle, holding them in place on her tongue and she stared straight ahead. There was a three-sixty degree shot that showed she was staring a sign that read,

Milledgeville. The sign was ancient and covered in moss, rust making it almost impossible to read.

I knew without a doubt that the eyes were Anderson's—and that he'd been a guest inside Blackstone.

The whites were blood red, destroyed. Evidence of whatever they'd been using to mind-wipe them or to control them, like they'd done with Chaundry.

The rest of him was outside the abandoned remains of a massive building.

"I know that place," Chang said quietly. "It's where I was tracking all the energy diversions."

Damon said nothing so I looked at him.

"Massive amounts of energy, all pouring in there. For no reason. It's been abandoned for years—was used as a hospital for the mentally ill before there was a...reform in how humans treated their fellow citizens with mental issues. Like leaving so many of them homeless and wandering the streets." Chang's lip curled.

"No reason to power an empty building."

"I take it that's Anderson," I said, pity stirring inside for the dead man. His head rested on a stump of a neck, the hand of the remaining arm placed on the scalp, almost as if he was puzzling something through.

There was a small note nailed the man's forehead.

Come and get me, Kit. Before I kill some more of your Alpha's stray pets.

Another doll rested against the head.

"It could be a ploy," Chang said, keeping his voice calm although his eyes had gone pure gold.

"It is." Rana had circled around to stare at the phone and I knew she'd seen every image, and the message. "It's a ploy to get the Alpha and Kit out of Orlando where the bulk of the strength is. He'll likely make an attempt to grab Kit, assuming that perhaps Damon will try to leave without her and Kit will follow."

Chang smoothed a finger across one eyebrow. "It could be a possibility—if Damon didn't know Kit well. She'd never be left behind."

"No," Rana said softly. "She wouldn't."

"Again, I really don't like being talked about like I'm not here." Leaning forward, I stared hard at the image and then turned to the media screen. "I want maps."

Then I looked at Chang and Damon. "I think we should let him think he's getting what he wants."

Chapter Twenty-Seven

The cat wasn't even trying to be subtle as he raced along ahead of us.

I grimaced at the destroyed Milledgeville sign as I climbed out and stood next to Chang.

Rana was with us, once more clad in the concealing, misleading cloak. She eyed the claw marks down the sign and then turned to look at the girl, still staring in our direction with her ruin of a face.

Flies had gathered around her and the stink was horrid.

"You will come back and care for them?" Rana asked softly.

"Yes."

"Come on." Chang moved to stand next to me. "He's moving too fast for you to keep up with him, and we'll have a hard time catching up if we linger."

With a nod, I gestured for him to lead on. "Show me the way, good and trusty guide."

He frowned at me but settled into a light jog—for him. I was moving at an all-out run. If I didn't have to keep the pace up for long, I'd be okay. Rana moved in time with me and she shot me a look that I read with more ease than I liked. *Do you think this will work?*

Frowning at her, I just gave a shake of my head—not to say no, but to convey I didn't want to discuss this. It didn't occur to me that she probably wouldn't get it. But her heavy sigh seemed to indicate she understood.

We hadn't gone too far when somebody stepped out from behind a tree. Rana and I both parted, each of us darting to opposite sides of the road. Chang simply came to a halt in the middle and stood there, arms akimbo and in the span of a blink, his slim form began to...grow. The hair on his hair began to thicken, becoming almost mane-like.

I couldn't make out anything more than that before it was over.

I had my hand on my gun—that and the sword were the only weapons I had visible.

There was another, waiting for me. Her blood-soaked song wept in the back of my head, letting me know she was ready. *Eager.*

But not for this.

Nova stood in front of me, his face thinner than I'd ever seen. But the smile he shot me was as crooked and crazy as ever, and there were no shadows under his eyes. "I guess you got the message."

"Yeah. Next time, the bastard should just send email. It's a lot friendlier and a lot less evil." I hesitated for a moment longer and then rushed across the space separating us, flinging myself at him. "You crazy bastard. Leaving without saying good-bye."

He hugged me. "Hell, Kit. I suck at good-byes. Said too many of them anyway. But it wasn't time yet. I knew that."

Shoving back, I balled up my fist and punched him on the shoulder. "I didn't. Jerk."

"Things to do, Colbana, and not much time left to do them." He said that simple statement in a no-nonsense sort of way, and I knew that summed it up for him. That was Nova, plain and simple. Life, for him, was all about the mission. Just like his death.

"Nova."

Chang stepped up to join us.

The psychic gave him a short nod. He touched the shifter's shoulder briefly, eyes intent. "Can't say I'm surprised to see you."

Chang returned his stare and for a moment, there was nothing but taut silence.

Then Nova let his hand fall and he shook his head. "Figured after I saw the pieces of that cat all over...well." He shrugged and looked back over his shoulder. "I saw the big guy. You all trying to run him down?"

"Yes." Chang didn't elaborate. Neither did any of us.

"Well, there's a problem. He tore straight inside, didn't bother to get the lay of the land or anything else. Ended up barreling straight into one of the traps and our friendly neighborhood bad guy has him. Afraid I haven't been able to help—there are other...issues." His lips twisted in a scowl. "Timetable and all. And there are kids, some others you might find on some missing persons list. I get the feeling there were more here, too. Dunno what happened."

Chang directed a look at me. "I'm getting the children. You do

227

what you have to. I told him we needed to focus on our missing and our young."

"Did I say otherwise?" I demanded.

"It's not about what you say." Chang cracked his neck one way, then the other. "It's about his insane, infernal need to protect you above all things, including his people. Try to stay in one piece. I won't be coming back for you."

Nova watched everything with great interest, brows nearly disappearing under his hair. But he didn't say a word.

"Fine. Go on then," I said, shoving past Chang. I drove my shoulder into his chest as hard as I could. It felt like I'd shoulder-bumped a rock—and the rock won that round. Fighting the urge to rub at the sore spot, I started up the crumbling stairs. I had no idea where I was going, but I'd figure it out.

Or…Nova would figure it out for me.

"Well. Trouble brewing back home?" he asked, jogging to catch up to me. Rana was somewhere behind us, melding into the shadows like she owned them.

"Shut it." I stopped at the top of the stairs and looked around. It didn't take long to see where something ugly had happened. "Oh, no…"

I took off and came to a stop nearly a hundred yards away, skidding to the ground on my knees. The scent of blood was overwhelming, fairly recent but not fresh. "You big, stupid bastard."

"We told him, Kit. We warned you both," Rana said as she emerged from the shadows cast by the massive shadows of the ruin. "This was nothing more than a ploy to draw the two of you here. We should get you out while we still can. Save the young and—"

"It's too late for that."

The voice sounded even more unsettling in person than it had on the phone.

Slowly, I turned.

Robin Goodfellow came drifting toward us. Behind him, floating in mid-air, was the broken, battered body of a big cat. Blood dripped from a pelt so mottled with blood, it made it hard to see the gold under it.

"You son of a bitch." I started to lunge forward.

Buy time…have to buy time…

Both Nova and Rana grabbed my arms, Nova's hands icy cold,

Rana's clad in their concealing gloves. "No, Kit."

"But he…he…" The words caught in my throat.

"*He…he…he…*" Robin said mockingly. Then, with a cool smile, he lifted his arm and swung it toward me in an arc.

"No!" Nova and Rana let me go, but it was useless.

I couldn't catch the massive weight of the cat and if I had, it likely would have knocked me to the ground. Blood splashed my face as his big body hit the ground just in front of me. Smoothing my hands down bloody fur, I pressed my palm to his neck. A heartbeat—steady enough, but slow and weak.

"You evil son of a bitch."

"Language, Kitasa." He came to the ground, his naked feet big and brown, toes curling into the stone as if he craved the feel of the earth beneath him. "You know, in my day, women didn't speak like that—in fact, some didn't speak at all. I didn't like for my women to speak, for example. I'd often cut out their tongues if they did it too often."

Drawing my gun out, I pointed it at him. "Why don't you try that trick with me?"

"You think that little toy would do you any good?" Brilliant blue eyes glowed against his golden skin. There was something incredibly *alien* about him, incredibly other. His head was larger than it should be, eyes the same, while his body was slender, almost stretched out. He was muscled though. And despite how bits and pieces of him looked wrong, he was compelling—one might even consider him beautiful, if you could overlook the madness in his eyes.

He was in my face so suddenly, I nearly dropped my weapon in surprise. *Oh, dear…you dropped your guard…* A manic laugh burbled at the back of my throat but I swallowed it down as Robin leaned in until we were practically nose to nose.

"Shoot me with it, Kit darling. Shoot me. See how much good it does you."

So I did.

He'd guided the muzzle to his throat and I squeezed the trigger—once, twice, three times.

He blinked, almost lazily the first time.

But the second and third, he stiffened.

He shoved me away hard enough that I slipped in the pool of blood congealing under my boots. He lurched away, a hand to his throat. There had been iron in the ammo I'd fired into him. Specialty stuff, that ammo. Not pure iron, but a fair amount. And I'd been right. It had hurt him.

Hurt him just enough to piss him off, probably, but he was bleeding. If he bled, he could die.

A wet, thick cough escaped him as he turned to face me. "I always wondered," I said, smiling. "Was there any truth to the fey not liking iron? Looks like there was."

"I'm not *fey*." Robin sneered, almost looking insulted. And the injury was gone. "You cannot fathom what I am."

"Well, I heard all about the Robin Goodfellow bullshit. Sounds like *fey* to me. Just the darker side of it. You've got the good fairies and the bad fairies…you're from the side who lost in the battle for heaven, aren't you..." I smirked and added, "Hobgoblin."

An ugly noise escaped his still-healing throat.

"I've messed with fairies before and iron is pretty much straight poison." I leveled the gun at him. "Wanna go again?"

He snarled and lifted a hand. The gun was ripped away with so much force, I had to swallow back a gasp of pain.

"Stupid wench."

He backhanded me.

Blood filled my mouth. I could taste it as I crashed into something hard and narrow. I figured out what a few moments later. The remains of a concrete bench crumbled around me as I shoved upright onto my hands and knees.

As Robin drew near, Nova's voice flooded my head. *Chang's found the cells.*

Good. That was… I blinked as a rush of pretty stars filled my vision.

"You were so stupid, coming here. You, your man…his second best. So far from home and you left those ignorant cats back down in Florida. What do you think would happen if somebody decided to go and wreak havoc?" Robin knelt down next to me.

"I'd feel…very…sorry for them."

I'd cut the inside of my cheek on my teeth. Wincing, I swallowed blood.

"Save the pity. Others need it more…like yourself. The children who will die wailing and gnashing their teeth and screaming for their mummy to save them." Robin fisted his hand in my shirt, hauling me up. "Screaming for their useless Alpha. But he will be here, trapped in my little hell. You know where you are yet, Kit? I had to kill all of the handlers, of course. But I know how they managed what they did. I have their research. In a few years, we'll just start it up all over again." He stroked my cheek with his free hand. "You were so desperate to find Blackstone. And you did—welcome, Kit. Welcome to my latest pet project. It's hidden, down beneath this old travesty. They used to send their crazy people here. Ironic, isn't it? People were signing over their *perfectly healthy family*...little sis or Cousin Max... all because Max could make fire or sis got bit by a werewolf. And by the time my people were done? We had *made* them crazy." He cupped my jaw and started to squeeze. "And you, you little bitch, you went and fucked it up for me."

"You're welcome." I shoved upward with my blade, trying to gut him.

The sword didn't make contact. But that was what I'd expected.

A voice in the back of my head tickled my fogged brain and I had to concentrate so it would make sense. Nova whispered, *Thirteen kids, Kit. Need some time. Don't die. I've never been wrong yet. Don't want to start now.*

My pain-filled brain had the bleary understanding that I needed to distract Robin—and I also had to figure out some other way to do it than acting as a punching bag.

I needed to find another way to distract Robin, something that *wasn't* just me getting turned into a punching bag. Thoughts were muddled, though. Too muddled. I couldn't think and...

I shoved him away when he bent down and licked at the blood trickling from my brow. "You taste of fear and deception, Kit. What are you withholding from me?"

"My complete and utter contempt. Oh, wait...I think you know that by now." I shoved against his grip, kicked at him.

"Robin." It was the sound of Rana's voice, calm and composed, almost...bored.

Robin's head cocked, his eyes narrowing shrewdly as he stared at me. But it wasn't my face he saw.

"Well, well, well." He carefully lowered me to the ground, smoothing his hands down the sleeves of my shirt, fingers lingering. "You truly are a child of surprises, aren't you, Kit?"

"I don't know why you're surprised." Swiping blood from my

mouth, I managed a smile. It was probably as ghastly as it looked. "You saw her there when you called the Clan. Did you think she was just hanging around for kicks and giggles?"

He shoved me to the ground and turned, staring at my aunt.

I guess I didn't matter so much anymore.

"What is your queen going to do with you?" He clicked his tongue and shook his head, a look of mock pity on his strangely beautiful face. "You have made a mess for yourself, girl."

Rana's lips curved, her amusement clear. "You think she is more than a paper queen at this point? She could barely lead a few aged fools who continue to cling to the old ways. We're a dying people because of her." Now Rana shrugged. "She couldn't lead our armies if she tried. Because of *her*, our armies are woefully lacking. She isn't *fit* to be queen now."

"Oh, this is lovely." The words were practically a purr and Robin smiled, clapping his hands. "Dissension in the ranks. Why didn't I realize that before? I should have come to *you* for help."

"Had you tried, I would have taken a blade and rammed it straight up your bloody ass." Rana swung hers in a pattern so fast, it became nothing but a blur.

"Now, Rana. I understand why this ignorant whelp here doesn't understand the way of things. But you..." He shook a playful finger at her.

While he was busy with her, I shoved myself upright and took a deep breath, taking stock.

Rana noticed. She never looked away, but she noticed.

"You should know better. You were trained... But poor Kitasa...she's just...unfinished. That's why I set all of this up, you know. She's untrained, uneducated. I thought I'd make use of her abilities, but she was more clever than I gave her credit for." He looked at the ground—for me—then frowned when he saw that I wasn't there. "Aw, look. So stubborn, Kit. You know, it's a pity they didn't do better with you. You wouldn't have made a half-bad warrior if they'd given you a chance. Consider what you've done! Even untrained, you dealt with my firestarter and all the blocks she threw your way. And I know you were the one responsible for freeing the witches in South Carolina." He gave me a roguish wink. "It's just us now. You can admit it."

"Bite me," I suggested.

"I just might." The look he gave me froze me to the core. "It's been a while since I've indulged so. But first, you'll all suffer." He gave Rana a bored look. "Does your old hag of a queen have any idea what a prize she threw away with this one? I've a mind to keep her alive. If I break her mind..."

"I'd die first."

As he turned glowing blue eyes my way, I stared him down, despite the fact that his gaze was one of the most unnerving I'd ever beheld. It was enough to sicken me, sucking me in and showing me years upon years of degradations and cruelties the likes of which I'd never imagined.

"But we would have so..." He blinked. The connection broke and I sucked in a breath. Time shuddered and when it stopped, he was closer.

I backed away, all but falling on my ass in an effort to get more distance.

"Much...fun." He trailed his fingers down my cheek.

The cold struck the very core of me and I reacted out of instinct, calling my blade and striking out. I shoved her metal deep, deep inside him and he screamed in fury.

Big furred arms came around me, hauling me back a split second before Robin would have caved my skull in with a brutal fist.

A heavy weight pinned me to the ground and I looked up into golden eyes for a split second before the shifter pulled away and rose. He stood there next to me on hind feet, his half form a lean meld between cat and man, golden fur no longer dripping with blood although the stain of it was still there.

"Stay behind me," he growled.

"Aren't you dead yet?" Robin asked irritated.

The only answer was a low, rumbling sort of growl.

"Robin," Rana said tauntingly. "We weren't done talking."

He took another step toward me, but Rana moved between us, her blade upright, no more than an inch from his neck.

"That silly little pig-sticker couldn't harm me if you tried." Robin sneered. "There are only a few weapons in existence that can do me any damage. Precious, you *know* this."

He shot me a scathing look. "If you had done your job, I would have had one more of them. Instead..."

"Did somebody take something from the Black Anni, Robin?"

Rana asked softly.

The noise that left him then was so abnormal, so...*unnatural*, it sent chills down my spine.

He lunged for Rana and she slashed up with her short sword.

"You little *bitch*! Where is it!"

Rana laughed as she twisted and whirled out of his way. Oh, she was fast. I'd forgotten how fast. "Like I would tell you. Come on, puck. Let's see how much blood I can draw from you with my little pig-sticker. You are looking rather...porcine of late, you know."

He snarled, another one of those unnatural, rumbling noises that sounded of tumbling rocks and broken glass, all smashed together.

"It's been a long time since I've broken a warrior, Rana. You'll regret this...but I'm going to *enjoy* it." He held out a hand and I watched as a fiery length formed there, in his hand.

A blade, I realized. A stench filled the air, one of sulfur and rotting dead things.

He swung the blade through the air and the stink became worse, the blade trailing wisps of putrid smoke in its wake.

As he brought it down toward Rana's head, she brought hers up.

A shower of sparks exploded.

Kit. Nova's voice echoed in the back of my head, hard, cold...emotionless. *We have the kids out. But the adults who were here—they are gone—just about* all *of them. And he had a lot more than I thought. I think he sent them south.*

My stomach twisted—and it wasn't only because the puck had just sent the blade in a deadly arc that came way too close to Rana's neck.

We'd worried he'd had something lying in wait for Orlando. We'd egged him into it, even. That was why...

Hell. That was why we were playing things out the way we were. The big cat loitered at my side protectively, ready to lunge at a moment's notice.

We were prepared for him to try for Orlando. *We're ready,* I thought, pushing those words out. *How many?*

A lot, Kit. I don't know how many and I can't risk reaching out. Look...I haven't mentioned this because I didn't want Justin knowing and trying to do anything about it on his own, but one of the people left here...Justin told you about him. I have to take him out. There are two witches here that can't be left alive and those are the only two still here.

I frowned, not sure what he was talking about.

Then Nova nudged my memories.

Justin, in my office, as he told me about the terrible weight of his new abilities, and the consequences that had almost happened. What Banner had almost done to him. Banner…and its connection to this awful place. Banner—because it was a federal entity and the fucking fake *president* had corrupted everything.

"They took me to this…I guess you can call it a hospital, but it's more like a jail. That's where I met the other witch who had a gift for metallurgy. He was strong…I could feel him from miles away. You've met those kind before. Like a storm coming on… When they finally caught up with him, he was using a human girl for a pincushion. He was using metal shards to penetrate that girl's body, over and over. She was still alive when they first arrived. She bled out before they could take him down."

Justin had looked haunted when he told me about the other metallurgist, one who'd been born evil and the onslaught of the new gift had just made him even crueler, made him thirst for blood that much more.

The other one is an offshoot. I don't know what he is, but they keep him in a pit and toss him the remains from prisoners who died in experiments. *He can't get out, Kit. He hurts my brain and that's just the start of it.*

I knew what he was trying to tell me.

Bad things would happen if the messed-up NHs got to Orlando— and bad things would happen along the way—but even worse things would happen if the two still left here got free. *Do what you have to, Nova. Deal with those two.*

And Mr. Goodfellow.

"No," I said softly. "He's mine."

There was a faint sense of…acceptance. Then, Nova said, *Kit…duck.*

He was gone from my mind in the next moment and I ducked, rolling to the side just as Rana came flying through the air.

A lean, muscled form, its pelt a warm gold caught her and eased her to the ground, keeping her from smashing into the crumbling stone of the hospital. "Oh, bollocks," Robin muttered as he came striding toward us, swinging his sword up and settling it on his shoulder.

We're clear, Kit. Chang has reached the cover of the woods and they are moving off. He's secured a vehicle and will be out of range in minutes.

I acknowledged that and began to slowly move back.

"You're like some annoying garden pest—I take one of you down and the other pops back up." He pointed his sword at the warrior-form of the cat as he rose protectively over Rana. "You. I'm just going to kill you. I'd planned to skin you and nail you to a wall so you could watch while I cut into your woman. Now? I think I'll just make you change back and cut out those pretty gray eyes. They can sit on a shelf while I rape your bitch."

He held out a hand.

Wind swept through the clearing and Rana lunged, throwing her body over mine and taking us both down as the wind grabbed the shifter and threw him into Robin's hand.

"How does that sound, you worthless animal?" Robin asked as he grabbed the powerful shifter's body and flung the cat to the ground. "Not like you have a choice, but do you want to live a few minutes more or just...die?"

The low, ugly snarl was full of menace, but Robin just laughed as he tightened his hand around the cat's thick, muscular neck. "Come on...oh, you really are quite alpha, aren't you?" He licked his lips, his blue eyes glowing brighter for a brief a moment. "Change, my strong little cat. Maybe I'll let you live. *You* can be my toy."

He slammed the cat down and by the time his furred head struck stone, the pelt had begun to recede.

"I'd...make...a very bad...toy...you son of a bitch."

The cat finished his shift—almost completely and Scott, Damon's second strongest man, surged to his feet, a half-demented smile on his face. Then he struck out, driving his clawed hand—the one part of his body that had yet to shift back—into the puck's stomach. Then, with a sickening, wet sound I'll never forget, Scott wrenched the spine and tore it out. For a brief moment, Robin just stared.

Then he faltered and stumbling, collapsed.

For a minute, I thought maybe it was over.

Maybe.

CHAPTER TWENTY-EIGHT

"You didn't really think we'd leave Orlando unprotected, did you?" Scott stood up, his face a mask of matted fur and blood.

Then he spat on Robin's still body as he came over to us, one leg moving awkwardly.

Rana shoved upright onto her hands and knees and spat out a mouthful of blood. The right side of her face was nothing more than an ugly map of bruises, some of them already so swollen, it was hard to tell where one stopped and the next began.

One eye was swollen shut.

The other was clear, though. Clear, hard and focused.

"Can you call?" Her voice was thick and raspy and when she got to her feet, I knew why. Robin had managed to get his hand around her throat, then he squeezed, squeezed, squeezed.

I moved to her side and helped her up while Scott stood in front of us.

He gave both of us a critical look before focusing back on the battered body of Robin Goodfellow. He was already starting to regenerate the spine Scott had ripped out—I could see the body twitching. "You should have ripped off his head, bought us more time."

"The more damage he has, the faster he heals," Scott said almost clinically. "I figured that out before I let him incapacitate me."

"You *let* him," Rana said, her voice still a raspy ruin of what it should be.

"Yes." Scott lifted a negligent shoulder. "He would have done it sooner or later and the quicker he did it, the quicker I would heal. He's a strong son of a bitch. Please tell me you know what you're doing. If he makes it to Orlando…"

Rana gave me that intense look again, one brow arching.

"We got this." I focused on the exposed spine—no. Back. His

back was whole and unmarked—

Oh, *fuck*.

Robin exploded off the ground, his blue eyes blazing so bright, it almost hurt to look at him. And he *did* explode—bigger, taller, wider. His clothes fell to tatters around him and heat emanated from him. I felt it leaking out to kiss my flesh.

He shot out a hand and we scattered.

I darted behind a tree. I grabbed a branch and monkeyed up. Height. I needed height.

"You will *die* for that, you pathetic excuse for a man," Robin shouted.

The shout was a lot farther off the ground than it had been. Yeah. He was bigger. The shout was much larger than it should be, too. I chanced a look at him as he swung out a massive hand, flattening several of the small, scraggly trees across the broken concrete pathway.

Scott in his half form leaped out from the shadows, holding…shit, it looked like a sign post, ripped out of the ground. He lunged upward and drove it into the puck's exposed testicles. Very big, hairy testicles. He was four or five times his normal size now and even more disproportionate than he had been, yet he moved with the same insidious grace.

Or he had, until Scott had dealt him a very sharp, painful blow to his balls.

As Robin howled, Scott dashed back off into the shadows.

Off in the distance, I heard a rumbling.

"You…all of you…are going to die…the slowest, most painful death…and I'll watch," Robin said. He crashed into the side of the building and flung out a hand, staring toward it. Waiting. "And *yes,* I'll be going to Orlando. You think I've forgotten about those mongrels you wanted to protect? I'll eat their bones now. Skin them while they scream."

Blood seeped down his thigh, no longer the heavy flow it had been.

A hand touched my ankle.

I tensed, but didn't move, recognizing Rana's presence.

Now. Her look communicated that as our eyes met.

I gave a single, jerking nod.

She'd warned me that he'd know the second I called the bow.

238

He'd feel it.

I settled into position, automatically taking the stance I'd need as I faded, letting the invisibility settle over me. Almost...almost...

His head swung in my direction and I panicked. Did he see me?

But there was another rumble and he looked back, bellowed. *"Salazar! Come!"*

I lifted my bow.

He looked at me again.

My gut sank.

I almost screamed as something—no—Scott launched himself out of the shadows once more, this time holding something more damaging than a street sign. It looked like...shit, was that a railroad tie? He drove it into one of Robin's eyes. But in doing so, he got too close, lingered too long.

Scott's pained scream as Robin caught him in both hands sent a hot, nasty spike into my brain and I almost leaped down—I couldn't see him—I needed a better view.

Don't! It was Rana's voice. In that small place in my head, I heard her voice clear as day. *You have to wait. You'll only have one chance!*

Something bloody went flying.

"I'll rip you apart limb from limb!" Robin howled as a river of red spurted from Scott's upper body.

An arm, I realized numbly. He'd ripped off Scott's arm.

There was another rumble in the ground.

Man, Nova had to do something—

"Why don't you put my man down and deal with me, you overgrown garden gnome?"

The sound of that voice made my hands clench.

Damon.

He wasn't supposed to here.

Orlando.

He was supposed to be in Orlando, him and Doyle, keeping the Lair safe.

He emerged from the shadows and as I stared at him, stunned into a stupor, he fired a cocky grin up at the puck.

"Well, well, well...ran away from your little cave, did you, cat? Are those little kitties all alone in the big bad city?" Robin winked and chuckled. "Nice to know. I'll have lots of fun with them—after I kill you." He hurled Scott's mangled, bleeding body in my direction.

He hit with a sickening crack and thud.

I looked—I couldn't stop myself.

Scott's lashes fluttered and he made a low, pained noise.

"You might have a little more trouble than you think." Damon threw back his head and snarled—by the time the terrible, awful sound had ended, Damon was no longer human—or at least, he wasn't wearing his human skin. He was *never* human.

Now he stood seven feet and stepped across the clearing. "You gonna to hide behind the steroids, hobgoblin?"

Robin laughed. Then he, too, took a few steps forward, shrinking with each step. The railroad tie still pierced his skull, looking obscenely huge and he reached up, casually plucking it out. Blood and gore smeared it as he swung it at Damon.

Damon moved out of the way, faster than anything I'd ever seen.

Robin made a humming sound under his breath. "That was a clever trick, sending the other one."

He swung again, faster.

The ground shook and he smiled at Damon. "But I've got a few tricks up my sleeve you can't even hope to match."

"Don't bet on it." Damon had moved again, his back almost toward me.

And Robin was almost *facing* me—

Damon swung out a clawed hand. It made contact and so did the next.

But Robin made contact, too.

And he was strong.

Much, much stronger.

I bit my lip to keep from screaming.

The ground rumbled again and Robin shot a look over his shoulder. "Salazar!"

The earth was vibrating almost constantly now and Robin paced forward, moving ever closer to my tree—and Damon and Scott—no.

Scott wasn't there.

I blinked, not sure what I was seeing.

But Scott wasn't *there*.

Robin didn't even notice.

"You think you've got me on the run, all four of you, making me spin like a top." He drew back a foot to kick Damon, but Damon caught his foot and twisted, moving with him.

At the same time, he drove claws up into Robin's gut, disemboweling him. That might have slowed down a lot of creatures. Robin just ripped out the trailing bits of meat and hurled them away, backhanding Damon as he shoved upright. "I *tire* of this. Sala—"

Another rumble and the door to the decrepit, ancient building blew open. A shadow appeared just as Robin turned, his face splitting in a brilliant smile.

"Ah, yes, there's my…"

The puck's voice faded as the shadow hurled something toward us.

"There…I think you wanted him." I recognized Nova's sly, good-natured drawl. "Will that piece do or did you want a bigger slice?"

Robin snatched the round object out of the air. I saw what it was as the puck stood there, holding it in his hands. A head. A dismembered head. I fought the urge to giggle, felt the bubble of manic, mad humor—people were losing their heads all over the place.

Slowly, Robin let the savaged piece of flesh fall to the ground and he lifted his gaze to stare at Nova.

I called the bow. Nocked the arrow.

Nova came barreling out and skidded to a stop, halfway between the puck and the open doors. Unerringly, his eyes found mine and his mouth hitched up. *Showtime, Kit. It's been fun. You need to make tracks.*

The very air seemed to freeze.

The arrow was nearly soundless.

Nearly wasn't good enough and Robin was on his feet, exploding back into that monstrous, giant like form as he spun away. The arrow planted itself into the crumbling building. Robin bent and grabbed the dismembered head—Salazar, I guess. One of the ones that Nova said had to die. Robin spun his body like an athlete at the mound. The head came flying toward us.

It hit the tree next to me with such force, half the branches shuddered and broke. The noise was like a sonic boom—*nothing* should be that strong. I fell, thrown off balance.

And when I fell, so did the veil of invisibility.

"No!" Robin shouted. "You cannot…*No!*"

I guess he'd felt the bow.

He came at us hard and fast as I lifted the Druidic bow, another arrow ready.

He stumbled to a halt at the sight of it, one hand lifted. "Loose the arrow and you die with me."

A pressure closed around my head, squeezing, squeezing...

Lights danced in front of my eyes.

Somebody screamed. It might have been me.

"Give me the bow!"

I loosed the arrow and it went wide. But the other arrow, the one still shivering in the wall of the building—I called it. And sent it home. Right in the eye of the puck.

That was where it wanted to be.

The air exploded.

Or maybe it was my head.

I only know I went flying—like a punch straight to my chest. I hurtled back, back, back... strong arms caught me.

"Nova," I said.

Damon pressed my face into his chest.

And then, everything went white hot.

A supernova, just like the man had once said.

The blast sent us hurtling back through the air and white light scored in the inside of my eyes.

That white light seemed to last forever.

But then, it faded and all I saw was black.

I woke alone and in the darkness.

My head was hurting so bad, I thought I might be sick.

"You didn't do too bad."

That voice was enough to send me scrambling for my sword—scrambling, because in the blur of pain and agony, I'd forgotten for a brief second.

Forgotten I could call her again.

Forgotten that this woman had fixed it.

Light flared, too bright for a moment and then it went soft, soft enough that I didn't fear opening my eyes to stare at the tall woman standing by the window and studying me.

"You," I said, my voice shaking.

"Me." Frankie—or whatever in the hell her name was—looking quite pleased with herself. "It took you long enough, but I take it you figured out what I did for you. Do you like it?"

I gripped my sword tighter. "I…yes. Thank you."

"Nice manners." She winked at me and came over to sit on the foot of the bed. "Why don't you join me? You look silly there, crouched on the floor like you're hiding from a monster."

"Am I?"

Her brows shot up almost to her hairline. "Girl, you have no filter."

Well, that was true enough.

"I like it." She started to smile, then to laugh. "Come on, honey. Sit down. I'm not going to hurt you, but I think you figured that out well enough."

Slowly, I shifted upright, taking care not to jostle my aching head.

The second I was mostly vertical, she reached up and touched the space between my eyebrows.

"Don't—"

I'd no sooner spoken than her hand fell away. "Don't be a crybaby." She flicked her hand away. "No reason for you to hurt and no reason for me to go hungry."

Flattening out my lips, I inched back.

"You know how that works, I take it. I feed from your pain." She lifted a negligent shoulder. "I don't like it, but this is the life I was given, so I live it."

She said it so bluntly, so matter of factly.

"Where am I? Why am I here? Where is…" Abruptly, I stopped, reluctant to offer any sort of information.

"You're at a hotel just south of the Florida-Georgia Line. Don't worry. You weren't abandoned. Your man is at the office—paying for the pizza." Frankie pursed her lips and pressed a finger to them. "Shhhh…don't talk too loud. I can keep him from hearing for a few more minutes."

I blinked at that. Then… "The others? Scott? And…"

"Rana? Your darling auntie?" She smirked at me. "Relax, honey. I'm not going to mess with her. I think she did right by you in the end. She's out and about—took care an errand, then I think she was going to make sure all is safe from the defiled ones."

"Defiled ones."

"You are a parrot, aren't you?" She lifted a brow. "The ones the puck broke. Defiled. He ruined them. A few were set loose, heading to Orlando."

"Damn it." I squeezed my eyes shut. "I *told* him—"

"Psh. Your man made plans. He contacted the Assembly—miserable group, for the most part. But they serve their purpose, I suppose. But the witches, his ally the wolf Alpha—even Banner, they've all been watching. And his young cub." Frankie smiled at me, amused. "He didn't leave the city unguarded. But Robin was quite a threat...you know that. So did your aunt. That's why you all came to deal with him."

"Since you know everything...how is Scott?"

She smoothed a hand across a tight braid. "He lives."

He *lives*. I wanted to yell at her, but it wouldn't do any good.

"Why are you *here*?"

She sighed then and rose, moving over to the window. "A friend of mine was...in the area."

"Nova."

Quietly, she said, "You shouldn't sound so surprised. Surely you've figured out he is...*was*...more than he appeared."

When I didn't answer, she turned to me. "He's gone, isn't he?" I asked.

"Yes." Frankie tipped her head back, staring up at the ceiling. "But don't hurt too long over him. He'd been bumping around on this miserable old planet a damn long time and he finally took out the last monster he was meant to take on, plus one more."

"The last?"

She shot me a quick look. "Sometimes special monsters need special killers. Nova was a very special killer. He's earned his downtime." She came closer and reached up.

I froze as her hand neared my face and stayed that way as she flicked my hair back. "You're not a monster killer, but you didn't do half-bad, Kit. Taking out Robin. That was impressive. And now his little hell-lab is gone too. Nobody else can make more monsters either. Well done."

"Gee, thanks."

"You're welcome. Again...nice manners." She smiled at me, so brightly, it took a moment to realize she was fading.

Fading into nothing.

"Hey!"

"Don't forget, honey…you owe me a favor," she said, her words echoing around me.

"Hey!" I shouted again.

But she was already gone.

The door flew open a split second later and Damon came rushing in.

And he didn't have a pizza.

CHAPTER TWENTY-NINE

Waking up was a sweet, sweet pleasure and at first, I couldn't figure out why.

Damon lay warm against my back, his thigh pushing between mine, a hard pressure against my butt making it clear that he was appreciating the overall morning experience as well as I was.

His hand pressed against my belly and pulled me back against him.

I arched my neck as he raked his teeth along my skin, bit me lightly.

I hummed in appreciation, a sound that quickly changed to a gasp as he pulled me onto my knees and came inside me.

There was no foreplay, little tenderness and I didn't care.

We'd gotten into Orlando late—he *had* been paying for pizza, then dropped it as he realized things weren't as they should be in the room he'd rented for us. So we'd had to get food on the way. I was exhausted. I'd probably slept ten or twelve hours. I still felt worn thin and stretched out.

Two of his men had seen us coming.

I didn't remember much after getting to the Lair. There was a blur of people talking, a shower, somebody shoving food at me.

Then bed.

Now…Damon.

His fist tangled in my hair, drawing my head back and I groaned as he brought my face around and stole a deep, drugging kiss from me.

Thick and hard, his cock pulsed inside me. He barely moved, content to rock against me, just *feeling* me, letting me feel him.

Right up until it wasn't enough.

And then he began to drive himself inside me, thrusting deep and hard, one arm braced at my waist to hold me still.

The climax was harsh and sudden and when it was over, I lay face down while he draped over me, his cheek pressed to the skin above my spine.

After what felt like an age, he stretched out next to me and pulled me into his arms. "He had a lot of monsters tucked away, probably released them as soon as he got there." A harsh noise of disgust left him. "I had a bad feeling in my gut over all of it, talked to the Assembly and the head witch over at the Road here in Orlando. And…"

Even more disgust worked its way in his voice as he shoved up onto his elbow.

I turned to face him and he cradled my face in his hand.

"I got in touch with Abraham, then Amund." Damon watched me, his eyes solemn. "All of them agreed it was in the city's best interest to…come together, for this at least. No more than a few hundred yards of the city was left unguarded—there were sentries everywhere. The Road reached out to Red Branch—the house by the state line and once they were alerted, they started watching, caught some stragglers and helped with patrols between here and there. The pack took out several. Doyle killed a few—got hurt, but he'll heal. The vampires had pairs watching from the air—the ones that could fly. Some of the leeches died but they were taking them out, too." His eyes glinted, an icy sort of rage compared to his normal fire. "Whittier House declined. Two of the…"

I hesitated, then offered, "The defiled?"

"Defiled." He frowned, something that might have been pity in his eyes for a moment. Then he shook his head. "Yeah. That works. Two of them got in and killed a few of their just-turned. Probably wishes they'd shown a little more concern."

He nuzzled my neck. "You ever going to spill everything that happened with this…Frankie, kitten?"

"No." Closing my eyes, I curled my arms around him and clung tight. We'd almost gotten into a row at the motel—he'd heard her, had known something was going on. Just like now. "No, I don't think I will."

"Figured as much." He grunted and rolled onto his back, pulling me with him. "I don't have all the numbers yet. I know we lost at least two—the pack lost one. None of the witches died—they're all pissed about Colleen and Justin."

Closing my eyes, I braced myself for the worst.

"One of them got to the Road here in the city. There's not enough of him left to identify." He traced a random path on my hip, his fingertip rough. "The other one...he almost made it here. Killed two of my people before Doyle took him down."

"I'm sorry."

"Don't be. That plan of yours..." His hand tightened on my hip, then he kissed my shoulder, moved in until he was kissing the bite mark hidden in the tattoo ink along my neck. "You were the one who had to kill him—it was the fucking arrow—but the threat wasn't just to the Clan. Others had to step up, too. And I needed to be there. Scott's strong, but he's not me and Chang's always going to protect the young."

"You're the Alpha. Your people needed you."

"My people were protected." He touched our foreheads together.

"How is Scott?"

"He's going to be fine. Apparently, Rana hauled him out of the line of fire and once she saw that everything was done, she got him home." His mouth went tight. "I think she wants to keep things level—doesn't like feeling like she owes me so she saved Scott."

"Could it be that maybe she just didn't want to leave him there?"

"*I* would have gotten him out." The look on his face was the kind that made think he'd swallow glass before offering anything else about Rana.

I couldn't say I blamed him.

After a few more moments, he said, "Chang got all the children here. We've got healers looking at them. Some have been missing for almost a year."

Squeezing my eyes closed even tighter, I tried to figure out what I could say to that.

"But they are alive."

Alive...

Damon slid his hands to my waist. "They're alive, Kit."

Justin hadn't stirred the entire time I sat there talking to him.

His leg had healed.

The witches caring for him told me that sometimes, he'd respond to their voices, but he hadn't opened his eyes.

And Colleen...

Now I sat in front of her.

They were both in the same room because when they tried to separate them, Colleen got violent—*violent*—she hurt herself and she tried to hurt others. The father of the Green Road house here, the largest in the entire state, was worried.

She's not a warrior. Something inside her is broken and she's trapped in the maze of her own mind, I fear. The longer she stays there...

"I didn't kill him hard enough," I said as Damon sat down next to me.

He rubbed the back of my neck. "She doesn't need to hear that right now, baby girl. Talk to her, okay?"

I fought the urge to scream.

Talk to her.

About *what*?

The fact that Justin wasn't waking up?

About the fact that we'd discovered the hospital? Or the graves of children Damon and Alisdair's people had uncovered?

Or *maybe* I could tell her about the news that had broken this morning—there was a bunker somewhere in Virginia that had been discovered. Two soldiers had guarded that bunker—and they *claimed* they had no idea why they were there, but they knew they had been there for over six years. They only ever had a handful visitors, and they were on a mission classified as top secret.

Guarding a prisoner, it turns out.

The president.

The *real* one.

He'd been rescued by Shanelle and company—she'd been in charge of questioning the one man we'd brought back from South Carolina. Apparently, she'd had a suspicion that had been planted by the discovery of that little camera and she'd gone to Damon. He'd told her everything. She hadn't exploded, though.

She'd turned her canny mind—and her vast resources—to finding the truth.

She'd actually *been* to that bunker.

The rescue op was headed by NH personnel and that was widely publicized. But whether or not it would shine favorably on us, nobody knew.

The president wasn't even the president now, though. He'd been missing during the actual election and his imposter had run.

It was a confusing mess and definitely not something to chat to Colleen about.

Sighing, I leaned over and touched her hand.

"Wake up, Coll," I said. "I miss you. I need you."

Dropping my head down on the bed, I tried not to cry, but the tears were there and they were going to come no matter what. Colleen continued to stare blankly at nothing. She *was* awake, in a way. But words had no impact, touch had no impact. Sound…nothing.

Fingers brushed my hair.

I froze.

It happened again.

Slowly, I looked up and saw Colleen's eyes flitting back and forth, never resting on me. But she was *looking* at me.

"Colleen?"

"Is she waking?" One of the witches in the healing hall came rushing over. "Let me…"

Her voice faded into a rush of noise as I caught Colleen's hand in mine. "Leenie, talk to me," I said, leaning in and trying to catch her eyes with mine.

"Kit." Her voice hitched. Broke. "Kit…"

"Oh…oh, my. Kit, Alpha Lee, you'll need to—"

Screams broke out. Harsh, unending peals of them. Magic exploded and knocked me back into Damon. Even he staggered under the blast.

"Get out, *now!*" the witch shouted as she rushed closer.

Or rather—she *tried*. She, too, was flung back.

Colleen huddled up in a ball on the bed, face pressed to her knees as she shuddered and shook and screamed. Magic boiled and swirled through the room.

I tried to go to her, but Damon tightened his arms around me. "Not a good idea, Kit."

"Let me go!"

The sound of my voice set off a shockwave. It shook the entire room and we were slammed flat.

Panting for air, I shoved against Damon, trying to get up. But he wasn't moving. His heart slammed against my back, thundering fast and hard.

"Just be still," the witch murmured.

She lay next to us, staring upward, seeing something I couldn't see. "I've called for the Father. He'll know what to do."

The swirling magic storm stole the words from her lips but I heard them, just barely.

"I—"

The wail of magic grew louder.

Damon's arms tightened. "Be *quiet*," he said, exasperation turning into anger. "She's reacting to you, baby girl."

Me?

There was a faint creak—the door opening.

Then a *thud*—as it slammed shut.

Were we trapped?

Oh, hell. Oh, *shit*—

Then, from one breath to the next, it ended.

"Coll."

The voice was tired and strained.

I drove an elbow upward, as hard as I could—and it was surprisingly easy because Damon had abruptly moved, coming to his feet and jerking me up.

Justin was upright, moving toward Colleen with a limp.

His hair hung lank and unkempt around his face, his normally golden skin sallow, his cheeks sunken in.

But he was awake.

And he only had eyes for Colleen.

She was still huddled on the bed, her face hidden.

"Colleen," he said gently, sitting down on the bed.

She flinched, but he didn't let that stop him. He touched his hands to her knees and she flinched again.

"Look at me, Coll," he said quietly. "You ain't wanting to do this. Look at me."

Colleen didn't look at him. But she did collapse against him and broken sobs escaped her. Justin pulled her in close, a weary sigh escaping him. His eyes came to mine. I took a hesitant step forward.

He smiled and nodded.

I went to the bed then and sat down.

Colleen's hand snuck out and gripped mine.

Curling my free arm around Justin, I leaned my head in and

rested it on his shoulder. "You're going to be okay, Colleen. We'll take care of you."

There was a letter waiting for me when I returned to the Lair late, late that night.

His arm slowly regenerating, Scott stood outside my door holding a note. I almost didn't accept it. I'd had…well, just about *enough* happen for the day.

Colleen had eventually slept and Justin had talked to me for a brief moment before he collapsed back into an exhausted slumber.

You know what it's like to be broken, Kit. That's how she feels. They tore her apart inside—unmade her. Unless you're a warrior, witches weren't meant to harm. And they used her for all sorts of harm, trying to break her. And they did…because she wouldn't let them kill me.

That was what it boiled down to. They'd used Justin against her.

If they weren't dead, I'd go back and kill them again, but slower.

I had no idea what was going to become of Colleen now, but Justin said he wasn't going to let her go through it alone. Neither would I.

But I was exhausted and all I wanted to do was sleep.

Not deal with…this.

Because I knew who that letter was from.

I opened it, though, cracking the heavy wax seal and taking a deep breath to steady myself.

Let your cat know I've dealt with the rest of the broken ones.

I'm leaving for now. I have matters back home that need seeing to. But I have unfinished business here as well.

I will return.

She knows you live, Kitasa, and for as long as she lives, that is a problem.

That is one problem I plan to rectify. Do not let your guard down.

Damon took the note after I'd finished reading it. As I turned away, there was a knock at the door and I moved to open it.

Doyle came in, looking young and fit and strong enough to take on the world.

Unfinished business.

"How's Colleen, Justin?" His eyes searched mine and I could see the worry, knew it was real.

"That's a loaded question." With a weak smile, I gestured for him to come inside. From the corner of my eye, I saw Damon fold the letter, tuck it inside a small box on our dresser. "You want to call down to the kitchen for a pizza or something? We'll talk about it."

"Yeah. Sure." He lifted a shoulder as he paced around a little, looking restless. His eyes bounced around the room for a few seconds before he turned and looked at me. "Where's your aunt?"

"Taking care of some business."

If I wasn't mistaken, he looked disappointed.

"But she'll be back, I think."

This time I wasn't mistaken. A gleam of speculation glinted in his eyes...and a hint of a smile.

Keep Up...Join the Newsletter
Visit shilohwalker.com & sign up for the newsletter and have a chance to win a monthly giveaway.

A Note To Readers

Thanks for your patience on this one…I know you waited longer than normal. Some of you are aware that I've been dealing with health issues and I didn't want to rush things and put out a book that just wasn't up to par.

I knew for a while I'd be bringing Kit's family into things and I also knew that at least *one* of them wasn't going to be a total troll. After all, somebody cared enough to give her the foundation she built her skills on.

Also…while there's nothing on my site yet…*nooooo*…

This isn't the last book.

Now…if you wanna know more about Frankie and what happened with her and Kit? Read on.

BIO

J.C. Daniels is the pen name of author Shiloh Walker.

Shiloh Walker has been writing since she was a kid. She fell in love with vampires with the book Bunnicula and has worked her way up to the more...ah...serious works of fiction. She loves reading and writing anything paranormal, anything fantasy, and nearly every kind of romance. Once upon a time she worked as a nurse, but now she writes full time and lives with her family in the Midwest. She writes romantic suspense and contemporary romance, and urban fantasy as J.C. Daniels. You can find her at Twitter @shilohwalker or Facebook (AuthorShilohWalker) and read more about her work at her website, www.shilohwalker.com.

MORE JC DANIELS' TITLES

Blade Song #1
Night Blade #2
Broken Blade #3
Edged Blade #4
A Stroke of Dumb Luck (Tor)
Bladed Magic (A Kit Colbana Novella)
Misery's Way (A Kit Colbana Novella)
Final Protocol

LOOK FOR OTHER TITLES BY J.C.'S OTHER HALF, SHILOH WALKER

The Grimm
Urban Fantasy Romance
Candy Houses • No Prince Charming • Crazed Hearts
Tarnished Knight • Locked in Silence • Grimm Tidings
Blind Destiny • Furious Fire

The FBI Psychics
The Missing • The Departed • The Reunited
The Protected • The Unwanted • The Innocent

The Hunters
Paranormal Romance
Hunting the Hunter • Hunters: Heart and Soul • Hunter's Salvation
Hunter's Need • Hunter's Fall • Hunter's Rise

And more

Misery's Way

"Have you scouted out the next spot?"

Saleel lifted one shoulder. "Yes. Montana. I tire of the heat."

"Montana?" I grimaced and mentally shuddered. Summer was rapidly drawing to a close. That would mean cold. Snow. Worse … ice. "I hate the cold."

I'd spent many of my earliest years in the muggy heat of America's south—or in the heart of Africa. There were a handful of years that had been spent … elsewhere, but I try not to think about that.

Heat was simply bred into my bones. I could handle the cold, but that didn't mean I liked it.

Saleel's teeth flashed white in the faintest of smiles when he glanced at me. "Then perhaps next time when I ask you if you have a preference, you should give me an answer. Instead, you say, *Do whatever you want, Sal.*"

He managed an imitation of my voice that was almost dead-on.

I stuck my tongue out at him.

He went back to staring into the tent. "Offer your tongue again, my angel, and I will make use of it."

Yeah. Right.

The two of us were like gasoline and fire and we both knew it. Combustible—and dangerous.

"Promises, promises," I said lightly, and then I eased closer, bracing my shoulder on the lightweight metal of the doorframe, gazing deeper into the tent.

Saleel was right.

I was restless.

But I hadn't yet figured out why.

A hot summer wind caressed the back of my neck. I enjoyed it while I could. Once I got inside, the air would be stifling. Already, I was dreading it. I could smell the heat of too many bodies and the air was thick with sweat. Heavy with despair.

Hope clung to many of the people who awaited me, but hope was a capricious bitch. I could all but hear the cackling, gleeful laugh as she darted from one person to another, crooning, *You don't really think this will work, do you? You're going to die … You're all going to die ...*

Fans churned from all corners, laboriously whirring away. They did little to cool the temperature, but at least the air kept moving.

It wasn't the heat, though, that plagued me. It wasn't even the promise of death. People died. It was simply part of life. It wasn't the despair or the misery—the hunger inside me reached for that, but that wasn't what made me restless.

"It's time," Saleel murmured.

I nodded.

But still, I didn't move, searching inside the tent.

"Frankie?"

"I'm going." I took a deep breath and reached deep inside for the well of calm that would carry me through when I took another's pain inside me. I craved pain—fed on it.

That didn't mean it was pleasant.

The twisted duality of my nature made me crave the misery even as I knew it would later cause me plenty of my own misery. My body already dreaded it. My stomach knotted and my muscles tensed and my legs tried to resist my head's commands to move.

As I moved to the simple podium set up on the dais, I did a brief scan of the crowd. If there was anybody in there with a bad heart or other such frailty, I'd deal with them first. Maybe that's all it was—somebody could be hovering right on the edge of life. I'd had that happen before.

There were plenty of those who did—or claimed to do—what I did, and they would have thrived on healing somebody with a failing heart or stopping a stroke in action. It was pure drama.

But I wasn't there to cash in on dramatic moments or inspire awe.

Terrible as it sounds, I was just there to feed.

My quick scan told me everything I needed to know. An elderly woman up front needed to get her pacemaker checked, but she wasn't in immediate danger—still, I'd do what I could tonight before she left. Hearts were always tricky.

"Welcome!" My manager, Jody Wilson, lifted her hands and waited for the applause to die down.

I paused a few feet from my spot and waited. The crowd was deafening. Despite the cacophony, I could hear just fine—including the scattered mutters of *She's a fraud, Man, look how tall she is, I would kill to have those cheekbones ...*

The curtain at the back opened and as a couple of people slid in, I cast them a casual glance.

They might as well have brought an electrical storm with them, and my second glance wasn't so casual. Tension shot through me. I felt like I had a leash around my neck and I was being jerked right toward them.

You ...

The restlessness I'd felt all night suddenly made sense.

It hadn't been the heat. It hadn't been boredom.

I'd been *waiting*. And I'd been waiting for *them*.

But I couldn't let myself get too distracted, not at first.

I still had a job to do, and I had to feed. It had been over a month since the last meeting, and while I could go a fair amount of time between feeds, the last one had been minimal. Most of the people had been there either for kicks or because of things that, sadly, I couldn't fix. I wish I could help all of them and not just because of the rush I get when I take in the suffering, or the peace I find when pain is alleviated.

Suffering, to put it bluntly, sucks.

Tonight, the air was thick with misery, so thick I was choking on it and if I wanted, I could feed until I was drunk from it. It was everywhere, all around me. And ... to my surprise, one of those so quietly hurting was the woman who'd entered in silence from the back. One who crackled with the wild energy of somebody who wasn't entirely mortal.

I blocked her out, again. And focused on a young woman in the front. She was pregnant—and she had cancer.

My heart twisted as I moved closer, my gaze resting on her. She stared at me, her eyes beseeching.

Her friend was glaring at me as she tried to tug her away.

"Come on, Cici," she said, her voice cutting through the chaos churning inside me. She watched me with disgust.

I slid a look around, studying the faces of the sea of people. In the back, I noticed the blonde woman—the latecomer. Her cat-green eyes held a flicker of distaste.

She glanced at her companion and the two of them shared one of those unspoken conversations. I shifted my attention to him and arched a brow. Oh ... *helllloooo* ... pretty, pretty man.

His eyes were narrowed pensively as he took in his surroundings, his gaze never once connecting with mine.

The two of them looked highly out of place, though. They looked … bored.

You won't be bored much longer.

I smiled at them both.

44116076R00157

Made in the USA
Middletown, DE
28 May 2017